white picket fences

**Center Point
Large Print**

Also by Susan Meissner
and available from Center Point Large Print:

The Shape of Mercy

**This Large Print Book carries the
Seal of Approval of N.A.V.H.**

white picket fences

SUSAN MEISSNER

CENTER POINT PUBLISHING
THORNDIKE, MAINE

This Center Point Large Print edition is published in the year 2009 by arrangement with WaterBrook Press, an imprint of The Crown Publishing Group, a division of Random House, Inc.

The text of this Large Print edition is unabridged. In other aspects, this book may vary from the original edition. Printed in the United States of America. Set in 16-point Times New Roman type.

ISBN: 978-1-60285-601-1

Library of Congress Cataloging-in-Publication Data

Meissner, Susan, 1961-
  White picket fences / Susan Meissner.
    p. cm.
  ISBN 978-1-60285-601-1 (library binding : alk. paper)
  1. Family secrets--Fiction. 2. Redemption--Fiction. 3. Large type books. I. Title.
  PS3613.E435W45 2009b
  813'.6--dc22
2009028965

It is necessity and not pleasure
that compels us.
—DANTE, *The Inferno*

one

The chilled air inside the Tucson funeral chapel suppressed the punishing heat outside. Amanda shivered as she took a seat on the cool metal chair. She leaned over and whispered to her husband in the chair next to her. "A sweater in Arizona in September?"

He nodded casually, apparently unfazed by the abrupt temperature change from scorching to polar. Neil had worn a suit, though she told him she didn't think he had to, and she envied his long sleeves. He quietly cleared his throat, opened the program he'd been handed when they walked in, and began to read the obituary of the woman whose casket sat several feet away—the woman neither of them had ever met.

A generous waft of newly refrigerated air spilled from the vent above her head, and Amanda instinctively turned to her niece on her other side. The teenager's arms were bare under a flamingo-hued halter dress. Amanda wondered if the foster mother had given Tally any advice at all on what she might want to wear to her grandmother's funeral. Amanda again turned to her husband.

"I think we should've come yesterday." Her voice was barely above a whisper.

Neil looked up from the program. "It wouldn't have changed anything," he replied gently.

"Besides, we got here as quick as we could. It's not your fault you didn't know she was here. Your brother should've told you."

Neil reached for her hand and gave it a squeeze. Amanda looked down and noticed a thin line of wood stain under one of his fingernails, evidence that he had cleaned up from his latest wood-working project in a hurry. Neil turned back to the program, and Amanda looked over at her niece.

"You doing okay?" She hesitated, then placed an arm around Tally's shoulders.

The girl flinched and glanced at Amanda's arm before turning back to face the casket. The six-teen-year-old shrugged. "I didn't really know my grandma." The words were laced with casual regret, as if she knew people were supposed to know their grandparents, but what could she do about that now? Amanda intuitively pulled Tally closer. The girl stiffened at first and then relaxed, reminding Amanda that Tally barely knew her either.

Amanda hadn't seen her niece in nearly a decade. A handful of phone calls over the last few years, including one from a Texas jail and one from a château in Switzerland, had confirmed that Bart was still alive and that he still had Tally. Bart tended to contact her only in desperate times. And most of the time he didn't recognize his own desperation.

She had always felt like the older sister when it

came to Bart, the one who watched out for him, the one who tried to keep him out of trouble, the one their parents expected more from. It had always amazed her that Bart was just fine with that arrangement. She had been in junior high when he left home at seventeen, and he'd come home only twice in the years before she graduated from high school. Bart missed their parents' quiet divorce. Missed their mother's remarriage to an Australian man who had no intention of living anywhere but Melbourne. Missed her wedding to Neil and the births of her two children. Missed their father's last agonizing days of pancreatic cancer. In thirty years Bart had missed just about everything, including all opportunities for his family to get to know Tally.

The opening notes of the organist's ballpark rendition of "Shall We Gather at the River?" startled her, and she barely heard the buzz of her husband's vibrating cell phone. Neil pulled the phone out of his suit pocket. "It's a text from Delcey," he said. "She wants to know if she can sleep over at Mallory's house tonight. They want to go to the beach."

Amanda crinkled an eyebrow at the thought of her daughter not being home when they flew back to San Diego. "Tonight?"

Neil looked at her. "Maybe it's a good idea."

"No. Not tonight, Neil. She can go to the beach but she should be home tonight. Don't you think?"

"I guess."

"Which beach? How's she getting there?"

"Encinitas. Chase said he'd take her," Neil said, looking at the tiny screen on his phone.

Amanda wondered for a moment how Chase would feel about making the thirty-two-mile round trip to the beach. With Delcey out of the house, Chase would have the place to himself until she and Neil returned that evening. Their quiet seventeen-year-old probably couldn't wait to get his chatty younger sister out of the house. It hadn't passed her notice that her children were the same ages she and Bart had been when Bart left home. Chase's introspective nature and stark Teutonic features were similar to Bart's, but beyond that he was nothing like her brother. And Delcey thankfully did not have to mother Chase like she'd mothered Bart. "Tell her she needs to be home by six thirty," Amanda said. "I want her to be at the house when we get back tonight."

Neil punched in the message on the tiny keyboard. He nodded to the funeral program as he sent the message. "Did you know Virginia was a nurse in Vietnam? In the Army Reserves. She was in Saigon when it fell." He cocked his head as if waiting for a response and slipped the phone back in his pocket.

"I . . . I didn't know that," Amanda whispered back, pulling her thoughts back to the funeral chapel.

"She had medals from the army." Tally's head was turned toward Amanda, resting at an angle—like she had been a silent and interested part of the just-finished conversation about Delcey. "I saw them on the wall in her bedroom. But I didn't get a chance to ask her about them."

"I'm sorry, Tally." Amanda stroked the child's shoulder.

"I don't think my dad knew that about her. That she was in Vietnam. They didn't get along, actually. My dad and Grandma. She blames him for what happened to my mom." Tally swung her head back to face the front. "But you probably already know that."

Amanda opened her mouth but said nothing in response. Tally's mother, Janet, whom Bart hadn't even been married to, had died of an overdose of sleeping pills when Tally was an infant. Janet was alone when it happened. Alone by choice. Bart was nowhere around. She was about to tell Tally that Bart had never said much to her about Virginia, which was true, but a minister with a white checkerboard square at his throat and a tiny black book in his hands had come to stand next to Tally. Amanda closed her mouth.

"Is there anything you would like to say during the service, Tallulah?" the minister asked.

"Me?" Tally's voice was edged with astonishment. "Um. No. No, I don't want to say anything."

He patted her arm. "I understand," he soothed.

"This is a very difficult time. My prayers are with you, child." The minister smiled, turned to the next row of chairs, and approached a woman whom Amanda had met outside the funeral home ten minutes earlier. Virginia's only surviving child, Jill. Janet's younger sister. Tally's other aunt.

Amanda watched as the minister bent down to speak to her. The woman wore a charcoal gray suit, with a silky burgundy scarf frothing at her neck and black stilettos on her petite feet. She had flown in from Miami that morning, probably having made the funeral arrangements by the iPhone she now held in her left hand. Jill shook her head. Jill's husband and twin teenage sons shook their heads as well. Amanda couldn't remember which twin was which.

Tally also appeared to be watching the exchange of hushed words between her aunt and the minister. Amanda leaned in. "Do you know your aunt Jill and your cousins very well?"

"I met them once," Tally whispered back. "When I was four. My dad and I were in Tucson the same time they were. I don't remember them, though."

Amanda gently touched the girl's arm. "Not many people can remember things that happened when they were that little."

"I remember your kids, though."

This surprised Amanda, though she knew it

shouldn't. Tally was eight the last time Bart had swung through San Diego on his way to somewhere else. Certainly old enough to remember at least a little of that trip. But it wasn't Tally's words that had surprised her. It was the tone. It was hopeful, like Tally was relieved she had memories of her California cousins. And they appeared to be good ones. "I'm glad to hear that," Amanda said. "Chase remembers you too. Delcey was too little. But she likes the idea of having a girl cousin."

Amanda was about to tell her niece that Chase and Delcey had wanted to be here at the funeral today, which wasn't completely true, but the organ music stopped at that moment. The minister stepped onto the carpeted platform next to the casket. Amanda took a quick peek over her shoulder to see how many others had gathered at the chapel to say good-bye to Virginia Kolander. Thirty or so people sat in the chairs behind her. As she turned to face the front, Amanda noted that Tally's outlandishly fuchsia dress and matching streaks in her hair offered the only speck of rainbow in the tiny sea of gray and black shoulders. The girl's ankle tattoo, a ruby-throated hummingbird with its wings extended, was the only divot of extraordinary in a lineup of charcoal pant legs and nude-toned hosiery. Tally crossed her legs and Amanda involuntarily tensed. The movement gave the illusion that the hummingbird was now poised for a beautiful escape, that it was peeling away from Tally's skin and about to take flight. Amanda pulled her gaze away and exhaled softly, remembering that Bart confessed to buying that tattoo with money Amanda had sent him for car repairs.

The minister cleared his throat to speak, but he paused as the door at the back of the chapel opened. Every head turned to follow the latecomer inside. The dark-haired woman held an iced coffee in one hand and a briefcase in the other. Her white button-down blouse clung to moist skin.

"That's Nancy. My social worker," Tally said, toneless. "She's the one who called you."

The social worker hurried inside, mouthing the word *sorry*. She declined a chair offered by the funeral director, choosing to stand against the back wall instead. She tipped her head toward Tally and then smiled at Amanda as she pushed a pair of sunglasses up on her head.

Amanda nodded to the woman she'd met over the phone two days earlier, the same woman who told her that Bart Bachmann was missing—somewhere in Warsaw, they thought—and that his daughter Tallulah was homeless.

two

The minister had made a joke about his name when he'd introduced himself to Tally before the funeral began. She'd been standing in the foyer with her aunt and uncle as heat shimmered off the stained glass. He told her his name was Reverend Holly and that he was one letter short of being holy. Tally had smiled out of politeness, and he said she favored her grandmother when she grinned. "It's going to be okay, Tallulah," he said, before he moved away to talk to the funeral director.

She wondered how he could know something like that about someone he had just met. Tally shifted her weight on the chair as Reverend Holly began to pray from the podium. At the movement, Amanda gently removed her arm from around Tally's shoulders. Tally hadn't meant to hint that she wanted the arm off, though it had unnerved her some having it there. She looked up at Amanda, but her eyes were closed. So were the eyes of her uncle.

Tally studied them, using the precious seconds that she wasn't under any scrutiny to stare at the couple who had agreed to take her home with them until her father returned from Europe. Her aunt Amanda had her father's gray eyes, the single dimple, the ashy brown hair. She had a gentle voice and an easy smile. She was a reading teacher. Neil was taller than her father and quiet; he wore rimless glasses and very shiny shoes. He was a financial planner, whatever that was. Bart told her once that her uncle Neil was the calmest, most mind-numbing wet blanket he'd ever met and that sweet Amanda was just like him, though not as wet. She had asked him if that meant they weren't nice people, and he'd said it meant they were as delightful and daring as doorknobs.

She wished now that she had asked, "But are they *nice?*" Because now it mattered. With her dad off treasure hunting in Poland and no way of reaching him, it would've been smart to have asked. All she had to go on was the memory of one visit to the Janvier house when she was eight and the hour she had just spent with them.

Amanda and Neil had come to the foster home that morning to pick her up in their rental car rather than having the foster parents or Nancy bring her to the chapel. Evelyn, the foster mother, had told her that was a very nice thing for them to do. Tally responded that she really didn't know her aunt and uncle that well. And Evelyn said, "But they're your family," as if those four words were the answer to all life's problems.

Nancy, the social worker who'd come for her when the hospital realized she planned to hitch-hike home to an empty house the day Virginia died, said going to stay with the Janviers was a very good arrangement. "It's always better to be with family," Nancy said. "Trust me on this."

"But my dad won't know I'm in San Diego," Tally countered. "I think I should be able to stay in my grandmother's house until he comes back."

Nancy told her the county couldn't let a minor stay alone. And besides, the house belonged to Virginia's daughter Jill now, and she planned to sell it.

"But my dad said he'd be back in a few weeks. He's coming back to Tucson for me. I need to be here," Tally said.

"Well, Tally, if we could reach your father, we'd tell him your grandmother has died and that you're waiting for him at your aunt and uncle's in San Diego. The fact is, we can't reach him. No one knows where he is. Isn't that right?"

"I told you he's in Warsaw."

"But you don't know where, you don't have a phone number where we can reach him, and you don't even know why he went there. That's what you told me."

"I know what I told you," Tally said quietly. "It's nobody's business why he's there. And I *don't* know where he is. He's going to call me at my grandma's. That's what he said. And now I won't be there when he calls."

"But you also said he was going to contact you when he got there. He's been there more than a week, Tally. No call."

The minister said her name at that moment, and Tally jerked her head up. The remembered conversation with Nancy flitted away. She wasn't aware that Reverend Holly had finished praying and was now giving the eulogy. "You filled Virginia's last days with delight and purpose, Tallulah," he said. "Virginia often spoke of you to me and how much she missed watching you grow up. I know it meant a great deal to her to have you here these last few days. You were a brave girl, and I know you did everything you could to save her."

Tally blinked. She had lived with Virginia Kolander a total of eleven days, the full extent of their personal experience with each other. Her connection to Virginia had been casually sutured over the years, with only a shoebox of faded photographs and scattered birthday cards stuffed with flannel-soft five-dollar bills. She'd visited her grandmother when she was four, but she had no memory of it.

Her father never wanted to come to Arizona when it was time to move on. Tally knew why, though she never let on to him that she did. She'd twice overheard her father tell the play-by-play of his falling out with Virginia Kolander: five years ago to the underwear model whose penthouse they shared during those six magical months in Manhattan, and a few years later in Dallas when he warbled it to the owner of Luigi's Pizzeria the winter they lived in its basement and beer was cheap.

According to her grandmother, Bart should've intervened when Janet's postpartum depression ballooned into despair. Her father had argued it was pretty tough to intervene, considering he and Janet weren't married or even living in the same house.

"She was sick," her grandmother had said.

"I didn't know it," her father replied.

"You should have been there for her!"

"Well, maybe you *should've been."*

"She didn't want to see me!"

"She didn't want to see me either, Virginia."

"Because she was sick!"

"I ain't no doctor."

Her father had been a little on the intoxicated side both times he told this story, and Tally wasn't entirely sure how much of it was true.

Except that it sounded true. When he was sober, her father had half a dozen stories explaining the heavenly whereabouts of Tally's mother. All good ones. He only told the sad story of her mother's overdosing on sleeping pills when he'd swallowed enough alcohol to loosen his tongue and when he believed Tally was nowhere within earshot. His favorite explanation was that Tally's mother was really a fairy princess who left her on his doorstep so he'd have someone to make him chili and Rice Krispies treats.

When her father announced he was taking her to Arizona to live with Grandma Virgie while he took care of some business in Poland, she asked if she couldn't just stay with their friends Carrie and Joe, considering his opinion of her grandmother had never been that high. But her father replied he'd unfortunately burned a bridge with Carrie and Joe that still smoldered and made people's eyes water. After a two-day drive from Texas and the tense first day at her grandmother's house, her dad left with a nod to Virginia, a kiss on Tally's cheek, and a whispered promise that he'd buy her a red Corvette when he found the gold and diamonds his father had hidden from the Nazis.

Tally's gaze now fell on the piano-brown casket in front of her. The minister said Tally'd been brave. That wasn't true. She'd been scared out of her mind when she came home from the second day of school to find a hot teakettle with no water left in it glowing on the stove and her grandmother collapsed on the kitchen floor, her skin cold and gray and her eyes unmoving.

Tally's fingers trembled as she dialed 911. Her voice quavered as she gave her name and address.

"Is your grandmother breathing?" the woman said.

"I don't know," Tally answered, though she knew her grandmother most certainly was not breathing. "Maybe."

"It's all right, honey. The paramedics are on their way. Okay?"

"Okay."

"Tally, are you alone?"

She had looked at her grandmother's lifeless eyes staring back at her. They were the eyes of a stranger.

"Yes. I'm alone."

The minister's cottony voice again plucked her back to the chapel. He was giving a benediction. The closing prayer. "Amen." The minister closed his little black book.

Aunt Jill shoved her handkerchief in her pocket and stood up. Men came from the back of the room to prepare the casket for its journey to the family plot in Ohio. Nancy stepped away from the wall and reached into her purse for her cell phone. A man seated behind Tally asked the person next to him if there was going to be coffee and at least cookies, and several chairs made soft scraping noises as the handful of people rose to their feet. Amanda reached for Tally's hand and squeezed it.

Tally's eyes were dry.

three

The Tucson airport was quiet for a late Friday afternoon. Amanda handed Tally a strawberry smoothie and sat down in the molded chair next to her. Most of the other chairs in their row were empty.

"Thanks." Tally sipped from her straw and looked away, toward a window and the Arizona landscape. Amanda turned to Neil and offered him a sip of her cinnamon latte.

"No thanks, hon." He held the sheaf of legal documents that allowed them to take Tally, temporarily in the custody of Pima County, across state lines. He'd already read them once before, in Nancy's office. He now pored over them again, as if on a hunt to find a slippery sentence that could somehow foist permanent custody of Tally on them. Nancy had assured them it was nothing like that at all. His brow creased as he read.

Amanda sipped the latte and leaned back in her seat. Neil still seemed reluctant for them to step into the role as Tally's caregivers—even now in the airport with their niece sitting next to them— but Amanda wondered if it wasn't mostly because she'd said yes to it before she'd even asked him.

The call from Nancy Fuentes had come while she was making supper just two days before.

"Is this Amanda Jan . . . Janvier?"

"It's ZHAWN-vee-ay. Yes."

"This is Nancy Fuentes from Pima County Human Services in Tucson, Arizona. Your niece, Tallulah Bachmann, is here in temporary foster care and she really needs a place to stay."

"Why? What's happened? Where's my brother?"

"That's the problem. He's in Europe. Poland, we believe. But no one knows how to reach him."

"Poland! What's he doing in Poland? And why is Tally in Tucson?"

"Well, we don't know exactly why he's there, nor can we confirm that he is, in fact, there. Your niece said that's where he is, apparently looking for family members. Tally has been staying with her grandmother, Virginia Kolander. I'm sorry to say Virginia died yesterday of a heart attack. So Tally's alone here."

"Is Tally all right? Where is she?"

"She's fine. She's in a temporary foster home here in Tucson. Look, it would be nice if Tally could stay with family until we can track down her dad," Nancy continued. "We're wondering if you'd be willing to come to Tucson and get her. I know it would mean a lot to her. It wouldn't take long to get the paperwork done since you're family. You could take her home after the funeral on Friday. I think she'd like to be here for that . . . Mrs. Janvier?"

"Did Tally give you our number?"

23

"Ah, no. She gave me your names, though. I had to look you up. Look, you're all she has for family. There's just one other aunt. But she and her husband live in a condo with two teenage sons in Miami. She doesn't have an extra bedroom. She . . . It wouldn't work. And it's too far away for my liking. I know you have kids about the same age as Tally and one of them's a girl."

"Did you look that up too?"

"Your niece told me."

Neil, smelling of Right Guard and linseed oil, came in from the garage as she hung up the phone. He nodded to Amanda, walked to the sink, and began to wash his hands. The waxy odor of oil fusing with apple-scented hand soap swirled around her.

Her husband grabbed a dishtowel to dry his hands, and Amanda waited for him to ask who'd called. He had to have heard the phone ring. The garage was one wall away. When he didn't ask, she cleared her throat.

"Virginia Kolander died."

Neil draped the towel neatly on the handle of a nearby cabinet. "Who?"

"Tally's grandmother. Janet's mother."

"Oh. Too bad. Did we know her?" He opened the fridge and grabbed a bottle of lime-flavored water.

"No. Not exactly."

Neil opened the bottle and took a long drink.

When he pulled the bottle away, he said nothing.

"Tally was with her when she died," Amanda continued. "Neil, she needs a place to stay."

Neil frowned. "Where's Bart?"

"He's not in jail, if that's what you're thinking. He's on some trip to Europe. No one's really sure where, though. That's the problem. He hasn't called."

"Europe?" Neil's tone was incredulous. "Bart's in Europe?"

"Yes."

Her husband's eyes widened behind his rimless glasses. Neil made no attempt to hide his surprise. "What for?"

"I just know he's not here and no one knows how to contact him. Tally doesn't have anywhere else to go."

"Who told you all this?" A slight frown rested on Neil's lips.

"A social worker in Tucson. That's who I just got off the phone with. She said Tally told her Bart is in Poland looking up our relatives."

"Looking up *relatives?* You've got to be kidding. Do you even have any over there anymore?"

"I don't know. Maybe. I don't know, Neil."

Neil looked away and took another drink. He set the bottle down on the counter behind him. "Tally doesn't even know us. We don't know her."

"I've sent her a birthday present every year—at least when I know their address—and a gift at

Christmas. We're not complete strangers to her. And she was here once."

"That was ages ago," Neil said. "And what about Delcey and Chase?"

"What about them? Tally's their cousin. This is what families do. They help each other out when times are tough. It wouldn't be so bad for them to see that life isn't always easy."

There was a momentary pause.

"You already said yes, didn't you?" Neil finally said.

She felt her face flush. "It's just for a few weeks at the most. Bart's going to come back for her. I know he will. He would never abandon Tally. He's got a long list of faults, but that's not one of them. He would never leave her."

"Where's she going to sleep?"

"We can put her with Delcey," Amanda offered, her confidence returning. "There's room for another twin bed in there. And if that doesn't work out, she can have my sewing room. It's just for a little while."

He was silent for the next moment. She sensed he was doing some kind of calculation in his head. It unnerved her.

"What?" she asked.

"All right. We'll do what we have to do. But you really shouldn't get your hopes up. You can't undo in a couple weeks what Bart has spent years doing. You'll only end up disappointed."

"What do you mean?"

"You know what I mean." Neil turned and headed back to the garage and the bookcases he was building.

"So you're okay with this?" Amanda called after him. "Can I tell the kids, then?"

"Definitely tell the kids. They need to know what to expect."

He opened the door to the garage. A whiff of wood shavings met Amanda's nostrils as he left the kitchen and the door swung closed.

Neil reached for the latte. She handed it to him. He took a sip, grimaced, and handed it back. "Whoa. Too sweet for me." She noticed the stain under his fingernail again.

He'd been up past midnight staining the bookcases he was donating to a local nursing home for its fiftieth anniversary and the opening of a residents' library. He was supposed to be done with them by the weekend. The hastily planned trip to Tucson was cutting into that deadline, but she knew he would find a way to get them finished. That was just his way. He would finish them and they would be beautiful. Neil had lately made quite a name for himself as the soft-spoken financial planner who made stunning furniture in his spare time and donated it all to charity. The last project he had done, a grandfather clock for a local multiple sclerosis foundation, had netted more than two thousand dollars in a raffle. It was an impressive timepiece, as was the headboard he'd made for a couple who'd just returned from the mission field in Ghana.

She'd been surprised by Neil's ability to give away so much. He had always been careful with money, including how much he put toward charitable causes. But lately he gave away nearly everything he made in his shop.

"You've got a little bit of wood stain under your fingernail," she said.

"I was kind of in a hurry last night. I can't put the finish on the shelves until the stain is dry."

"You'll finish them in time."

"Have to." He stood and stretched. "I'm going to find a restroom."

Neil walked away, and Amanda noticed that Tally followed him with her eyes. Amanda made a stab at small talk. "Your uncle Neil has a wood-shop in our garage," she said. "Makes the garage kind of messy but he builds really beautiful furniture. He's making bookcases for a nursing home. They're going to be so lovely." She leaned in. "I wish we could keep them."

Tally didn't turn her head. Her gaze was on Neil's back, now many yards away. "He doesn't really want me to come home with you, does he?"

Amanda involuntarily sucked in her breath. "Well . . . of course he does. Tally, Uncle Neil is just . . . He's kind of a quiet man. Not at all like your dad." She laughed. "That's probably why I married him!"

Tally didn't laugh in return. "I don't really want to come home with you either. No offense. I'd rather just go back to San Antonio."

Amanda swallowed the sting. The girl hadn't meant to hurt her, she knew that. "You liked it there?"

"We had a nice trailer. Double-wide." She turned to face Amanda. "We weren't living in our car anymore."

"Oh. Well. A double-wide. That sounds nice."

"Dad had a job driving some rich guy around. It was a nice car. He liked driving it."

"So he was a chauffeur," Amanda said.

Tally seemed not to hear her. "And I really liked the school I was going to. And my friends."

Amanda considered putting an arm around her niece, but she couldn't decide if Tally would want her to after she'd tried it at the funeral home. "The school where you'll be going is a really good one. One of the best in the state. They called me yesterday. Nancy got all your records faxed to them from San Antonio . . . and from the few days you were here in Tucson. So you're all set to start on Monday. Chase will show you where everything is. It'll be okay. And I'm sure it'll be for just a little while."

Tally said nothing.

"Chase is kind of quiet too. Like his dad. Half

the time you have to guess what he's thinking. But he's very artistic. Very talented. He's into making videos. You know, home movies? I think he might want to go into filmmaking. He wouldn't want to be an actor or anything. He doesn't like being on the other side of the camera."

Tally took a sip of her smoothie. "He has blond hair?"

"Oh! Well, it's sort of like mine now. Darker. But still curly. Delcey's hair is still blond, though. Delcey's your typical thirteen-year-old. She loves to talk to people and go to the mall and chat with her friends about boys. You know."

Tally exhaled softly.

Amanda risked the rebuff and put her arm around Tally's shoulders. "We've put a guest bed in Delcey's room for you," she said. "I hope you won't mind having her for a roommate. We only have one other room, the sewing room, and it's a bit of a mess. Well, actually it's a *huge* mess. Will that be okay?"

Tally shrugged. "Whatever."

"Hey, on Sunday there's a picnic at our church. You'll be able to meet some girls your age. Chase will show you around. The food's always good. They have a huge barbecue. And a pie contest. Oh, and a silent auction. Uncle Neil's made this darling cradle for it. It's really cute. I think it'll be a lot of fun. Does that sound all right?"

She shrugged—one shoulder this time. "Sure."

30

Amanda paused and then leaned forward. "Tally. If you knew where your father was, you would tell me, wouldn't you?"

Tally nodded silently and without hesitation.

"He's not . . . Bart's not in some kind of trouble, is he?"

"He's not in trouble," Tally said quickly, leaning away from her.

"Do you know why he went to Poland? I mean, why now? What does he want?"

For a moment Tally seemed to ponder an answer. Then she stood up. "You can ask him yourself when he comes back. I'm done with my drink." She walked over to a trash receptacle and tossed it in.

four

Broadway and Union during the evening rush. A homeless man in tattered denim sauntered next to a young executive in Italian leather and Armani, and neither was aware of the other. It didn't get more real than that.

Chase Janvier repositioned his tripod for a new vantage point across the intersection in front of the U.S. Courthouse. He opened up the lens of his video camera and zeroed in on a head shot of a tailored woman in stilettos, busily tapping at the tiny keys of a BlackBerry as she walked. She clutched a half ring of bagel in the hand that held the device. The woman didn't look up to get her bearings as her heels staccatoed the sidewalk. She knew where she was going.

The woman's pace overtook the tattered man who'd stopped to poke at a candy wrapper on the pavement with his foot. Chase pulled back the zoom as she passed him. Would the man catch a whiff of her perfume and turn his head as she walked by? Or would she would be as invisible to him as he was to her?

Slowly the man in rags swiveled his head in the woman's direction. Chase leaned forward, itching to capture a remnant of the man's earlier civility, his ability to appreciate beauty. The man's eyes locked on the woman's hands—delicate, pale, and jeweled. He took a step toward her, the candy wrapper forgotten. Chase filled the viewfinder with the man's face and at once saw what the man was staring at: not the graceful features of gentility but the half ring of bagel. The man pivoted and took another step toward the woman, then quickened his pace to match hers. If Chase didn't move, he'd lose them in the crowd.

He grabbed his tripod by its legs and dashed across the intersection, the blast of a punched car horn following him. Once across the street he held the camera to his left eye and zeroed in on the retreating figures. The footage would be jerky, wild. He smiled. The erratic images would add a layer of expediency to the recording: life in motion on the streets of San Diego. He liked it.

Chase closed the distance, settling into a stride behind the homeless man, who shuffled several feet behind the woman. At the street corner a waist-high trash receptacle came into view. The woman shifted the BlackBerry in her hand as she worked the bagel free from its place in her palm. The homeless man accelerated his pace.

A gust of wind from a passing Metro Transit bus caught the woman's honey gold hair and lifted handfuls of it across her face. As she reached with the hand that held the BlackBerry to sweep her hair away from her face, she stretched her other arm forward. She misjudged the distance to the trash can, and the half bagel tumbled to the pavement. The woman clacked away unaware. Chase took a step toward the curb and leaned against a lamppost to stabilize his shooting arm. In the viewfinder he saw the man bend down and close his fingers around the half bagel. He squinted at the bagel as he straightened. Poked out a raisin. Frowned.

He tossed the bagel in the trash can.

The homeless man turned, and his eyes met the lens of the camera. Chase raised his head, ready to bolt if the homeless man confronted him. But the man smiled, revealing shiny pink gums and one front tooth. Chase smiled back and kept the camera rolling.

The homeless man shuffled past him and disappeared into a sea of silk, iPhones, and agendas.

Perfect.

Chase stopped recording and looked at his watch. Nearly six. His parents would be home soon, bringing with them a cousin he barely knew. They'd be ticked if he wasn't home when they arrived with her.

It surprised him that his parents were letting Tally come just like that. His parents never did anything on the spur of the moment. Especially his dad. And it annoyed him just a little that he was expected to be her tour guide at school. She was a year younger than he was. They wouldn't even have the same classes.

He'd wanted to know how long she'd be staying. His mother said she didn't know.

Chase grabbed the tripod with the camera still attached and broke into a jog for C Street and the trolley line. It would take him fifteen minutes to get to Old Town where his car was parked and another thirty to get home. He would barely make it home before his parents, assuming traffic was moving along I-15.

The trolley pulled into the Civic Center Station, and Chase dashed the last few yards to board before it headed north. He slid into a seat and began to detach his camera from the tripod, wondering for the tenth time that day what it was going to be like to have weird Uncle Bart's daughter living with them. Chase barely remembered Bart; he'd been a little kid the last time he saw him. He remembered a tattoo of a dragon, the aroma of tobacco and limes, a leather jacket that squealed when Uncle Bart hugged him, and the curly twirl of his uncle's ponytail. He remembered even less of his cousin Tally. She'd hung around with Delcey, though she was closer in age to him. He remembered that Tally smelled faintly of tobacco and limes too, that she ate her Lucky Charms dry, that she'd never heard of the television show *Full House,* and that she didn't run to anyone when she fell on their patio and skinned her knee. She just got the garden hose and, with tears in her eyes, rinsed away the blood and gravel.

Chase had overheard snippets of conversations his parents had since that long-ago visit. Uncle Bart was in Manhattan. Uncle Bart was in jail. Uncle Bart was in Switzerland. Uncle Bart was living in his car in San Antonio. And there was the unspoken understanding that wherever Uncle Bart was, Tally was with him, except, of course, when he was in jail.

And this time was apparently an exception too. Tally wasn't with him this time. Uncle Bart was in Poland and Tally was homeless in Arizona.

Homeless. The image of the toothless man rose up in Chase's mind as the trolley shuffled through Little Italy.

He doubted Tally and Uncle Bart had been tempted to eat discarded bagels off the streets.

Had they? Chase half-consciously moved his fingers across the slim body of his video camera, wondering.

This could be interesting.

This could be very interesting.

Chase shifted the tripod onto the seat next to him and noticed a matchbook peeking out from the seat back. He paused a moment and then reached for it. Duncan's Sports Bar and Grill. It felt thin in his hands, empty. Chase frowned and opened the matchbook anyway. It wasn't completely empty.

He stared at the lone match for a moment, then ran his finger up the match's smooth cardboard body and the cat tongue–textured head. The trolley zipped along the tracks as he folded the cover and stuffed the matchbook in his back pocket.

five

A copper sun was just beginning to slip into the horizon as Neil turned onto a wide landscaped street and into a neighborhood of stucco homes in creamy beiges, corals, and tans. The houses were all storied and stately, their green lawns bordered with rock, ornamental cactus, and flowering shrubs. Swaying palms lined the sidewalks and front yards, stretching past red tile roofs and trellises of bougainvillea. Porch lights began to wink on as they drove past. Chandeliers inside the houses gleamed through the slats of white plantation shutters. After a few turns onto streets with melodic Hispanic names like Corte las Brisas, Amanda announced to Tally that they were home.

Tally peered out the car window as Neil pulled into an expansive driveway. Three white garage doors with orange-slice windows were in front of them, but her uncle didn't open one. He slowed to a stop next to a silver sedan, put the car in park, and cut the engine. Tally opened her door.

The color of the Janviers' house reminded her of Texas sand, an overcooked beige. A flagstone path lit by amber footlights led up to an iron and glass front door. Flanking the entry were scarlet geraniums in enormous terra-cotta pots.

Tally reached for her duffel bag on the other side of the backseat. "Someone's here?" she asked, looking at the sedan next to Neil's car.

Amanda shut her car door and turned to look at the other car. "Oh. No. That's mine. Neil and I park our cars out here in the driveway. Neil has his woodshop in the garage. Chase is the only one with a parking place in there." She smiled.

The front door opened, and a cocker spaniel came bounding out. In a halo of porch light a young man stood at the threshold. "Sammy!" the young man called.

"This is our dog Samantha," Amanda said, leaning down to grab the dog by its collar. "And that's Chase." She nodded toward the front door. At that moment a second figure appeared in the doorway. "And that's Delcey."

Neil reached down for the dog. "I've got her."

"C'mon." Amanda draped an arm around Tally's shoulder.

They walked in the direction of the front door. Her cousins hesitated at the doorway, watched her take her first steps toward them, and then stepped onto the porch.

Chase was tall like Neil, but Tally thought he looked more like her dad than Neil. The blond hair she remembered had darkened to a shade of dark honey, and it hung in waves to the edge of his collar. Delcey had her father's features: large eyes, a slender nose, and dimple-less cheeks. The girl held a phone in her hand, and as Tally walked up to her, Delcey held up the phone and snapped a picture. Amanda said her daughter's name, disapproval in her inflection.

"All my friends want to see what my cousin from Texas looks like!" She took a step toward Tally. "I'm Delcey. I love your pink highlights. That is such a cool color."

"Thanks," Tally said.

"And this is Chase," Amanda said.

The young man nodded. "Hey. Nice to meet you. Again."

Amanda smiled. "That's right! You remember when Tally and Bart visited us before."

"I don't," Delcey chimed in.

"Yeah," Chase said. "I remember."

"Nice to see you again too," Tally said. They closed the distance to the front door, and Sammy barked at her as she crossed the threshold.

The tiled entry led to an open and spacious kitchen with high ceilings and granite countertops. Opposite the kitchen was a living room and, beyond that, a staircase with a landing that led up to the second floor.

"How about if we show you around? Neil can order a pizza, and then you can settle in. Does that sound okay?" Amanda said.

Tally nodded. "Sure. Whatever."

"This is obviously the kitchen," Amanda said. "That door over there leads to the garage and Neil's woodshop."

"And my car," Chase added.

"Yes. And we keep that door closed," Neil added as he poured water into the dog's dish and set it down. "It keeps the dust out of the house, and there are a lot of flammable items in there."

"Okay," Amanda went on. "The laundry room's just down that hallway past the door to the garage. You can put your duffel bag in there if you want to do some laundry before you put away your clothes. I know you left your grandma's in a hurry."

"Oh yeah. Sorry about your grandma," Delcey said.

"Yeah, thanks," Tally replied.

Delcey leaned in close to her. "You really found her dead?" she whispered.

"Dels, get a clue." Chase had heard Delcey but apparently no one else had. Amanda was pointing to a door by the laundry room and telling Tally that was her messy sewing room. Neil was washing his hands after handling the dog's dish.

What? Delcey mouthed to her brother.

Chase shook his head.

"Yeah. I did," Tally murmured.

"What was that?" Amanda turned to face them.

A couple seconds of silence followed.

"Oh. Delcey was just asking me a question," Tally finally said.

"Okay. So if we go this way, here's the dining room, and through that doorway is the family room and the den. There's a computer in there if you . . . want to, you know, e-mail your friends or do homework. If you can get Delcey off of it, that is."

"That's why I need my own computer," Delcey moaned.

Neil came up behind Delcey and put his hands on his daughter's shoulders. "We are not having *that* conversation tonight," he said. He gave his daughter's shoulders a gentle squeeze.

Delcey wriggled out of his grasp. "Dad! All my friends have their own laptops. All of them. And don't ask me if all my friends jumped off a cliff would I want to jump off a cliff too." She turned to Tally. "I hate it when he says that."

"Well, I'm sure you and Tally will find a way to share the computer, Delcey," Amanda said. She looked at Neil. "Maybe we should order the pizza?"

"Sure." Neil turned to her. "Tally, what do you like?"

"Get Canadian bacon and pineapple," Delcey said, the longed-for laptop forgotten for the moment.

"Let her pick, Dels," Neil said.

Tally shrugged. "I like any kind."

"Canadian bacon and pineapple!" Delcey chirped.

"Let's get a couple, Neil." Amanda walked toward the stairway to the upper floor. She motioned for Tally to follow.

Neil turned to his son. "How about mushroom, red onion, and avocado?"

Chase nodded. "Sure. That'd be great."

"Ugh. That is so gross." Delcey grabbed Tally's arm. "C'mon. I'll show you my room. We put a bed in there for you."

Tally fell in step with Delcey, and Chase turned to follow them as well. "Mushroom, red onion, and avocado?" Tally said to him over her shoulder.

"I take it you've never had it."

"Omigosh. Just wait till you see it," Delcey

groaned. "It's like something out of a horror movie."

They began to climb the staircase. Amanda was already at the top and heading into a bedroom. Family portraits hung on the wall to Tally's left as she climbed the stairs. She passed a large family picture of the four Janviers, a couple of Chase and Delcey alone, and several of people she didn't know. At the turn on the landing was a portrait of her father and Amanda when they were little. Tally recognized the photo. She had a smaller copy of it in her shoebox. Then she saw one of her, when she was in sixth grade. It was the only year Bart decided to get school portraits. Actually it was an old girlfriend of Bart's who had sent her to school with the order form and a check: Mellanie with two *l*'s. Rich and beautiful Mell. Tally stopped on the landing. She hadn't seen that school picture in a long time. In the photo she wore a blue cashmere sweater and tiny diamond earrings that Mell had loaned her. A few months after the photo was taken, Mell had moved to Paris.

Delcey pointed to it. "That's you."

"I think she knows who that is," Chase said.

"I *know* she knows!" Delcey retorted. She turned back to face Tally. "I like this picture."

Tally said nothing.

"My mom says you were living in New York when it was taken," Delcey said.

Tally nodded. "Manhattan."

"You are so lucky. I want to see New York." Delcey began to ascend the rest of the stairs.

"Yeah, it's pretty cool."

"So . . . ," Delcey said, taking the next step slowly. "Did you, like, scream when you found her?"

Tally stopped midstep. "What?"

"When you found your grandma. Did you scream?"

"Delcey!" Chase sputtered.

Tally told them she hadn't.

six

Chase stood at the doorway to the laundry room, his eyes fixed on the palm-sized, shimmering rectangle resting on the edge of the tiled counter. Tally was fishing clothes out of an army surplus duffel bag as the glass of the front-loading washer sloshed a bleary eye at her. At her feet were two small piles of dark and light clothes.

Tally was older than Delcey, but shorter. Slim. Prettier. She'd seemed distant when she arrived a few hours earlier, like she was already contemplating an escape. After the awkward family reunion and pizzas for dinner, his mother told Tally she was welcome to settle in by taking a nice relaxing shower and washing her clothes before she put them away. *Way to go, Mom. Tell the homeless cousin you want her cleaned up before she lays her head down on one of your pillows tonight.*

Reddish brown hair now hung in damp curls around Tally's face. Streaks of purplish pink peeked out from the wet strands. Two earrings glittered on one ear, five on the other.

The shimmering rectangle was a cigarette lighter, and it had been removed from the bag only a second earlier.

"You smoke?" Chase asked.

Tally jumped. She obviously hadn't seen him standing there. "What?"

Chase nodded toward the silver lighter gleaming in a patch of moonlight on the counter. "That yours?"

Tally followed his gaze and then her shoulders seemed to relax. No, not relax. They drooped. "It's my dad's. He asked me to hold on to it for him." She went back to her task.

"Looks old. Is it real silver?"

Tally shrugged.

"My mom won't let you keep it in your bedroom."

Tally looked at the slim case again and then at Chase. "I'm not going to be using it."

He shrugged. "I'm just saying she won't let you keep it upstairs."

"Why not?"

"Because you might start a fire."

44

"But I'm not going to be using it."

"So do you smoke?" he asked.

Tally reached over to the counter, enclosed the lighter in her hand, and slipped it into the back pocket of her cutoffs. "Do you?"

"No."

His cousin bent over the duffel and lifted out a pink halter dress. She hesitated and then dropped it on the pile of dark clothes.

"Why didn't your dad take it with him?" Chase leaned against the doorjamb and crossed his arms.

"I don't know." A pair of green socks. Darks.

He didn't believe her. He bet she knew why her father had left the lighter with her. It was probably to be a talisman of some sort. To remind her of him while he was away. To assure her he would return. To comfort her if he didn't. Chase suddenly wanted to film the scene he'd just witnessed. The girl digging through the rumpled clothes, finding the lighter, placing it on a streak of moonlight, the sudden challenge of a bystander, and then quietly slipping the lighter into a pocket, hiding it from sight.

If he ran up to his room to get his camera and came back, she'd be done, probably not even in the laundry room anymore. The best moment had already passed anyway: the second she looked at the lighter and her shoulders sagged.

It was a moment lost to him.

"I'll keep your secret," he said.

"It's not a secret." She didn't look up.

It most certainly was a secret. And he thoroughly intended to keep it. But he raised his voice a few decibels and grinned at her. "So you want me to tell my mom you have a lighter?"

"I don't want you to do anything." Again, she didn't look up. She dropped a pale yellow tank top onto the pile of lights.

"I could tell her, you know."

She raised her eyes. They revealed nothing.

For a moment, their eyes were locked. "I'm not going to tell her," Chase finally said.

Tally bent down and plunged her hand back into the duffel bag. He waited for her to thank him. She didn't. She lifted a lacy orange bra out of the duffel, and Chase looked away.

A mix of irritation and fascination swelled within him. "You're welcome," he said, turning his eyes back on his cousin.

Tally reached into the bag and pulled out another bra. This one was purple. Chase forced himself not to turn his eyes away. "You want me to thank you for minding your own business?" she mumbled, oblivious to his efforts to avoid staring at her underwear.

Chase laughed. "I heard you."

"I wasn't whispering." The purple bra landed on the pink dress.

He couldn't decide if he was fascinated or annoyed by her boldness. He itched to have his camera in his hands. "This is how it's going to be?"

Tally sighed. "I'm only going to be here a few weeks. I promise not to burn your house down."

Again their eyes were locked. Chase sensed Tally was like him somehow—no, that he was like her. She was waiting to break free, just like he was. "What if your dad doesn't come back?" he said softly.

"He'll come back." She said it easily, without looking up at him.

Chase moved away from the door frame and took a step inside. "Look, you won't be able to keep that lighter a secret from Delcey. She's going to go through your stuff. She'll find it."

Tally blinked. Her eyes seemed to widen a bit. "Your parents let your sister go through things that don't belong to her?"

"They don't know her like I do. I'm telling you, she'll find it. She'll say something."

"Why don't they know her like you do?"

Was she serious? "Because they're parents. Let me keep it for you. I promise I won't say a word."

A few seconds ticked by before Tally answered him. "Why would you do that?"

Chase took another step inside. "You probably think we don't have a thing in common. But you're wrong."

His cousin opened her mouth as if to say something and then shut it.

47

"Let me keep it for you."

For a long moment Tally stared at him. Then without a word she reached into her pocket and pulled out the lighter. Chase took a step toward her and opened his hand. She pressed the lighter into it.

"It was my grandfather's. Our grandfather's. It's the only thing my dad has of his." She didn't look up.

Chase closed his palm around it. "I'll keep it safe."

"How do you know Delcey won't find it in your room?" Tally raised her eyes to him. They had lost their sheen of defiance.

"I know how to keep things hidden from Delcey. And I'm not sharing a room with her."

"What do you have to keep hidden from Delcey?"

He slipped the lighter in the front pocket of his jeans. She watched it disappear.

"I have secrets, same as you." He turned and walked out of the laundry room.

seven

The bedspread, freshly laundered and smelling of lemon verbena dryer sheets, had headlined the year Delcey was addicted to purple.

"Brittany Bolton's favorite color was purple, so everybody's favorite color in second grade was purple." Delcey lay on her stomach on her own bed with her bent legs crossed behind her. Tally stood across from her, pulling folded clothes out of a laundry basket and placing them on the vast lavender expanse that covered a rollaway bed. "That bedspread's from when I was, like, seven."

Tally nodded. "Yeah. Thanks."

"Well, it's not like it's mine. I don't even really like purple anymore." Delcey swished her legs behind her. "I wonder where the butterfly pillows are."

Tally looked up from fishing out a pair of socks. "What?"

"There used to be butterfly pillows. Pink and purple and turquoise. Guess my mom didn't keep those."

"I'll be okay without them."

"I liked them then, but they'd be so ugly now. I am so over purple. I like melon. This is melon." Delcey spread her hands out over the coral-hued comforter underneath her and smiled.

Tally wanted to close her eyes and wish herself back to San Antonio. To the trailer with no air conditioning. To her own bed. To a pantry of six cans of Hormel chili and not much else. To Twinkies for breakfast. To the sound of her father playing his guitar outside on a fruit crate and singing with urban crickets as his chorus. To the life she had before Dad read the letter.

If he knew where she was, he'd come for her. If

he'd wanted her to stay with Aunt Amanda, he never would've brought her to her grandmother's. He would've brought her here instead.

But he hadn't wanted Amanda to know he was going to Europe. Amanda would've either tried to talk him out of going or would've wanted her half of the treasure. The buried jewels belonged to her father's and Amanda's grandparents. Neil would probably insist Amanda get her half. Her father hadn't wanted to deal with that.

"Yeah. Melon's a nice color," Tally replied.

Delcey grabbed her cell phone off a bedside table, glanced at the tiny screen, and sighed. "I sent Mallory a text ten minutes ago! Where is she?" She tossed the phone back onto the table. "Who's your best friend?"

Tally opened her mouth, unsure what to say. Her circle of friends in San Antonio was small. Marcella and Julio. PJ. Dan. Chelsea. Her friends didn't even know where she was. Dad had insisted they leave in the middle of the night. She was used to quick exits, but she wasn't used to leaving without saying good-bye. Bart thought it would be best if no one—not even friends—knew where they had gone, and he asked her not to talk to anyone in San Antonio until he came back and things had cooled down. That's usually the way it was when they left in a hurry.

Amanda walked by the open bedroom door at that moment and poked her head in. "Do you need another drawer, Tally? I'm sure Delcey can make some room in her dresser if you need more space."

Tally lifted her head. "No thanks."

"Do you need anything else? Anything at all?"

"I'm good."

"You'll let me know if you think of something?"

"Sure."

Amanda walked away. Tally opened a drawer on a small bedside dresser and placed socks and underwear inside, the question about who her best friend was apparently forgotten. Delcey reached again for her cell phone and looked at it. A second later she tossed it back onto the table.

In the corner of the drawer, Tally saw a shimmer of metal. A gold heart-shaped locket on a chain. She picked it up and held it toward Delcey. "I think this might be yours."

Delcey crinkled her eyebrows, doubtful.

"It was in the top drawer." Tally extended the necklace to her.

Her cousin peered at the chain in Tally's hands. "Oh. I don't wear that one anymore."

Tally's arm stayed aloft.

"You want it?" Delcey's eyes brightened with what appeared to be a sudden burst of generosity.

Tally shook her head gently. "No. Thanks anyway. It's yours."

"But I don't wear it anymore. You can have it."

Tally slowly turned and put the necklace back in the drawer where she found it. She laid a short

51

stack of folded T-shirts and tank tops on top.

"So you don't have any brothers or sisters or nothing?" Delcey sounded bored.

"No."

"Yeah, I just have Chase. He's so weird. I used to want a sister."

Tally placed a pair of jeans in the drawer and said nothing.

"You are *so* lucky you don't have a brother," Delcey continued.

A pair of capris went into the drawer.

"It's so weird that my mother has a brother and he's your dad and that your dad is Uncle Bart."

Tally looked up from the basket.

Delcey continued. "That means my mom is like me and your dad is like Chase. Uncle Bart is like Chase. That's just so weird."

"Why is that weird?"

Delcey shrugged. Then she sat up on the bed, and her gaze traveled down to Tally's foot. "My parents would so freak out if I got a tattoo."

Tally glanced at her ankle. "Really? My dad picked this one out."

"I'm so sure!"

Tally lifted her head. "He did."

"Your dad *made* you get a tattoo?"

"I never said he made me. He asked me if I wanted one. I said yes. This is the one he liked best."

Tally turned back to the diminishing pile of

clothes. Another pair of jeans. A gray hoodie. Her bright pink dress.

"Why did your dad want you to have one?"

Tally shrugged. "I guess 'cause he was getting one. A new one. He already had a couple."

"Didn't it hurt?" Delcey rubbed her own ankle lightly.

Tally's eyes drifted back down to the bird in flight. "Yeah. A little. But he told me it would. And he told me it would stop hurting."

Delcey swung her legs around and tilted her head. "You really don't know where your dad is?"

"He's in Europe."

"But you don't know where."

Tally hesitated before answering. "Not today."

Delcey got up from the bed and flopped onto a beanbag chair by a window. The foam beads squealed. "What's he doing there?"

"We've got relatives there. He's looking them up."

"So they're, like, my relatives too. Right?"

"Yeah."

Delcey leaned back and toyed with an earring. "But it's not like they're going to know him, right? I mean, does your dad know any language besides English? How's he going to talk to them?"

Tally inhaled and let her breath out slowly. "The relatives he's looking for aren't, they aren't . . ."

Delcey sat up straight. "They aren't what?"

Tally hesitated. She was saying too much. Her

dad was actually hoping he wouldn't talk to anyone he could call family. The treasure was a secret. "They aren't alive anymore. He's gone to see where they're buried."

"How come?" Delcey breathed.

A voice startled them. Chase was at the doorway, leaning on the frame as if he'd been there for several seconds. Had he heard Delcey compare him to her father? "Mom says her brownies are out of the oven," he said. "She wants us to come downstairs and have one."

"All right." Tally grabbed the empty laundry basket and followed Chase out.

"Brownies? At ten o'clock at night?" Delcey exclaimed, still inside the room. "Cool!"

"My mother's messy sewing room must be looking pretty good, eh?" Chase said as they headed for the staircase.

She didn't have time to come up with a reply. Delcey was behind them in seconds.

eight

Amanda sat back in her canvas chair and sipped lukewarm lemonade from a plastic cup. Neil stood several yards away, protected from the late afternoon sun by the splotchy shade of a eucalyptus. He was talking investments with another churchgoer. She could hear snippets of their conversation.

The man was probing Neil for insights on a carefree retirement. Oh, the irony. She noticed a physician friend of theirs leaning against a picnic table across the lawn, deep in conversation with a woman who was rubbing her neck, then rubbing her forearm, and then pointing to her toes. Why did people think they could get free advice from professionals at social events? It didn't matter what kind of party or picnic or sporting event they went to; as soon as word got out that Neil the financial planner was there, he'd be cornered by some hapless, inquiring soul, never to emerge until it was time to eat or time to go.

Neil caught her eye and winked. She smiled back.

He was just too accommodating, that's all. Neil expected the interruptions and had started tucking business cards in his pockets whenever they were out socially.

Today he'd put on a salmon-colored Henley and khakis instead of the carpenter shorts and T-shirt that she'd laid out for him. Amanda hadn't said anything. She liked that shirt on him. The slight gray at his temples accented the rosy orange hue. He looked very handsome.

But still. No one came up to her at parties and picnics wanting to know how to get their kids to read better. She'd stuff her pockets with business cards if she thought they would. Maybe that's why Neil didn't mind chatting about business at social events—it didn't feel like business. Likewise, she loved her job in the remedial lab at the elementary school. Every day she saw miracles. An unmistakable veil lifted when a kid finally grasped the concept of words on paper and at last the world of books lay before him like the threshold to the universe. Everything about the child's countenance changed. It was like Helen Keller at the pump, understanding that the wetness on her hand had a name.

She sat up in her chair, looking for the kids and Tally. The picnic was well attended. Groups of people milled about, awaiting food from the hissing gas grills. A volleyball game intensified at the far end of the parking lot, and young kids tossed water balloons across the far lawn.

"Wondering where your kids are?"

Amanda looked up. Gina Kliever stood beside her, holding a can of Coke. Her daughter Kelly was the same age as Delcey, and Gina had been to their house many times to drop her off or pick her up. "Oh. Hi, Gina. Yeah. I've kind of lost track of them."

"May I?" Gina pointed to Neil's empty chair beside Amanda.

"Be my guest. I don't think Neil will be coming back anytime soon."

Gina plopped down on the chair and eased her feet out of her flip-flops. "I think a bunch of teenagers went inside to play basketball in the gym. Kelly did. Delcey and Chase are probably in there too."

"Mmm. I just . . ." Amanda searched the crowds of people for Tally's fuchsia-streaked hair. She didn't see her. "I'm just hoping they haven't forgotten about their cousin. She doesn't know anybody here but us."

"You have family visiting you?"

Amanda turned to face her friend. "Just my niece. My brother's daughter. Her name is Tally."

"Tally? That's a very unusual name."

Amanda grinned. "I have a very unusual brother. It's short for Tallulah."

"Wow. Now there's a name you don't hear too often. Is this the brother you've mentioned before? The wild and mysterious one?"

"Yeah. That's Bart."

"Darn. I would've liked to have met him. He's got something going on this weekend, huh?"

Amanda exhaled. "You could say that."

Gina hesitated and then nodded. "I see . . . He kind of dumped her on you this weekend?"

"Not exactly."

Gina waited.

"He's off again on one of his schemes. I'm sure it has something to do with fortune or fame. It usually does. He's in Europe somewhere."

"Really? He goes off to Europe a lot?"

"No. He just likes to *go off.* Usually he takes Tally with him, but not this time."

"How old is she?"

"Sixteen. He left her with her maternal grand-mother in Tucson but—get this—she died unexpectedly early last week. Heart attack. No one's heard from Bart, and he didn't leave us a way to get ahold of him, which is typical. So now we've got Tally until he decides to come home."

"I take it there's no mom in the picture?"

"Tally's mom died when she was a baby. Accidentally overdosed on sleeping pills. So they say."

"Too bad."

"Yeah."

Gina took a sip of her own drink. "How long's your brother been gone?"

"We're going on two weeks."

"And no one's heard from him?"

"No."

A trio of grade-school girls skipped past them, laughing. "Do . . . do you think something's happened to him?" Gina's tone was soft.

Amanda sighed. "I don't know. Bart's gotten himself in and out of more sticky situations than I care to admit. I'm not worried yet. But I do wonder if maybe he's trying to disappear for a while. I'm not entirely sure what Bart was doing for money just before he left. I wonder if maybe . . ." She didn't finish.

"Maybe he's running from the cops?" Gina said.

"Or from people you just don't mess with."

"So he's purposely not contacted his daughter . . ."

Amanda shrugged. "I don't know. He told Tally he was going to look up our relatives in Poland, which is the lamest thing I've ever heard."

"You don't have relatives in Poland?"

Amanda shook her head. "No, I'm sure we do."

"So?"

"I don't see how he'll find them. My grandmother immigrated here after World War II when my dad was a kid. She was Catholic but she'd married a Polish doctor. A Jewish man, actually. But then the war came, and, well . . . I'm sure we have distant relatives, but they're going to be impossible to find."

"How come?"

Amanda ran a hand through her hair. She didn't often talk about what she knew about her father's side of the family. The little her father had shared of it wasn't pleasant. "My grandparents were sent to the Warsaw Ghetto when the Nazis invaded Poland. My grandfather wasn't a practicing Jew, but that didn't matter. The two of them had been hiding my grandfather's mother and sisters during the first six months of the occupation, which of course didn't sit well with the Germans when they discovered them. They were all sent to the ghetto. Somehow my grandmother and father escaped to England. My grandfather didn't, though. He died at Treblinka."

"Treblinka?"

"A concentration camp."

"Wow." Gina's eyes widened.

"Yeah. Kind of a sad story."

"You don't think any of the others survived?"

Amanda took a drink of the lemonade and grimaced. It was souring as it grew warmer. "I'd be very surprised to hear that any of my grandfather's family members are alive since they were all Jewish. My grandmother's family might've survived, but so many families scattered during the war. I honestly don't know how Bart expects to find any of them."

Gina poked at a dandelion with her toe. "So here you are—one-quarter Jew and one-quarter Catholic, at a Protestant church picnic." She looked up at Amanda and smiled. "Getting ready to eat grilled pork chops."

Amanda smiled back. "Very funny. You know, my dad never talked about his parents being so different from each other culturally. And my grandmother never talked about her deceased husband at all. Well, maybe she did. Her accent was always so strong, I could hardly understand her. She sounded like Arnold Schwarzenegger in falsetto, back in his Conan days."

Gina threw her head back and laughed.

Amanda grinned and then continued. "I was kind of scared of her growing up. She always had this faraway look in her eye, like she didn't really feel she belonged here."

"She never remarried?"

"She did, when my dad was a teenager. And the funny thing is, I was closer to her second husband than I was to her. To me, that man was my grandpa, not the Jewish doctor who died in the concentration camp. I've never really considered my Jewish heritage, you know? That part of my past seems like someone else's." Amanda tossed her lemonade onto the grass.

Gina was quiet for a moment. "What's she like?"

"What?"

"Your niece. What's she like?"

"Oh. She seems okay. She came complete with magenta streaks in her hair, multiple piercings, and a tattoo."

Gina's eyes widened. "Are you serious?"

"Yeah, but actually she's very quiet. Polite for the most part. A little distant. But that's to be expected. I think she knows more than she's telling me about why Bart's in Europe."

"Really?"

"Not that her telling me why he's there would help much. I don't think Bart left her with any way to contact him. If she knew how to do that, she wouldn't even be here."

Gina nodded. "Meaning she's not thrilled about staying with you?"

Amanda shrugged. "Yeah. Go figure. She finally has a nice roof over her head, decent food to eat, a safe school to go to, and people her own age to talk to, and she can't wait to go back to a rented trailer in the worst neighborhood of San Antonio."

Gina stretched her legs out in front of her. "Maybe the white-picket-fence lifestyle's not for everybody."

"I guess."

The two women were quiet for a moment. Then Gina sat up in her chair, her eyes squinting into the sun toward the row of barbecue grills. "Hey," she said. "Isn't that Chase?"

Amanda sat up and followed Gina's line of vision. Twenty yards away Chase stood in the shimmering heat of a grill. Her son leaned forward, and he seemed to be studying—very intently—the fire that pranced crazily around sizzling pieces of meat. He was facing her, but she was sure he didn't see her. His lips were moving as he stared at the flames. An aproned man standing in front of the grill grabbed a squirt bottle, and Chase took a step forward.

"What's he doing?" Gina asked.

Amanda barely heard the question. An arm of fire shot up from the grill, and the man took a step backward and squirted a jet of water. But Chase didn't move, and the man turned to her son, a mixture of surprise and concern on his face.

"Amanda?"

Amanda stood up, turning her head to see if Neil was seeing what she was seeing. Half turned away from her, Neil was fully engaged in conversation, arms gently crossed across his chest, nodding to the man pouring out his nest-egg woes. She swung her head back around. The aproned man was saying something to Chase. But Chase just stared at the flames going about their merry charring business. He seemed to be speaking to them.

He was not listening.

The blissful sounds of the picnic fell away, and her mind flooded with alarm. *He can't possibly remember.*

nine

Chase was the last to come downstairs for breakfast Monday morning. He'd had trouble falling asleep the night before and overslept.

"I was just about to come up and see if you were okay," his mother said as he stepped into the kitchen. She smiled at him. It looked forced.

"Didn't hear my alarm." Chase grabbed a glass out of the open dishwasher, aware of his mother's eyes on him. She watched as he poured himself a glass of juice.

He moved to the table to sit next to Delcey as she slathered Nutella on a bagel. On his other side, Tally munched on dry Cheerios, eating them from the bowl with her fingers. Neil was mostly hidden by the newspaper but said good morning to Chase from behind the business section.

Amanda set a half-circle omelet down in front of him, and again her gaze lingered. Chase leaned toward his food, away from her.

His mother had approached him at the grill the day before, as he began to step away from it. She asked him nervously if he knew where Tally was. He didn't know where Amanda came from. She seemed to materialize out of nowhere. It took him a second to answer. His heart was hammering in his chest as the moments at the grill pinged around inside his head, poking into the darkest corners of his memory.

"She's with Delcey. I told you Delcey wanted Tally with her."

"Yes, but . . ." She faltered then and bit her lip.

"I don't see what the big deal is, Mom. I'm sure she's having more fun with Dels than she would with me. I'm, like, the only person here my age, in case you haven't noticed."

"You're not having fun?"

" 'Fun' is not the word I would use, no."

"Matt couldn't come, then?"

"His family went to the beach."

"So . . ." She looked back at his father, chewed on her lip some more, then turned back around. "You think Tally's okay, then?"

"Yeah, Tally's fine. Can I go now?"

"You mean leave?"

"I mean, are we finished here?"

She'd held his gaze for a second. "Sure."

Chase reached for his fork.

"Did you sleep well?"

Chase peered up at his mother. Her hands rested on the back of Tally's chair, but her eyes were on him. "Uh, yeah. Sure." He took a bite of the omelet.

She nodded, her gaze lingering a second longer. He could feel her unease. Again he looked away from her.

She had seen him transfixed in front of the flames.

She had seen it and didn't know what to make of it.

Chase shoved a large forkful into his mouth and raised his head. Their eyes met. She said nothing.

His mother slowly turned to Tally. "It's no trouble for me to go with you this morning, Tally, and get you settled. First hour is my prep time, so really, it's no trouble at all."

"I'll be okay," Tally said.

"Well, all right. Your schedule's waiting for you at the front office. They told me someone would be waiting to give you your books and get you to your first class."

"You told her that already, Amanda," Neil said from behind his paper wall.

"I'll be fine. I've been to new schools before." Tally stood and took her cereal bowl to the sink.

Delcey glanced up from her bagel and looked at Tally's bowl. "How come you don't use milk?"

Tally shrugged. "I just like cereal without it."

Chase shoved the last bit of omelet into his mouth and grabbed his phone to look at the time. "We gotta go."

Amanda turned away.

Tally nodded and grabbed the worn backpack she'd brought with her from Arizona. She had declined his mother's offer to buy her a new one.

"Okay, so you two have your lunch cards?" his mother said.

"Yep," Chase said. Tally nodded.

"Did you put air in the passenger-side tire?"

Chase turned around. His father's face was now peeking out from the open newspaper.

"I'll do it today after school," Chase replied.

The face hovered and then disappeared behind newsprint. "You don't want to let that go, Chase. It's not good for the tire, and it's not safe for you. Or Tally."

"Yeah."

Neil lowered the paper. "Oh. Chase, you'll be able to help me deliver those bookcases today when I get home from work, right?"

"Sure."

"I'll be home a few minutes before five, and we'll do it then. Tally, you can come with us if you want."

Tally blinked. "Um. Okay."

The paper returned to its normal resting height. Chase and Tally headed to the garage. They worked their way past wood projects in progress to Chase's Toyota. Chase opened the last of the three garage doors, and they got in. He backed out, then threw the gear into first and took off.

He glanced over at his cousin. "I can come to the office with you if you want."

She shook her head. "It's all right."

He shifted gears. "You're really not nervous?"

Tally cocked her head. "I'll be outta here in a couple weeks anyway. I'm only going because the state makes me."

"Right." He shifted into third. "I'll come with you anyway. My mom would like it if I did."

Tally exhaled heavily in silent acquiescence. "Your mom is . . ." She didn't finish.

Fourth gear. He waited. "You can say whatever you want, Tally."

"Nice. She's very nice."

Chase looked at his cousin. "I guess."

"You probably don't notice it because you're around her all the time."

Chase shifted his gaze back to the road. "I never said I didn't think she was nice."

"Does she always worry so much about people being okay?"

A split second of silence hung between them. "Not always," Chase replied. He was glad she didn't seem to care what he meant. "How did you like meeting all of Delcey's little friends at the picnic?"

She glanced over at him. A slight smile rested on her mouth. "I think I've had more fun getting sent to the principal's office."

"The principal's office! You're a troublemaker, are you?"

She turned her head away. "No. Not really."

"So why'd you get sent to the principal's office?"

Tally hesitated a moment. "To be told things."

She didn't elaborate.

Chase pushed Coldplay into the CD player, and they rode the rest of the way blanketed by drums, bass, and guitar.

ten

The woman in the admissions office was tall and round, and she smelled of roses soaked in aged vanilla. Chase sneezed when she asked him if he'd like to be the one to show Tally where all her classes were.

"Uh, sure. I can do that." He sneezed again, and she issued a benediction upon him.

"All righty, then, Tallulah. Here are your books." The woman pointed to a stack on the counter between them. "You have till the end of the week to get covers on them, dear. And here's your locker number and combination. And your schedule. Your records from Texas indicate you've already had psychology—that's what most of our college-bound juniors take—so we've put you in sociology instead."

Chase leaned over and looked at the schedule in Tally's hand. "Hey, you're in my class. I have sociology that hour too." He looked up at the woman behind the counter. "Did you guys know that when you did the schedule?"

The woman smiled and shrugged. "The guidance counselors do the schedules for transfer students, hon."

Tally let her eyes rove over the schedule. American history. Pre-calc. World lit. Sociology. Anatomy. Ceramics.

Chase shook his head. "Oh man. You've got Carruthers for American history. Dead people have more personality than that guy."

The woman cleared her throat. "You have a few minutes before the first bell. So maybe you should help Tallulah find her locker?"

Chase grinned at his cousin. "By all means, Tallulah, let's go find your locker." He turned and headed for the double doors that led to the campus. Tally grabbed the pile of books.

The campus was awash in generous sunlight. Lilies of the Nile protruded from every patch of landscaping, shaded by mature sycamores and towering California fan palms. As they walked to her locker, Chase pointed out the buildings by department. All around them the cosmos of high school life played itself out as hundreds upon hundreds of students descended upon the open-air hallways. When they got to Tally's locker, the first bell rang and the swell of people seemed to multiply.

"I'll meet you in front of the library at lunchtime, okay?" Chase said. "That's where I'm meeting Matt. And then we'll go to the caf. We have sociology right after lunch. Matt's in that class too. You gonna be all right?"

"Yeah." Tally tossed the books for her afternoon classes into the locker and slammed it shut.

"Okay, so the history department's right over there," Chase gestured toward a stucco building across the sea of people.

"I got it."

"All right. Well, see ya." Chase turned and half jogged away. Tally studied the map in her hand to make sure she could find her locker again and then headed for the history building and the teacher whose personality, Chase claimed, was easily trumped by cadavers'. The second bell rang as she stepped into the classroom.

The morning passed quickly.

Mr. Carruthers turned out to be slightly more engaging than a corpse. And at least his class wasn't at the end of the day. Her pre-calculus teacher seemed pleasant enough, but Tally wasn't that great in math. Her father once said that math was either art or a foreign language to you. When she had asked him what it was for him, he said art—but nothing he'd ever want to hang on a wall in his house. She was glad she wasn't going to be at Chase's school long enough to fail. The world lit teacher had a nervous tic but a kind smile and calming voice. When he asked the class if anyone had read *The Rubaiyat* before, Tally wanted to raise her hand, but instead, she did the same thing she always did when she transferred to a new school—blended into the existing fabric. By the time the lunch bell sounded, Tally was ready for a break.

She located the library on the map and found Chase a few minutes later, leaning against a wall covered in climbing vines. Next to him was a guy with dark hair, olive skin, and a slightly crooked smile. He wore jeans and a faded Quiksilver shirt.

"Got through it okay?" Chase asked when she reached them.

"It was all right."

"Tally, this is Matt Santino. Matt, my cousin Tally. I mean, Ta-LOO-lah!"

Tally sneered at him and then turned her eyes to Matt. "Hey."

"Hey." Matt nodded to her. "Magenta's my favorite color."

Tally looked down at a lock of streaked hair resting on her shoulder and then raised her head. "Making fun of my hair?"

"It really is his favorite color." Chase began to walk toward the cafeteria.

Matt smiled at her as he and Tally fell in step with Chase. "Pretty awesome first name."

"Yeah, right."

"Really. You're the first Tallulah I've ever met."

"I get that a lot."

"Did your parents make it up or something?" Matt continued.

"It's Native American. Choctaw. It means 'leaping water,' or something like that. I don't know. My mom named me."

"Cool. Is she Native American?"

"She's . . . No, she wasn't."

"Oh." Matt seemed to suddenly remember her mother was deceased. Tally wondered what else Chase had told him. "Sorry. Forgot."

"I wouldn't have expected you to know." Tally looked at Chase.

"It's not his fault. I asked," Matt offered.

Tally stopped walking. "You asked?"

"When he told me you were coming to live here, I asked where your parents were. He told me."

"Told you what?"

Matt looked from Tally to Chase and back to Tally. "That your mom had passed away and your dad was in Uruguay."

Tally looked at Chase. "You told him my dad was in Uruguay?"

"I told him your dad was in Europe. He's playing with you."

Tally turned back to Matt. He was grinning.

She resumed walking and the two young men followed. They arrived at the cafeteria to find the line snaking around the building.

Chase sighed audibly and turned to Matt. "What have you got today, man?"

"Turkey and avocado on sourdough."

Chase pulled out his lunch card. "Trade?"

Matt reached into his backpack, pulled out a sack, and handed it to Chase. Chase took the bag and handed him his card.

"See you on the back forty in about a zillion years." Chase walked away from them and disappeared into the throngs of students eating on benches, retaining walls, and concrete walkways in the midday sun.

"You can do that?" Tally said, watching him go.

Matt shrugged. "Who's gonna know? The caf ladies don't know our names."

"What's the back forty?"

"The quiet little nook where Chase likes to eat my lunches. Don't worry. I know the place."

Tally turned back to face him. "You gave up turkey and avocado on sourdough for school food?"

Matt smiled. "My parents own a sandwich shop. I've pretty much OD'd on every kind of sandwich there is."

They moved forward a step or two in line. Someone waved to Matt from across the quad, and he waved back.

"You been friends with Chase a long time?" Tally asked.

"Just since last year. I wouldn't call that a long time."

"Is that when you moved here?"

"What? Oh, no. I've always lived here. That's just when I met him. We were lab partners in chemistry. I was in charge of the Bunsen burner; he did all the math."

They took a few more steps in line.

"You seem like good friends."

"Yeah. Sure. Chase is all right. Clever dude. Did he tell you he makes movies? They're all pretty deep and weird. He'll probably be famous someday. His stuff is just the kind to win awards because it's so mysterious, it has to be good, you know?"

"Amanda told me about the movies," Tally replied. "Chase hasn't said anything."

"Yeah, I guess he's kind of protective of them. I've only seen a couple, actually."

They moved forward several steps. A girl walked by and said hi to Matt. He nodded to her.

"What do his other friends think about his movies?" Tally said, watching the girl walk away.

Matt hesitated a moment. "Chase kind of likes to be on his own. I think he likes being able to look at everything from the vantage point of, you know, a detached observer."

Tally looked out over the masses in the direction Chase took off. He was nowhere in sight. "So he doesn't have any friends besides you?"

"Well, not friends he'd show his movies to. That's different."

"But he showed some to you."

Matt grinned. "Hey, you gotta have one friend you can show your weirdest ideas to."

"Yeah, I guess."

They took several more steps, almost inside the building now.

"How long is your dad going to be gone?" Matt asked.

Tally adjusted the weight of her backpack. "I don't know."

"You should see if you can join Chase and me on our sociology project for this quarter. Gimble's going to put you with somebody no matter how long you're here."

"What . . . what kind of project is it?"

"Everybody has to do a special assignment this quarter; it has to be a video or PowerPoint thing—big yawn—or a research paper or . . . I can't remember the other one. It has to be on some significant social issue that transcends its own time; you know, something that's happened before in another time and could maybe happen again. You should do it with us. We're going to do a documentary on the Holocaust. Your great-grandfather died at a concentration camp, right?"

They had finally reached the food. Matt grabbed a tray and handed it to her.

"How do you know that?" Tally asked.

"Chase told me a while back. He once showed me a movie he made about warring ants, and it was supposed to be some dark metaphor for how the strong oppress the weak. I thought it was kind of a cool movie, in a sad way. That's when he told me about your great-grandfather. I think we could use that for the project. You could help me convince Chase to do an angle on your great-grandfather. I think it would be good. And we wouldn't have to spend hours upon hours researching stuff."

"I don't know anything about my great-grandfather."

"But you've got Chase's mom right there. Family photos. Documents. People save that stuff. And besides, Chase knows these two old Polish guys at some nursing home around here who lived in Poland during World War II. They were at the same concentration camp as your great-grandfather. The same one. He met them last year or something. He told me a long time ago he wanted to go back and film them. It's the perfect setup for us. He's going there today to help your dad deliver something, and I think he should ask them."

"What if the teacher won't let me do it with you?" She took the tray.

Matt made a face. "Gimble won't care. He's

already told us we can work in teams of three as long as everyone does at least a third of the work." He grabbed a cardboard basket of breadsticks and a container of marinara sauce and put them on his tray. Tally copied him.

"I don't know how long I'm going to be here," she finally said.

Matt snagged two minicartons of milk. "Well, nobody ever really knows *that*." He offered one of the cartons to her. "Milk?"

She took it. Matt waved Chase's lunch card in front of the scanner and smiled at the attendant nearby. "We'll ask Gimble. Okay?"

"I guess so."

He gestured to the tray in her hands. "Lose it."

Tally scanned her card and grabbed the lunch items off her tray as they walked out of the lunch line and into the sunlight.

eleven

A manda's classroom radiated quiet. She flipped a switch, and the fluorescents above her hummed to life. She sat down at her desk, which was neatly cluttered with books, papers, colored pencils, and pads of happy-face stickers. She moved a trio of glitter markers and set down her coffee mug.

Amanda looked at the nearly empty desktop across from hers. Becky, her partner in the remedial classroom for the last six years, was on maternity leave and had taken the contents of her desk home with her at the end of the summer. Gary Shelley, Becky's long-term substitute, hadn't brought much with him, at least not much he cared to display on his desk. On his desktop were an open desk calendar, an NBA cup filled with mechanical pencils, a Barbie-sized wooden man, and framed photos of his two grown sons, one in a football uniform and one holding an electric guitar.

A few years older than she, Gary was likable and witty, wore cartoon character ties every day, was recently divorced, and spent his weekends studying for a master's in project management. As they were getting their room ready for the first day of school, Gary told her that this was his last year teaching. After twenty years in the classroom, he was ready for something new, which is why he didn't want a permanent teaching position this school year. She wondered if what he really wanted was to reinvent himself after his divorce, which he'd told Amanda was not his idea. She sensed a hunger for change in Gary that at odd moments of the day she envied. Amanda hadn't worked alongside a male teacher before, and she found his presence in the room a bit disarming. Neil never shared as much in an eight-hour period as Gary often had in the three weeks since school began.

She liked Gary as a person and he was easy to talk to, but she missed Becky's longstanding company. Especially today. It would've been nice to talk over her troubling weekend with a trusted friend before the first round of students came.

She let her eyes rove to the tree-shaped climbing structure in the corner that Neil had made. Pillowed niches for reading were hidden among the leafy boughs made from Bubble Wrap and green felt. The students called it the Sherwood Forest, though it was only one tree.

Neil had made it in one weekend a couple years ago, after she had described in the vaguest of terms what she had in mind. It was the envy of all the other teachers in her hallway. They said she was lucky to have such a talented husband.

She began to gently massage her temples.

Neil hadn't wanted to talk the night before about what happened with Chase at the picnic. Not when Chase was just in the other room, he'd said. She'd persisted.

"Neil, he was *talking* to the fire!" Her low whisper was riddled with tension. They stood on opposite sides of their king-size bed at a little after ten at night.

"How do you know he was talking to the fire?" Neil's muted voice was fringed in doubt.

"Because I saw him."

"Well, when you went over there, did you ask him? Did you ask him if he was talking to the fire?"

"Of course not."

"That's my point exactly." Neil had yanked off his Henley and tossed it toward the open laundry hamper. It landed half in and half out.

Amanda walked over to his side of the bed. "You didn't see it. You didn't see what I saw. He was standing at the grill, staring at the flames, and his lips were moving. It was like he was under a spell."

"But you said you talked to him a few seconds later and he seemed fine."

"Yes, but before that . . ."

"Before that he might have been practicing how to ask if he could take the car and go home. He didn't want to come to that picnic. None of his friends were there. But you insisted that he come."

"Please don't change the subject and make this about me. Yes, I wanted us to go as a family. Yes, I want to do more things as a family. But this is not about that. Neil, I think he remembers." Her voice broke.

Neil hesitated, breathed in slowly and then breathed out. "Remembers what? What could he possibly remember? He was four. What do you remember from when you were four? I don't remember anything from when I was that age. Nobody does."

"But traumatic events are different. I've read about this. A traumatic event can stay with a child."

"Then why would he just now act like he remembers? That fire happened thirteen years ago. Don't you think we would've picked up on it before now? That he would've clued us in? For God's sake, Amanda, don't open up something that you have no right to drag out of the past. We agreed a long time ago—we made a promise— that we wouldn't."

"But I'm not the one dragging it out. He is!"

"You don't know that."

"I saw him talking to the fire!"

"You saw him standing by a gas grill and his lips were moving."

She slumped down onto the bed. "You didn't see it."

Neil sat down beside her and gently put an arm around her shoulder. "Listen to me. Think about what you're saying. There's no way Chase could grow up remembering the fire. If he had, we would know. That child psychologist we saw back then told us what signs to look for, remember? Nightmares. Mood swings. Obstinate behavior. Remember?"

She remembered.

"Chase is a good kid on the brink of the rest of his life," Neil continued. "We have less than a year with him and then he's off to college. Do you really want to dredge this up right now when he's so close to leaving his childhood behind him?"

"I'm not the one dredging it up. He—"

"He deserves for you to back off. If there's something up with this, and I don't think there is, we're going to know. How could we not?"

"I just . . ."

"We promised we'd give him every chance to live his life like there never was a fire. We agreed that's what we'd do. He doesn't need to be confronted with what happened that day. Let it go for right now. It's the right thing to do. We'll wait and see what happens. If there's another thirteen-year stretch before the next momentary recall, then he'll be thirty the next time this happens. *If* it happens."

"Don't you think maybe we should ask somebody about it?"

"Like who?"

"Like Penny Ryder. The school psychologist at work. I could ask her."

Neil exhaled. "Go ahead, ask her. Tell her what you saw for ten seconds this afternoon and tell her what we've seen together over the past thirteen years. See what she says. But I want you to promise me—and I mean this, Amanda—I want you to promise me you'll say nothing to Chase about this and that you won't make an appointment for him to see someone about it. Don't do that to him. Not unless we're forced to."

Several seconds passed before she said okay.

He caressed her shoulder. "I just don't want to spoil things for him. He has his whole life ahead of him."

She nodded. And Neil rose from the bed, walked into their master bathroom, and began to floss his teeth.

Amanda sat forward at her desk, dropped her head in her hands, and rubbed her temples. What Neil had said made sense. But if Chase truly didn't have troubling memories of the fire, why had he stood glassy eyed at the grill, staring at the flames as if hypnotized by them?

She wished for the millionth time that she had been there that day, that she could've seen what Chase saw. Then she'd know. She'd know if what happened to him could've stayed with him and been smoldering there in his memory all this time. If it had been her turn to pick Chase up from the baby-sitter's that day, he wouldn't even have been there when the fire started. But she'd been eight months pregnant with Delcey and had a doctor's appointment that afternoon. She and Neil had traded. By the time she found out about the fire, it had already swallowed the baby-sitter's house.

A hand touched her lightly on the shoulder, and Amanda jumped in her seat. She pulled her hands away from her face.

"You okay?" Gary stood over her.

She smiled awkwardly. "I didn't hear you come in."

"I could tell."

"I'm . . . I'm fine. I just have a few things on my mind. That's all."

Gary set his Starbucks cup onto the desk opposite hers, sat down, and switched on his computer monitor. Today he wore Marvin the Martian on his tie. "How was the funeral? Everything go okay bringing your niece here?"

"Oh yes. Everything went fine."

"How is she?"

"What?"

"Your niece. How is she?"

"Okay, I guess. She's quiet, a nice kid, but kind of aloof. She doesn't want to be here."

"And no word from your brother yet, I take it?" He reached for his coffee and took a sip.

"No."

Gary nodded and set his cup down, laughing lightly. "I thought maybe she was already giving you a run for your money, the way you looked when I came in."

Amanda absently put a pencil back in its holder. "I kind of wish that's all it was."

"Oh?"

Amanda felt her face color. She hadn't planned on saying anything to Gary about what she saw at the church barbecue. "I don't . . . It's not something . . ."

"Hey, none of my business." Gary opened his briefcase and took out a lesson planner.

"No, it's all right. It's just . . . Neil and I . . . I'm worried about Chase, actually."

"He's your oldest?"

"Yes."

"You think he's in trouble?"

Amanda shook her head. "No. Nothing like that. Neil and I don't . . ." Her voice fell away.

"We don't have to talk about this, Amanda. I shouldn't have asked." Gary opened the lesson planner and withdrew a mechanical pencil from the NBA cup on his desk.

Amanda suddenly very much wanted his opinion. Gary could be objective, even more so than Becky could've been. He didn't know Chase or Neil. And he had raised two sons. He'd already shared that he had weathered a few rough times with his boys. He could tell her if she was making too much of the incident at the picnic and lose nothing by telling her.

"Actually," she said, "I think I'd like your opinion on this. You've raised two sons."

"Uh . . . okay. Sure."

"Neil thinks I'm blowing this out of proportion, but I don't think I am. I really don't."

Gary casually folded his arms across his chest. "Blowing what out of proportion?"

Amanda exhaled heavily. "Okay. First, no one else knows about what I'm going to tell you. It happened a long time ago when we lived in Orange County. And we just don't talk about it."

Gary's facial features softened with concern. His eyes encouraged her to go on.

"When Chase was four, our baby-sitter's son lit a cigarette in his upstairs bedroom. His room caught fire. The upstairs smoke alarm wasn't working and the fire spread. Chase was asleep with two other children in the master bedroom. He and one of the other kids managed to crawl out into the hall, and they were rescued. But there was a baby in a crib . . . Nobody could get to her."

Gary shook his head. "That's too bad."

"I know. It was terrible. Chase was taken to a hospital for smoke inhalation, and he was fine physically after they gave him oxygen. Neil got to him while he was still in the ER. I was pregnant with Delcey and at the doctor's office when all this was happening. By the time I got to the hospital, the doctors were ready to send Chase home."

"I'm glad he was okay."

"Oh my goodness, so were we. I felt so bad for the parents of that baby. Her name was Alyssa." She paused for a moment. Even after all these years, she still ached for the baby's parents.

Gary looked thoughtful. "So had the baby-sitter's kid left the cigarette burning in his room? I mean, if he was upstairs already, why didn't he save that little girl?"

"He told the police he was outside on the balcony with his cigarette—so his mother wouldn't smell it—when he noticed that his curtains were on fire and he couldn't get back in. Personally, I think he was lying. I think he fell asleep on his bed with that cigarette, his room caught fire, and he just got scared and hightailed it off his balcony. I think he wasn't thinking about anybody but himself."

"And where was the baby-sitter? How come she couldn't get to her?"

"Carol was out front with two older kids, talking with the woman who lived across the street. She told the police she had taken the older kids outside so the younger ones could rest, and that she just went across the street for a few minutes so the kids could see the kittens in the woman's garage. Carol's next-door neighbor was the first to notice smoke and flames pouring out of the upstairs windows. By the time Carol turned around, the whole upstairs was on fire. Carol told me later she had bought the new batteries for the smoke alarms. They were sitting right there on her kitchen counter."

"You wonder how she could forget to take care of something like that."

"I don't know. She was a nice person, never yelled, and Chase liked her. I liked her. She wasn't what I would've called irresponsible. She was devastated."

"No doubt."

"Afterward, Chase kept asking about the baby. He kept asking me where Alyssa was and telling us his clothes smelled like smoke. For days and days afterward. The neighbor who rescued him heard the baby crying. So the boys had to have heard her too."

"What did you tell him? About the baby."

Amanda shrugged. "What can you tell a four-year-old? We told him she was with Jesus."

"So sad."

"The thing is, a couple of months afterward, Chase just stopped talking about it. We thought it was a little strange, so we asked a child psychologist about it, and she told us kids that young have a different grasp of reality than adults do. She gave us a list of behaviors that would indicate Chase needed help processing what he'd been through. But he never exhibited any of those behaviors. It was like one day he just started living as if it had never happened."

"Well, he was pretty young."

"True. It was weird, though. After Delcey was born, he called her Alyssa a couple times, and each time he did, I didn't know what to say. But after a while he stopped."

Gary unfolded his arms from across his chest and reached for his cup. He took a sip and waited.

"Chase never mentioned the fire again." Amanda gazed at the warmly hued boughs of the tree Neil had made. "Not once. We moved here when Delcey was three months old, and Chase just never brought it up again. We were sure he had forgotten it. And we were okay with that because it was such a sad day. Neil and I didn't see any point in reminding him of what happened to Alyssa. He's always seemed a little cautious around fire . . . but no more than other kids I know. And like I said, he never mentioned the fire again, so we didn't either."

"I suppose I can understand that," Gary said vaguely.

Amanda turned back to face him. "Now I'm not so sure we were right."

"Right about what?"

She lowered her voice as if divulging a secret she didn't want the walls to hear. "This weekend at a church picnic, I saw Chase standing in front of a barbecue grill. Flames were shooting out. It was like he was in a trance. He looked like he was talking to the fire, like he was whispering to it. He had the oddest look on his face. I swear he was having a conversation with the fire. There was nothing normal or explainable about it."

Gary's brow puckered. "Does Chase know you saw him? Did you talk to him?"

"When I went over to him, he'd already started to walk away. I asked him a question and he seemed fine."

"You asked him a question?"

"I asked him if he knew where Tally was. It was a perfectly reasonable question to ask. And he gave me a perfectly reasonable answer."

Gary said nothing. He appeared deep in thought.

"I told Neil about it. I told him I thought perhaps Chase *does* remember the fire. But he thinks I'm jumping to conclusions, that there's a rational explanation for what I saw. He says we'd know if Chase had memories of the fire, especially disturbing ones."

Gary rubbed his neck. "Well, I suppose that's probably true. But why guess? Why don't you just ask Chase if he remembers it?"

"Neil doesn't want to. He says that if we drag this out now, we could unearth something that's best left buried. Neil doesn't want to mess with Chase's future by digging up a past he doesn't even remember. He made me promise I wouldn't say anything to Chase about it."

Gary leaned back in his chair. "To be honest, I can't think of a whole lot of things that are best left buried. Maybe you and Neil should go see a psychologist together and talk about what you should do . . . and maybe about what you should've done."

A wisp of regret spread across her face. "You think we should have asked Chase about it a long time ago."

He shrugged. "I just think if you had kept the line of communication open from the beginning, even when he stopped talking about it, you wouldn't be having this conversation with me. Chase would know he'd survived a fire where a baby died because he would've always known. And I don't get why you and Neil are afraid this would be too hard for him to handle. He's nearly an adult. Does he have emotional problems? Is he depressed? Is he deathly afraid of fire?"

Amanda was about to say no to all three questions when a thought slammed into her: Chase always closed his eyes when he blew out his birthday candles. Delcey—and every other kid she could think of—made a wish with eyes closed but would open them wide to blow out the candles.

Not Chase.

He always wished with his eyes open and then closed his eyes tight to snuff out the flames.

twelve

Chase and Tally stood in a swath of late after-noon sunlight as Neil backed the borrowed pickup into the driveway. Next to them, two solid-cherry bookcases glistened.

"Why is he giving these away?" Tally asked, touching the shelf nearest her and sliding an index finger across its smooth finish.

"Somebody at La Vista asked him to make them for a new library, so he did," Chase answered. "People are always asking him to make things and give them away. I don't really know why he does it." The truck stopped just in front of him. Chase moved forward to grasp the back of the truck and lower the tailgate.

"Maybe because it's a nice thing to do."

Chase glanced at the shelves. His father had carved vines and blossoms into the sides and edges, and the beveled wood shone under several coats of varnish. He said nothing.

Neil got out of the truck. "I forgot my cell phone." His father started for the front door and then turned. "Chase, there are some old blankets in that metal storage cabinet. You can pull those out and lay them on the truck bed. I'll be right back." Neil dashed inside the house.

Chase wordlessly walked to the cabinet on the far side of the garage and opened it. Tally followed him, and he handed her two army-issue blankets. He watched her gaze meander across the worktables, piles of lumber, saws, and sanders.

"Do you come in here sometimes and work on stuff too?" she asked.

Chase grabbed a third blanket and nudged the cabinet door closed. He tipped his head toward the workshop. "This is his thing, not mine. I make movies, and he makes furniture."

"You say it like you don't like what he does in here."

"You ask like you think I have to like it. He has his thing. I have mine. You don't see Delcey in here, do you?"

They walked back toward the open garage doors, and Tally nodded at Chase's car, parked inside the third stall. "How come you get to have the only parking place?" she said.

Chase tossed the blankets into the truck bed. "He hasn't asked for my spot yet."

They spread two of the blankets over the truck bed and were quiet for a moment. "Do you think those two men are still at this nursing home?" Tally asked. "The ones Matt thinks you should interview for that project?"

"Probably. I don't know. Josef's ninety-something. Eliasz, his roommate, is a few years younger. I haven't seen them since Easter. My mom sent me over there with cookies. *Easter* cookies. And Eliasz is Jewish."

Tally cocked her head. "But a cookie is a cookie."

Chase moved toward the first bookshelf. "Especially to a blind man."

"What?"

"Eliasz is blind."

"Did . . . did it happen at the concentration camp?" Tally asked.

"No. He was born that way."

"What *did* happen at the concentration camp?"

The door to the kitchen swung open and Neil stepped out.

"I've never actually asked him," Chase said, as his father walked over to them.

Neil motioned to the bookcase closest to Chase. "Okay. Let's get these loaded and go. I want to get them there before they start serving dinner and the halls get clogged with wheelchairs."

• • •

Chase had been to La Vista del Paz Assisted Care Facility twice before, starting when his father made a new podium for the dining room last year. A friend at church had told his father the facility needed some new furnishings and was having a fund-raiser to pay for them. His father had decided he would cross at least one thing off their list.

Chase met Josef and Eliasz the day he helped Neil deliver it. The two elderly men were sitting in the empty dining room with the newspaper's crossword puzzle between them when he and Neil rolled the new podium in. Josef was reading a clue to the puzzle aloud.

They looked like brothers. Silver white hair covered both their heads, elongated ears and noses disrupted their finely wrinkled faces, age spots polka dotted their sagging cheeks.

They smiled in unison, their thick Polish accents—even after decades in the United States—dovetailed, and they both wore cardigans in shades of blue. The eyes of the younger man were clouded and colorless. The other's eyes were clear and steel gray.

"Have you come to give a speech, then?" the sighted man had asked as they wheeled it in.

"Who is here, Josef? What are they doing?" The blind man's gaze followed the squeaking sounds of the hand truck's wheels.

"Looks like you have a new platform for lecturing the kitchen staff on how not to burn the bread, Eli."

"I smell new wood," the blind man said, craning back his neck and sniffing the air.

"I heard you needed a podium," Neil said. "I'm Neil Janvier, and this is my son, Chase."

"Very nice to meet you both. My name is Josef Bliss," the older of the two men said. "This is Eliasz Abramovicz."

His father said it was nice to meet them. Then he and Chase positioned the podium and released it from the hand truck.

"Did you build it yourself, Mr. Janvier?" Josef asked.

"Yes, I did. And please, you can just call me Neil."

The administrator came in at that point to thank them. Then she asked if Neil could step inside her office for a moment. Neil said he'd be right back.

"Very nice work," Josef said, sizing up the podium with his eyes. He turned to Eliasz. "Eli, what was the name of the furniture maker from Żyrardów that we met up with in the camp?"

"Jaworski. Does it look like something Jaworski would have made?"

"Yes. Yes, I think it does."

Chase found himself wanting to ask Josef what he meant. "Camp?"

Josef turned to look at Chase. "A concentration camp. Eliasz and I were at the same concentration camp. Outside Warsaw."

"Like a Nazi concentration camp?"

"Just like."

"So . . . so you're both Jewish."

"Eliasz is. I'm Catholic. You didn't have to be a Jew to be an enemy to Hitler." Josef smiled, but it was not an expression of amusement.

"How did . . . What did you do?" Chase asked.

"He made the Nazis angry," Eliasz spoke from beside Josef. "Josef didn't play by their rules in the ghetto."

"And you both survived a concentration camp?"

"Yes. Eliasz and I both escaped from Treblinka."

"Treblinka . . . ," Chase echoed.

"Yes. You know of it? It is in Poland."

"My great-grandfather died at Treblinka," Chase murmured, almost to himself.

"Almost a million people died there, son."

Neil and the administrator appeared at the entrance to the dining room, finishing their conversation as they walked back in. Neil looked at his watch and then motioned for Chase to come.

"I guess I have to go," Chase said.

"Well, you must come back and visit us sometime, Chase," Josef said. "Sounds like we have something to talk about."

Chase nodded but said nothing. As he walked away he heard Eliasz say surely it was time for tea and that the name Janvier sure didn't sound Jewish or Polish to him.

Chase came back only once after that—to bring Josef and Eliasz the Easter cookies. He had waited for Josef to bring up the concentration camp. But Josef did not. And neither did Chase.

A hall clock chimed five o'clock as Chase, Tally, and Neil stepped inside La Vista del Paz. Neil went to find the administrator, and Chase asked at the reception desk if Josef Bliss and Eliasz Abramovicz still lived there. She nodded.

"Tell my dad I'll be right back," he said to Tally, and he started down the B-wing corridor.

About halfway down the long hall, Josef sat in a wheelchair in a sunny alcove, reading a sports magazine.

"Chase!" Josef called out to him.

Chase stopped and stepped into the alcove.

"I thought that was you. Bringing more furniture today?" Josef asked.

"Bookcases. For the anniversary and the new library."

"Ah, yes. The anniversary. It's going to be quite the affair. Eliasz is resting up for it even now so he can dance the tango with all the nursing staff."

Chase nodded toward Josef's chair. "You've got a wheelchair now."

"It's what they punish you with when you fall too many times taking a pee."

"You all right?"

"This is just what happens when you hang

around too long, Chase." He patted the arms of the wheelchair.

The two were silent for a moment. Chase was suddenly hesitant to ask Josef if he and Eliasz would allow him to videotape them talking about the war. About Treblinka. The man might say no. Chase sensed a tiny part of himself hoped he would say no. He wasn't sure he really wanted to know what it had been like at the concentration camp. "Mr. Bliss . . ."

"Josef."

"Josef, I have a favor to ask. My friend and my cousin and I have a sociology project to do for school. We're thinking of making a video documentary and basing it on the Holocaust. We were . . . we were wondering if you and Eliasz would share with us what you went through during the war."

"So at last we will talk about this, eh, Chase?"

"What?"

"I was beginning to think you were never going to ask."

"I . . . I was waiting for *you* to bring it up."

"Why?"

Chase opened his mouth and then shut it. He didn't really know.

Josef tipped his head. "Come anytime. Bring your friends. Bring your camera. I have been waiting."

thirteen

"Okay, so here's how I see it." Matt lay on Chase's unmade bed with the one-page criteria for the sociology project lying across his lap. It was wrinkled and dog eared and stained with a splatter of Mountain Dew. "We can maybe open with some stills off the Internet. You know, pictures from concentration camps fading in and out, with our own commentary providing the prologue. Then we bring in pictures of Josef and Eliasz. And then we add their voices. And we can ask them questions, but not have it be part of the audio. Have it be a text image, white on black. We can add in stills of your great-grandfather as they're talking."

Chase leaned against his computer desk, arms folded across his chest. Tally sat on the floor by his feet, stroking the Janviers' snoozing cocker spaniel. He was about to tell Matt he had seen too many mediocre documentaries when Matt continued.

"Then we just let these guys go to town. I bet they can talk for hours about this stuff. So we just let them talk. We'll probably have a couple hours of footage for a fifteen-minute video, and the hardest part about the project will be trimming the content, not coming up with it. It will be a piece of cake."

Tally kept her eyes on the dog. "I really don't think this project will feel like it's a piece of cake."

"Okay. Bad word choice. But you know what I mean. It's not going to take hours and hours of our time. And I'm telling you, I've got two AP courses that are killing me. And a job and soccer practice. This will work out great."

"I don't want to use stills off the Internet," Chase said.

Matt sat up. "Why not? People do it all the time."

"I don't."

"Hey, even the History Channel uses other people's stuff."

"From museums and private collections maybe, but they don't go trawling the Internet for pictures."

"Chase . . . ," Matt began.

"Besides, that intro has been done to death. Old pictures fading in and out, dissolving to an old guy in a wheelchair, remembering."

Matt swung his legs around. "That's because it works. That intro works."

"I don't settle for what works; I want what makes an impression." Chase looked down at his cousin. Tally's hand still rested on the dog's back, but she was looking at him.

"I suppose you have a better idea for an intro?" Matt asked. "And no weird film-noir crap, either.

This thing has to have a point any ten-year-old would get."

"Of course I have a better idea."

"Let's hear it, then."

It had taken only a few moments of speculation to come up with an idea for the opening of their video. The idea came to him when he saw Tally looking longingly at the answering machine when they got home from school. She'd hoped it would be blinking. Without a word he knew she was hoping to hear from Bart. But there was no message.

"We open with nothing but violin, high and ethereal, like we're in somebody's dream," Chase began. "Then we fade to a man walking through a cemetery. We don't see the man's face, just his feet. We see him step through fallen leaves, and we see the trail he makes with his footsteps. He's looking for the headstone of his grandfather who died at Treblinka. He's been to many cemeteries. This is a man who's looking for truth. He wants to know the truth. His grandfather died behind a wall of oppression, and no one mourned. He wants to know the truth of what happened behind that wall, of what happened while everyone looked away and pretended there was no wall."

Chase looked down at his cousin. She was staring at him, mouth half open.

"That would be cool." Matt looked past Chase to a place in his mind. "That would actually be very cool . . . Oh. Hey, I get it. The man in the cemetery is your uncle Bart. Awesome. Yeah. That'd be awesome."

"No," Tally whispered, her eyes still on Chase.

Matt turned to look at her. "Yes, it would be awesome. Trust me. I know Gimble. He's going to love this."

Chase held his cousin's gaze. Something secretive hung there. "Why not?"

She shook her head, her eyes still locked with Chase's. "I don't want my dad brought into this."

"How come?" Matt asked. "It's the perfect setup."

Tally turned to look at Matt. "I don't want to make this about my dad. Let's keep it about the guys at the nursing home, okay?"

"It's about truth," Chase replied. "It's about what's true. Your dad is just one little part of it. You can't pretend he's not. His grandfather—our great-grandfather—died at the hands of the Nazis. That makes Uncle Bart part of it. Makes *us* part of it."

"If I'm part of it, then I want to make it an anonymous man who walks through the graveyard. We don't have to say it's my dad."

Chase just looked down on her, wordless. But Matt was quick to argue. "Yes, we do. It makes our project personal. It will stand out. We have to."

"No, we don't," Tally said. "There are probably tens of thousands of people like my dad who are looking or have looked for relatives who died during the war. An anonymous man can represent all of those people."

Matt shook his head. "No. I like it better that it's specific. This is what's going to set our project apart."

"But that's not why he's there!" Tally said angrily.

"Then what's he looking for?" Chase's tone was calm and measured.

Tally lifted her eyes to him. They were anxious, her eyes. He wondered again what secret she carried. He knew she wouldn't tell him.

"It has nothing to do with what happened in the concentration camp, okay?" she said.

"Then why's he there?" Matt's facial features were crossed with curiosity.

"He has his reasons." Tally resumed stroking the sleeping dog.

Matt hesitated a minute and then leaned toward her. "Is it illegal? Is that why you won't say?"

"Matt," Chase said.

"What? That would explain why he's missing."

"It's not illegal," Tally replied.

Matt turned to her again. "Hey, my uncle's a lawyer. And I'm not just talking an ambulance chaser. He's in international affairs. If your dad needs a lawyer . . ."

"I just told you it's not illegal!"

The dog awoke and lifted its head.

"Then why haven't you heard from him? What if he needs help?"

"Matt!" Chase raised his voice also.

"What?"

"Chill."

Matt raised his hands. "Fine. Just trying to help." He lay back on the bed and huffed. "A guy tries to be nice . . ."

"We can make the man in the intro anonymous, representative of everyone on the search for truth," Chase said evenly. "It's not going to make or break the project."

"Fine," Matt mumbled.

Tally looked up at Chase. She didn't smile or whisper a thank you. He half expected her to, but she didn't. Then she turned her head toward Matt, who was sprawled on the bed.

"He's not into anything illegal. This is just how my dad is, Matt. I'm used to it."

"Used to what?" Matt didn't look at her.

"Used to him not doing what everyone expects him to do. He's never done that."

Matt sat up halfway and spoke in a lighter tone. "He always does what people never expect?"

Chase saw a half smile on Tally's face materialize as she realized what she was saying. You could expect her dad to do the unexpected.

A knock sounded at his door, and his mother poked her head in. "Matt, would you like to stay for dinner? We're having manicotti. I know you like it."

Matt smiled. "Sure, Mrs. J. Thanks."

"Dinner in ten, then. You guys making headway?"

"Yeah," Chase said. "We've got a plan that will work."

"That's great." His mother smiled at him, her eyes lingering as if she wanted to say more. But then she turned to Tally.

"Tally, you want to come pour the milk?"

"Sure." Tally rose from the floor and followed his mother out of the room.

Matt flopped back down on the bed. "I'm telling you, dude. Your mom is Mother of the Year."

"Right. Mother of the Year." Chase turned around and started rifling through DVD cases on the shelf above his desk, looking for an unused one for their project.

"Hey," Matt continued. "Why do you think Tally won't say why her dad's in Europe? If it's not illegal, why won't she say? Think she doesn't know?"

Chase found a fresh DVD and began taking off the shrink-wrap. "No. She knows."

"You think?"

"I know."

"Why do you think he's there? It probably has nothing to do with your relatives, does it?"

He crumpled the shrink-wrap and tossed it into a trash can under his desk. The plastic immediately began to uncrumple itself. "No, that part is true, I think."

"So why's he there?"

"Why does anybody do anything?" Chase turned to his friend. "He wants something."

Later, just before ten, Tally came to his bedroom and leaned against the door frame as he powered down his computer. His mother was already in bed, Delcey was in the bathroom, and his dad was in his woodshop, where he'd been since dinner, sanding a rocking chair for the church nursery.

He looked up at her and waited.

"You already knew my dad's not in Poland researching the concentration camp, didn't you?" she asked.

"So? Anybody with a brain can see that. If he was just there to look up records in a museum, he wouldn't be missing."

"He's not missing."

"Nobody knows where is. Including you." Tally recoiled, and he wished he hadn't said the last two words. "Okay. Sorry. It's obvious your dad is looking for *something*. That's cool. I really don't care. And I don't care that *you* know what it is."

"It's nobody's business."

"I didn't ask." Chase closed his laptop and pushed it to the middle of his desk.

"He asked me not to say anything."

"Then don't."

Tally hesitated only a moment. Then she turned, went into Delcey's room, and closed the door.

fourteen

The concrete wall warmed Tally's back as she waited for Chase to get out of his last class. Around her, throngs of students laughed and chatted, either in groups or on their cell phones, on their way to parking lots and bus lines. They stepped around her, noting her presence without looking at her.

The third day at school was as unremarkable as the two before it. What she had hoped for was happening. She could be anonymous here. There were other brunette girls with magenta streaks in their hair who carried tattered backpacks and spoke in class only when necessary. She could actually blend in without any conscious effort.

There were probably a couple hundred girls like her at Chase's school: anonymous observers who earned average grades and flew below the radar. It would be very easy to leave here when her father came back.

She leaned her head against the wall and let the radiating heat massage the back of her head.

Sometimes when Amanda looked at her, she could tell her aunt was imagining what her life must be like with just Bart for a parent—and without a mother, since being a mother seemed to nearly define Amanda's existence.

There had been only a couple of times when

Tally thought perhaps a mother figure might enter her life. Both times it hadn't worked out that way. The first woman she could remember was when she was nine. Her father had taken a job as a doorman for a resort in Cape Cod, and the two of them lived in a cottage with three other hotel employees, including a woman who was the hotel's hairdresser. When she wasn't working, Connie would braid Tally's hair into cornrows or curl it into ringlets or tease it into a cone or dye it different shades. And whenever she fussed with Tally's hair, she'd tell her all the things she would do if she had a little girl like Tally. Tally remembered asking her dad if he was going marry Connie. After six months of Connie's affections, Tally had thought it was a pretty good idea.

Her father laughed and frowned at the same time. "You're a cutie, Tally-ho," he said. "But I can't marry Connie. She's already married. Besides, I don't love her."

Her father handed her a hot dog wrapped in a slice of Wonder bread—the menu for dinner that evening—and told her that Connie's husband had stolen money from his company and was doing time. Tally hadn't known what doing time meant, but she was more interested in why he didn't love Connie.

"It wouldn't make any sense to love a woman who's married to someone else, would it, Tally-ho? That's just asking for trouble."

Six months later Connie left the cottage to go live with her sister in Miami. Six months after that, her dad heard a new casino was opening in Reno and they were looking for blackjack dealers. Her father quit his job at the resort, bought a used car, and pointed it west. They never made it to Reno. The car broke down outside Tulsa, and by the time Bart had money to fix it, he had met some people who were opening a sports bar and grill and they wanted him to work there. They stayed in Oklahoma for two years until Bart met Mellanie, an underwear model from New York City who was in Tulsa for the wedding of her college roommate.

On the night of the rehearsal dinner, the wedding party came to the sports bar to unwind, and Mell and Bart fell into a conversation that lasted until dawn. After the wedding on Saturday, Mell came to their little apartment and invited Bart to come to Manhattan to be her bodyguard, valet, chauffeur, escort, and live-in assistant. Bart told her it sounded like a great job, but he couldn't come without Tally. Mell had winked at him and told him she only had a two-bedroom condo, but Tally was welcome to the guest room.

Tally had looked away. She knew what Mell meant. Even at twelve she knew Mell was asking Bart to share her bedroom. Her bed. She knew enough to be embarrassed by Mell's little wink.

After Mell left the bar, her dad made hot chocolate and asked her if she wanted to go live in New York.

"Do you?" she said.

"It might be fun for a while. Mell's got money."

"How long will we be there?"

Her dad shrugged. "You like Tulsa?"

"Not really."

"Want to see the streets of New York from the inside of a Jag?"

"Yeah."

"Then it seems to me it doesn't matter how long."

She'd sipped her hot chocolate and formed the next question in her mind as the hot sweetness stung her tongue. "Are you going to sleep with her?"

He hesitated only a moment. "You and I will be Mell's guests. We'll sleep in the guest room."

She never asked him about it again.

There were some nights during those six months in Manhattan when she'd wake up and the green-striped sofa across from her bed would be empty. She didn't know if her father was with Mell in her bedroom, and she really didn't want to know. Because, for the most part, the six months they lived with Mell in her high-rise off Fifth Avenue were enchanting. Mell bought her expensive clothes, enrolled her in a private school, let her try on all her fancy evening dresses, and sometimes brought Tally down to the studio to watch her work under a track of amber lighting with a dozen men standing around her while Mell wore nothing but a bra and panties.

Mell's attentions weren't motherly in nature, Tally could see that now. She had treated Tally like a favorite girlfriend's little sister. But at the time, she felt that the connection between them was maternal. Tally had grown fond of Mell and her spontaneous generosity and was nearly beginning to envision staying with Mell forever when she overheard her father tell Mell, after he'd consumed far too much of her expensive whiskey, that Virginia Kolander blamed him for Janet's death.

"Who's Janet?"

Tally picked up on the tentative tenor in Mell's sultry voice even from behind her closed door.

"Tally's mother! The woman I was going to marry!" The words were slurred but the tone unmistakable: Bart Bachmann was still in love with Janet Kolander, Tally's mother, dead twelve years.

It wasn't long after that evening that Mell announced she was moving to Paris and was not taking any of her New York staff.

Her father had enough money saved to buy two one-way tickets to Nashville, where friends of his "from way back" owned a horse ranch and offered him a job in the stables.

"Sometimes you gotta be the one with the shovel, Tally-ho," he said after his first day mucking, the airy elegance of a Manhattan condo far behind them.

She sat at a rickety two-seat kitchen table and watched him pull off boots caked with manure and straw. "I miss Mell," she said.

"You miss having everything handed to you. That's a dreamer's life. It ain't real. In the end, you have to make your own way. It's okay to have a little vacation from reality, but you can't live like you're on vacation."

"Why not?"

He set his boots down by the front door to their minuscule apartment. "Because you wouldn't be happy."

"Mell was happy."

He moved toward her and knelt so that his eyes were level with hers. "Two things you need to know, Tally-ho. First, that was *Mell's* life we were living. She'd made that life for herself, and we were just visiting. Second, Mell was not happy."

"She looked happy to me."

"Money has a way of doing that. Think about it, Tal. Don't you think it was kind of weird she asked us to come live with her after knowing me for just one day?"

"But you went."

He put his hands on her shoulders. "I thought it would be a nice break, Tal. And I wanted you to see what money can buy and what it can't. I don't have any regrets about going to New York, and I sure don't have any about leaving. Look how quick she let us go."

Even now, with her eyes closed and her back warm against a tower of concrete far from Tennessee, Tally still winced when she remembered Mell zipping out of her life as quickly as she'd zipped into it.

There hadn't been any mother figures to intrude upon her life after that. Bart had dated a few women since: the manager at Luigi's who let them sleep in the basement when they arrived in Dallas with no money the year she turned thirteen. The manicurist at an upscale salon in Houston who bailed Bart out of jail when he was arrested for driving with no license, no registration, no insurance, and outstanding traffic violations from years past. The flight attendant who took them to Switzerland for Christmas two years ago.

But no one Tally itched to think of as a mother.

Amanda was storybook maternal, everything she'd seen from a distance when she watched other mothers: gentle, kind, generous, insightful, and protective. And she didn't seem like one to claim half an inheritance that had been left to someone else. But her dad didn't want to trust his sister. He didn't want to trust anyone.

• • •

He had come home early from his job as a chauffeur the day he decided to drop everything and go
to Poland. Tally had come home from registering
for her junior year, and he was sitting at the little
built-in table in the double-wide trailer they were
renting. Open on the table was a little cardboard
box he'd kept in the trunk of his car for the past
two years. "Just some of my father's stuff," he'd
said of the box, which she knew contained the
silver lighter, a pocket watch, her great-grandmother's wedding ring, and a letter from his dad
that he'd never opened.

The letter lay open on the table.

"You're home early," she said.

He turned toward her, and his face looked weary
and energized at the same time. "I'm not working
for Mr. Charles anymore."

She leaned against the door frame, mentally
preparing for whatever he planned to tell her.
When her dad quit a job, there was always a new
plan. "Why not?"

"There are some things I just won't do, Tally-
ho."

A moment of silence hung between them as she
weighed the chances of staying in San Antonio.
"What happens now?" she finally said.

"I'm going to Poland." He picked up the letter
and waved it. "All this time I thought this was
either a lecture or an apology. I didn't want either

114

one. It's really the map to treasure, Tal. All the gold and jewelry my father hid in his backyard from the Nazis? I know where it is. It's all here in the letter."

She heard him, every word. But she still whispered, "What?"

"When he was just a kid, my dad hid the family's gold and jewelry before the Nazis came for them. He buried it in the backyard. My grandfather told him to."

"But . . ."

"It's probably still there. I'm going to go get it."

"But school starts next week . . ."

"I'm not taking you on this trip, Tal. You're going to stay a week or two with your grandmother in Tucson. It's all arranged. When I get back, we can live anywhere we want."

"But, Dad . . ."

"We can't stay in San Antonio, Tal."

In that moment she knew that whatever Mr. Charles asked her father to do, it was illegal. And now he knew too much. She let her body slide down the closed door until she rested against it on her bottom.

"Sorry, Tally. I really am. But we can't stay."

For a long moment, she said nothing.

"When are we leaving?" she finally said.

He stood. "Now would be a good time."

He let her sit there for a few moments before extending his hand to help her up. "You can pick the next place, Tal. Anywhere you want. You want to go back to Manhattan, we'll go. Anywhere you want. Except Texas."

"Why Grandma Virgie's?" She reached for his extended hand.

"Because she'll be so glad to see you, she won't ask questions. This is our little secret, Tally. My dad told no one about this except me. He told me it was my decision whether or not to do anything about it. Well, I want you to go to college and have a nice house to live in. So I'm doing something."

She watched him grab the wedding ring and pocket watch, knowing their first stop out of town would be a pawn shop. "How long will you be gone?"

"A week, ten days. Two weeks, tops." He shoved the ring and watch into his pants pocket. "I'll be back before you know it."

An hour later, San Antonio was in their rearview mirror.

That was more than three weeks ago. He had promised to call. He hadn't.

She hadn't read the letter. She didn't know where he was headed, just somewhere near Warsaw.

"Hey."

Tally's eyes snapped open. Chase was standing next to her.

116

"Were you actually asleep? I said your name twice. Come on. Let's go."

"I wasn't asleep. I was just . . . remembering." Tally stood slowly, moving as if she had in fact been sleeping and was suddenly wrenched from a dream.

fifteen

Amanda closed the door to Penny Ryder's office and began to walk the tiled corridor to her classroom. Her heels drummed a beat on the hard floor, punching the quiet air with a steady cadence. She liked the halls better when they were teeming with children, when her footfalls were indistinguishable from a thousand other sounds.

Her classroom was hushed and empty. Gary had already left, and she was slightly disappointed that he had not waited to see what Penny would advise. Amanda slid into her desk chair and looked at the business card Penny had handed her from across her desk moments earlier.

"This guy's really good with young adults," Penny said. "He's pretty young himself. Twenty-nine, I think. But a fabulous psychologist. I think his age makes a difference. Young people trust him."

Amanda slowly reached for the card. "I don't think Neil is ready to do this yet. Call anyone, I mean."

Penny nodded and then laced her fingers gently. "Here's the thing, Amanda. If Chase has no memory of the fire, or if it's safely tucked away in a far corner of his mind that he's never bumped up against in all these years, then just mentioning the fire isn't going to open a floodgate. On the other hand, if the memory is resting just below the surface and if it's strong and powerful and building in pressure, then releasing it now will indeed open a floodgate. But don't you see? Now's the time for that to happen. Not a couple years from now when he's away from home and trying to handle college life, and not a few years after that when he's entering the workforce or marrying someone or becoming someone's father. If you really think there might be emotions and fears that Chase hasn't dealt with, you owe it to him to get him some professional help now."

"But what if he really doesn't remember it?"

Penny unlaced her fingers as if releasing a wisp of air. "Then your bringing it up will have no negative consequences."

Amanda thanked Penny and told her she'd consider everything she said. She now studied the name on the card: Brandon Pinelli. She tapped the corner of it on her desk.

Chase had seemed fine the last few days. He'd politely taken Tally to school, offered to help her find her way, included her on the sociology project, put air in the tire like Neil had asked, immersed himself in his video projects, teased Delcey, offered a dose of sarcasm when the opportunity presented itself, left his clothes lying around, and spent most of his free time quietly engaged with his own priorities. It had been an unremarkable week.

Still. Those fifteen unexplainable seconds at the picnic gnawed at her. Penny said she and Neil should gently ask Chase directly if he remembered the fire. There would be no wondering about those fifteen seconds if they did.

But she'd already imagined that conversation. She'd already seen it played out in her mind with several scenarios—none of which put her at ease.

"Chase, do you remember the fire at the babysitter's house when you were four?"

"Fire? What fire? Why? What happened?"

What would she tell him then? Everything? *"Remember the flames? The smoke? Crawling out of the room where you'd been asleep? The screams of the baby no one could reach?"*

Or Chase might reply, *"The fire? Oh . . . oh yeah. The fire . . . No one came for me. I had to crawl out of a burning room. There was a baby . . . What happened to the baby?"*

Or, *"Of course I remember the fire. Don't you?"*

Then he'd ask why they'd never said anything until now. All those years and they'd never said a word. Why?

Amanda inhaled deeply and stroked the card in

her hand. *God, what am I supposed to do?* But the room was silent.

The beeping of her cell phone split the quiet. Delcey was texting her, reminding her that she needed to be picked up from dance team practice. Amanda picked up her book bag and walked out of her classroom, still holding the card in her hand, oblivious to the sound of her clicking heels.

Dinner was a subdued affair. Amanda made a lasagna toss, which apparently none of the family really cared for but was a quick fix on busy days. Delcey picked at it, Chase opted for salad and bread, and Neil ate his without comment. Only Tally ate what was given her without complaint.

Neil stood up as soon as he was finished and wiped his mouth with his napkin. "I've got to take the rocker over to the nursery tonight." He picked up his plate and began to take it into the kitchen.

"You want to go with him, Chase?" Amanda asked.

Chase looked up from his salad. Neil was already in the kitchen, putting his plate on the counter.

"Do you need help with it, hon?" Amanda called out to her husband.

"Chase can come if he wants," Neil said as he tossed his napkin into the trash. "You don't have to if you've got better things to do, Chase. I understand. It's just one chair. You decide."

"I've got a physics quiz tomorrow," Chase said, chasing a cherry tomato across his plate with his fork.

"Well, I don't blame you, then. That's more important. See you all later." Neil disappeared from view. The door to the garage opened and closed, and he was gone.

"Can I be finished?" Delcey's cell phone trilled. She pulled it out of her pocket and dashed into the family room for privacy.

Chase stood as well and wordlessly took his plate to the kitchen. He looked up at Tally as he placed his plate in the sink, and then he left the kitchen through the archway to the living room. Amanda heard his footsteps on the stairs.

She turned to Tally. "Guess it's just you and me with the dishes."

Her niece stood. "I don't care. I like doing dishes. Your plates are pretty. They all match."

Amanda smiled, lifted the pan of pasta, and stepped into the kitchen. She moved a dishtowel off the phone dock to set the pan down and saw a blinking light indicating a voice message. She hadn't noticed it earlier. She pressed the Play button, and a woman's recorded voice filled the room.

"Hello, Mrs. Janvier. This is Nancy Fuentes from Pima County Human Services in Tucson. Just checking in to see if you've heard from Tally's father. We haven't heard anything here, so if you could give me a call sometime tomorrow, that would be great."

The woman gave her phone number. The machine beeped and then fell silent. Amanda looked up at Tally. Her niece had stopped inches from the kitchen counter with two plates in her hands. She stared at the sink.

Amanda reached for the plates Tally held. "I'm sure your dad's just lost track of time. He's probably finding it harder to locate our relatives than he thought, you know? And he doesn't speak a lick of Polish."

Tally raised her head. A faint sheen of disappointment glistened in the girl's eyes.

Amanda wanted to pull her into her arms. Instead, she put the two plates in the sink and tried to think of something to reassure her niece that somehow everything would turn out okay. "Did your dad ever tell you about the time he and I got lost when we went camping?"

Tally blinked and shook her head.

Amanda walked back into the dining room, and Tally followed her. "We were camping in Yosemite. I was eight and he was twelve, and our parents let us go on a little hike on our own. They told us to stay on the trail, but of course Bart never liked to color inside the lines. He heard a waterfall off in the distance, and we walked off the trail so we could find it. It was a beautiful little waterfall, but as you can probably guess, when we turned around to go back, we couldn't find the trail."

Amanda handed Tally a bottle of salad dressing to put away.

"What happened?" the girl asked.

"Well, after about an hour of trying to find it, I started to cry. I was sure we'd never be found, that we'd freeze to death or starve or be mauled by bears. Bart told me to stop crying because he'd heard that wild animals can sense fear. And he said he was sick and tired of trying to find the trail so he was going to look for Indian arrowheads instead. So we started looking for arrowheads instead of the trail. And a couple of hours later, we found it. We found the trail when we weren't really looking for it. We met a search party on the way back, and I remember Bart got a talking-to for going off the trail. And our mother couldn't stop touching us, as if to reassure herself that we were actually there. We fell asleep in our sleeping bags that night with her hands on our backs."

Tally looked down at the dressing in her hands.

"Maybe your dad is just, you know, looking for arrowheads instead of the trail and he's lost track of time," Amanda said.

"I know what he's looking for," Tally muttered.

Amanda felt her pulse quicken. "You do?"

Tally nodded.

"Why don't you tell me what it is? Then maybe we could find him. We wouldn't have to wonder where he is or if he's all right."

123

Tally said nothing.

"Is he in trouble, Tally? Is that why you had to leave San Antonio in such a hurry?"

Nothing.

"He made you promise not to say anything, didn't he?"

"Yes."

Bart. She could strangle him. Putting his daughter through this for his own gain. He probably told Tally not to cry too, so no one could sense her fear. Amanda took a step toward her niece and laid a hand gently on her shoulder. "It's okay to break a promise if that's what it takes to help someone. If your dad needs help, we need to be able to give it to him."

"I . . . I don't think he needs help."

"How do you know he doesn't?"

Tally shrugged. "If he needed help, he would get it."

"Can you tell me why you left San Antonio?"

Again Tally lifted and lowered her shoulders. "Dad has never liked to stay in one place for very long."

"Was he in some kind of trouble in San Antonio, Tally? Are the police looking for him? You can tell me."

Her niece looked away for a moment. When she turned back, her eyes glittered with anger. "Why does everyone think my dad is in trouble? He's not a bad father. I know that's what everyone thinks. But he's not."

Amanda swallowed hard. "Of course he's not."

Tally blinked, unconvinced.

"I don't think he's a bad father. And I won't ask you again to break your promise. But if you want to tell me what your dad is looking for, I'm here. And if you think it will help us find him so we can tell him where you are, then I'm here. I'd like for him to know that you're safe."

Being reminded that Bart didn't know where she was seemed to tug hard at Tally. The girl sighed lightly. "I didn't read the letter."

Amanda had no idea what her niece was talking about. "What letter?"

"The letter from his dad."

Their father had been dead for two years. "From his dad? My dad?"

Tally nodded once. "You sent it to him when Grandpa died. With your grandma's wedding ring and the other stuff. *That* letter."

In her mind, Amanda saw herself taking the little box her father had asked her to send to Bart to the post office. Her brother got nothing else from their father's estate, not that there was much to be shared. Still, it rankled Amanda that their father had left his entire estate to her and a little cardboard box to Bart. Perhaps in the few strained conversations her brother and father had over the last twenty years, Bart had made it clear he didn't want anything from their father's estate. She could quite easily imagine Bart saying something like that. The box was sealed when her father gave it to her the week before he died. She had no idea what had been in it.

"What did the letter say?" Amanda said, barely above a whisper.

"I just told you I didn't read it. But it's because of that letter that he went. He told me he was going to Warsaw. He didn't say where besides that."

"But why?"

"You said you wouldn't." Tally picked up more dishes and headed toward the kitchen.

"I wouldn't what?" Amanda followed her.

"Ask me again to break my promise." Tally set the dishes on the counter.

"I'm just trying to do right by you, Tally. I don't have to know why he's there. But it matters that we don't know where he is. It matters that he doesn't know where *you* are." Amanda put an arm around the girl and gently pulled her into the crook of her arm. "I don't want you to break a promise. Or get hurt. By anyone."

Her niece stood still within the one-armed embrace for only a second. A moment later, Tally pulled away.

sixteen

A nurse's assistant wearing maroon scrubs positioned Eliasz's wheelchair in front of the tripod.

Chase looked up at her. "Actually, you can turn the chair to face my cousin. She'll be asking the questions, and I'll film it from a slight angle. It will look a little more natural that way."

"Yes, don't make me unnatural," Eliasz quipped, his words etched with Eastern European inflection.

"But don't make him look better than me or I'll never hear the end of it," Josef said.

"Could we bring in a couple of those wingback chairs from the lobby?" Tally asked tentatively. "If that's okay, I mean. I think it would be nice if Mr. Bliss and Mr. Abramovicz could sit in, you know, regular chairs."

"Yes, yes, regular and natural, that's for me," Eliasz said, and Josef laughed.

"It's not a pretty picture when we're unnatural and irregular," Josef said.

The nurse's assistant said she thought that would be all right. Matt left to get the chairs.

Chase glanced over at Tally. "That'll look nice," he said, and she nodded.

Several minutes later, the two men were seated in rose-hued wingback chairs. Afternoon sun

127

shimmered on their downy heads from a side window. A grand piano far off in the unfocused background made a peaceful backdrop. Chase positioned a potted palm slightly behind Eliasz's chair.

"Just moving a plant behind you, Mr. Abramovicz," Chase said.

"Yes," the man said. "I smell it."

When everything was in place, Matt spoke first. "Um, okay, well, thanks for letting us talk with you guys. We really appreciate it."

"It was a feat, fitting this into our busy schedules, wasn't it, Josef?" Eliasz said.

Josef nodded. "Indeed. You picked a good day to come. Thursday would've been impossible."

The two men laughed.

"Lucky us, then." Matt turned to Chase. "Are we rolling?"

Chase nodded.

"Okay, so Tally here has a list of questions, and she'll ask them and . . ."

Josef held up a hand. "Pardon the intrusion, but how about if we just tell you our story, and then perhaps when we are finished, you will decide if you have questions? Yes?" He turned to Chase.

"I think that's a good idea," Chase said.

Josef turned his attention back to Matt. "How much do you want to know?"

"We need twenty minutes of footage," Matt replied.

"We need to know what impact the Holocaust—and in particular, the Warsaw Ghetto—had on history," Chase said, adjusting the lens and avoiding Matt's pointed stare.

Josef smiled. "You need two different things."

"Uh, we need to turn in a topnotch project in less than three weeks," Matt said.

"Why don't we just let them start talking and see where it takes us?" Tally laid the page of questions gently in her lap.

"I'm cool with that." Chase made another adjustment on the camera.

Matt pressed his lips into a thin line. "Okay."

"Where should we start, Eliasz?" Josef said, turning to his friend.

"The ghetto begins before there was a ghetto," Eliasz an-swered. "It begins here." He pointed to his head. "It begins with one mind, one idea, one man. Wouldn't you say, Josef?"

"Indeed. I met my friend Eliasz here a month before the Germans invaded Poland. It was early August 1939. He was fourteen. I was twenty-two. He seemed very young to me then. Here I was, an important government employee in charge of so much, and he just the young son of the Jewish family who owned a bakery on my street. I had just moved to Warsaw from Lódz when I got my new job. I was second in charge of the water-works. It was an important job. My parents, they wanted me to become a priest, but I was in love with a beautiful girl named Katrine, so there would be no priesthood for me. Katrine was a nurse."

Josef stopped for a moment. Chase zoomed in on the man's withered hands. Josef was spinning a gold wedding band on his ring finger.

"Would you like to hear how we met?" the old man said.

Matt hesitated. Tally quickly said yes, and Chase brought the focus back to the old man's face.

"I met Katrine several months before the Nazis invaded. She had lost a lovely butterfly pin that I found in a park near the hospital where she worked. It was a different kind of pin; I had never seen one like it. It was made of gold, I suppose, and it was an open-winged butterfly with a tiny chain affixed to it so that a second, smaller butterfly could be pinned above it or below it, wherever Katrine wanted. There were a few small sapphires and tiny pearls too. I don't think it was worth a fortune or anything, but it was distinctive. I found it in the grass under a bench. It seemed to me that whoever lost it would want it back. I found out later it had belonged to Katrine's late grandmother, and it was exceptionally special to her.

"I came back to the park every afternoon for two weeks, asking if anyone had lost a pin. I liked the park; I didn't mind doing it. One afternoon I approached two nurses who were strolling the park on a lunch break. One of them was Katrine, the other was named Sofia. Sofia was half Jewish. They were roommates. When I asked if either of them had lost a pin in the park, you can imagine how Katrine's face lit up. When I took it out of my pocket, she began to cry. She wanted to give me a reward for returning it to her, but I didn't want a reward. I wanted to take her out for coffee. She was so pretty and kind. She said yes, albeit a little hesitantly. That cup of coffee turned into a three-hour conversation, and I knew right away I wanted to marry her. I bought the engagement ring many weeks before I actually asked her. It was a lovely ring. An emerald, almond shaped, with two little diamonds on either side. She loved it. Those were the most magical days of my life, even though all around us was the threat of invasion. Magical."

Josef closed his eyes, and Chase zeroed in on a glistening line under the old man's closed lids.

"That's a beautiful story," Tally said.

Josef took his time opening his eyes. "Yes. But not what you came to hear. No?"

"Were you married to Katrine when you went to Treblinka?" Matt asked.

"No. No, I was not. But we are getting ahead of ourselves." He continued, "Now, when I moved to Warsaw, I didn't know anyone. I took an apartment across the street from Eliasz's parents' bakery. In the predawn hours the aroma nearly drove me wild. Eliasz's mother and father, they were very good bakers. I would go into their shop almost every day. Eliasz amazed me because he could make such beautiful loaves of bread, even though he could not see. You've never seen more beautiful challah than what Eliasz could make."

Eliasz smiled. "I told him, it is all in the wrist!"

Josef smiled. "Eliasz's family was very good to me. Invited me to their home to eat. Went out of their way to welcome me. They were very kind. But you know what happened in September, yes? The Germans invaded Poland in the west. And the Soviets to the east. The weak Polish army was powerless to stop either one. Within three weeks, there was no more Polish army. There was no more Poland. People tried to leave the country, and they could not. There was no gas. Cars, they were left all over the roads. People just abandoned them when they ran out of gas, left them there with their suitcases still strapped to the top. They walked away with whatever they could carry. But it did not matter. There was no escape. We belonged to Germany. To Germany and to the Soviets. Everything changed. Katrine's family left for Vienna, where they had relatives, before the invasion. Katrine stayed because I stayed. I should have insisted she leave with them. It is my lifelong regret that I did not."

Again Chase saw Josef spinning the wedding

band on his finger. He was quiet for several seconds. Then he went on.

"By October, I could see the Germans had awful plans for Polish Jews. Eliasz and his family, and all the other Jews in Warsaw, were told they had to wear the armbands with the yellow star. We non-Jews were told to stop buying anything from Jewish shops. Things got very bad as the months went on. Jews could no longer have their own bank accounts. Some had their property seized. They weren't allowed to buy food or medicine from non-Jewish shops. I tried to help Eliasz and his family, but it was very difficult. Risky. They lost the bakery. Then in 1940, the ghetto was born."

"What exactly was the ghetto?" Matt asked, leaning forward in his chair. Chase realized he was too.

"The Nazis sectioned off a small portion of the city, moved all the Poles out, and built a wall around it," Josef answered. "The wall was three and a half meters high and topped with pieces of broken glass and barbed wire. And they crammed the Warsaw Jews inside. Half a million Jews stuffed into sixteen city blocks. How many people lived in your apartment, Eliasz?"

"Five families lived with us in an apartment built for one family," Eliasz said. "The Nazis would come every day to take us to work, and if you could not work, you could not get food stamps, and without food you were as good as dead. We pretended I could see. My father, brother, and I worked at a quarry. As long as I could stand next to my father and dig where he dug, I could work. Sometimes a transport would come and take many away to go to labor camps. But we learned later they were taken away to be killed.

"But the ghetto itself was also a place of death. Every month, four or five thousand people would die from illness or starvation. Every mother who had a baby looked for a way to smuggle her little one to the outside. The mothers knew if their babies stayed with them, they would die. I had a baby sister in the ghetto. We did not know how to get Marya out. There were guards at the gate and strict rules about who could come out. So we prayed for a way. And then, one day, who should come into the ghetto to inspect our waterworks, but Josef."

Josef nodded. "I came into this apartment building with another inspector, and I recognized Eliasz and his mother, Raiza, but I told his mother with my eyes not to let on that she knew me. I knew I could not help them if the other man knew of my sympathies. Raiza, she squeezed Eliasz's arm tight so that when he heard my voice, he would not say anything. I told them I had to see their bathroom to look at the pipes. I wrote a message on the wall behind the commode with my pencil. I asked them how I could help them. I left my pencil there so Raiza could tell me. The next day I told my superiors there were many problems with the waterworks in the ghetto and that I had to go back. The other inspector didn't want to come, which didn't surprise me. I told him many times to be careful what he touched because of typhus and cholera. I knew if I could make him afraid to come, I could come back alone. So when I came back to the apartment, I asked again to see the pipes in the bathroom. Eliasz took me upstairs, and I could see that my message had been rubbed away. He knelt down and pulled me down with him. And with his hand he took my hand and lifted a brick from the wall. Underneath the brick was a written message, and in the spot where the brick was, my pencil. The message was this: *Please take Marya out of the ghetto.* I whispered to Eliasz, 'How?'"

"I put one hand on his mouth and the other on his tool bag," Eliasz said. "And I rubbed the tool bag gently so he would know he had to smuggle my sister out in his bag. I mimicked taking medicine and closing my eyes so he would know we would have drugs to make Marya sleep. We could not risk her crying in the bag when he left the ghetto."

"I understood then why my message had been washed away and why the new message and the pencil were hidden," Josef continued. "We could

135

not trust any of the other people in the apartment. We didn't know if any of them would turn me in. Everything had a price in the ghetto. Everything. So very loudly I said the pipes were in terrible shape and that I had to come back and fix them. I said I would come in two days. At ten in the morning. This is because many in the apartment would be on work details then.

"I wrote a message to Raiza that she must comment to the other people in the building that Marya was running a fever and that she was worried about her. And that after I take her, she must pretend that she has gone to seek medical help for the baby. And that when she returns without the baby, she must weep as if the child has died. I knew it wouldn't be hard for Raiza to weep when she came home without her.

"I put the brick back and leaned in to Eliasz and whispered, 'Where shall I take her?' I thought they had friends on the outside who were ready to take her. I thought all they needed was a way to get Marya out. So I said, 'Where shall I take her?' And do you remember what you whispered to me, Eliasz?"

Eliasz nodded. " 'Wherever God directs.' "

"They had no plan," Josef continued. "They were desperate. And I was the only link to the outside that they had. I saw Katrine that night, and my heart was troubled with how I was going to find a safe place for Marya. Katrine asked me

136

what was wrong, and I didn't want to tell her. I knew what had to be done was risky. But she pressed me and I told her, all the time wishing I wasn't saying a word. Her heart was too tender. The moment I told her everything, she said I was meant to share this with her, but I didn't understand. 'Come with me,' she said. We went back to her apartment, where Sofia was eating her supper. I had of course met Sofia many times after the day in the park. But when we went inside the apartment, Katrine bent down and whispered something to Sofia. Sofia's eyes got very big, and she turned to look at me. For a moment I thought she was angry with us. I learned that night that Sofia was involved in a smuggling ring to get babies out of the ghetto. It was incredibly dangerous work. Katrine had inadvertently learned of this sometime earlier and had sworn to keep it a secret. So Sofia was angry at first, but later not so much. And I will tell you why in a moment.

"That night Sofia agreed to help me. She was surprised and relieved to hear that we already had a plan to use my tool bag and sleeping powders. Her friends used similar tricks. We arranged a meeting place. Sofia told me she would take care of the rest. I asked her who would be taking Marya, and she told me it was better if I didn't know, but that the child would be safe. So that is what we did. Eliasz got sleeping powders from one of the many Jewish doctors in the ghetto. Just before ten o'clock two days later, Raiza gave the powders to Marya and I came with my tool bag full of potatoes. The sack of potatoes I gave to Raiza. She wrapped the sack in a blanket and held the bundle to her chest like it was her baby. Her eyes were shimmering with tears, but she refused to let them fall. I placed her sleeping child in my bag and zipped it shut.

"Then I reprimanded her loudly for causing so much trouble with the pipes, and I laid my hand on her cheek and whispered that her child would be safe. I left in a hurry. I didn't want to keep looking at her face.

"I went to the meeting place: the basement of a butcher shop several blocks away from my own neighborhood. Sofia was waiting for me. I handed Sofia the child, still fast asleep, and I heaved a sigh of relief and thanked her. And she looked up at me, and I could tell she was taken aback by the finality in my voice. 'Josef,' she said to me. 'There are hundreds of other infants in the ghetto who are doomed to die.'

" 'How many times do you think we can do this?' I was still trying to understand what she was asking of me. And Sofia said, 'How many times will you be able to let a baby die that you could have saved?' I knew the answer was zero. Zero. I knew God had arranged for me to meet Eliasz and his family *before* the ghetto so we could save these children.

"The next day I went back to the ghetto and left a note behind the commode in Eliasz's apartment, asking him if he and his family would help me get more infants out of the ghetto. It was never my plan to involve Katrine in any of the other rescues. I told Eliasz we needed more doctors willing to part with their sleeping powders. And would he find them for me?"

"We said yes, of course," Eliasz said.

"And did you find more doctors to help you?" Tally's voice next to Chase was soft and hopeful. She, too, had leaned forward in her chair.

"Oh yes. There were many doctors confined to the ghetto. Dozens," Eliasz said. "Maybe ten alone in the building where I lived."

Chase watched Tally nod and sit back. A question seemed to be poised on her lips, but she did not ask it.

Josef turned to Eliasz. "How many babies did we sneak out of the ghetto, Eliasz? Twenty-two?"

"Twenty-five."

Josef nodded. "Twenty-five. Twenty-five babies we saved."

Chase sensed a strange sensation in his chest as he pictured Josef whisking away infants from the clasp of death, over and over again. He pulled away from the camera as if he'd been nudged. Only Tally seemed to notice. He rubbed his chest gently and gradually leaned back toward the camera, pretending it was nothing but a stray hiccup that had jarred him. He had no idea why the image of the rescued infants pulled at him. Out of the corner of his eye, he saw Tally turn her head back toward the two men.

"Wow," Matt said. "Twenty-five. So did the war end then? Is that when you stopped?"

Josef smiled and shook his head. "No. That's not when we stopped. We stopped when we got caught."

"You were caught?" Tally said.

Josef nodded. "We were all sent to Treblinka, which they called a labor camp."

"It was a death camp," Eliasz murmured. "Chase, surely you know this, since your great-grandfather died there."

"And what happened to the smuggling operation?" Chase heard his own voice asking the question, though it seemed to spring from a place deep within him.

Josef hesitated a moment. "Our ring inside the ghetto was shut down. We were all caught. But you should know others still smuggled the little ones out after we were arrested."

"How many others?" the voice within Chase asked.

"How's that?" Josef asked.

"How many other babies were saved?"

Josef shrugged his sagging shoulders. "Why, hundreds."

seventeen

Tally stepped out into the blustery brilliance of a searing September afternoon with Chase and Matt just behind her. The cars in the parking lot at La Vista del Paz shone under the roiling heat of a Santa Ana wind. When they arrived at Chase's car, he opened the doors to let the oppressive heat escape into the kicking gusts.

"We're going to have to come back." Matt ran a hand through his dark hair as the warm air played with it. "They didn't even talk about the impact of the ghetto on history yet."

"Well, maybe that's for us to come up with." Chase opened the trunk and laid the folded tripod inside.

"What?"

"I think we're supposed to interpret their story into a takeaway that has sociological value. Gimble's not going to give us an A for sitting on our butts listening to two old men talk about hell on earth."

Matt frowned. "So you're saying we don't have to come back?"

"No. We have to come back. We need to come back for the rest of their story. But we can't expect them to tell us what their experience means to our generation. We're going to have to come up with that ourselves." He laid his camera bag up against the spare tire, cushioning it with an old blanket.

"I guess." Matt leaned against the car. "So . . . what does it mean?"

Chase shut the trunk and turned to Tally. "What do you think it means, Tally?" His tone was slightly sarcastic, but a quick look at Matt let her know he missed it completely.

A gust of wind skipped around them. "I don't think you can stand around in a parking lot ten minutes after talking to survivors of the Holocaust and just decide what it means," she said.

Matt looked at his watch and pulled his body away from the car. "Well, I've got to get to soccer practice. You two deep thinkers can meditate on this. Me, I think it means there's a ton of people in the world who are full of crap. And a ton of people who think people full of crap are brilliant. How else did the Nazis get away with what they did? C'mon. I've got to go. Tally, you can have the front. I have to get out before you."

Matt slipped into the backseat, and Chase and Tally took the front. The roar of the air conditioner on full and their contemplative thoughts kept the four-mile drive to the soccer field a quiet one.

"We can go again on Wednesday afternoon, but that's the only day next week I can go." Matt pulled himself out of the backseat and grabbed his gym bag when they arrived at the soccer field.

"Right. See ya," Chase replied.

"Bye, Tally."

"Bye."

Matt jogged away from the car and Chase pulled away. In the side mirror Tally watched Matt greet another player as they headed to the men's restroom to change.

When they were back on the open road, Chase turned to her. "Why'd you ask Eliasz if they found other doctors in the ghetto willing to help them?"

Tally returned his gaze. "Don't you know?"

Chase turned back to the road. "You wonder if our great-grandfather was one of them."

"Why not? He could've been. He was a doctor. He was relocated to the ghetto."

Chase tapped the steering wheel. "Yeah. So? Maybe he was."

"I think it was incredibly brave what Josef and Eliasz did. I'd like to know if my great-grandfather was a part of that. Wouldn't you? I saw how you reacted to the number of babies they smuggled out."

Chase drew back as if she had misread him.

"You pulled away from the camera when they said how many children they had saved," Tally continued. "I saw it on your face. You were moved by what they did. When Josef told us they had to stop when they were sent to the concentration camp, you asked what happened to the smuggling ring. You didn't ask about them."

"So?"

Tally stared at him. "So there's nothing wrong

with that. I thought it was cool that you wanted to know what happened to the rest of the babies in the ghetto. I don't see why you don't want to admit that."

"Admit what?" His tone was dry, like the hot wind outside the car.

She stared at him. "What is with you?"

Her cousin looked at the road, wordless. Tally turned back in her seat and faced the passenger-side window.

"I don't know why," Chase mumbled a few seconds later.

"Why what?" Tally mumbled back.

"I don't know why hearing how they saved those kids affected me that way."

Tally swung her head back around. "You act like it's silly to be impressed by what they did."

Chase exhaled and shook his head. "No, that's not what I mean."

"What, then?"

He was quiet for a moment, his eyes on the road but unfocused. "Something felt strange inside me when Josef was talking to us, when he started telling us how he saved that first baby girl. Something . . . fell away." He was talking to her, but his voice and concentration were elsewhere.

"What do you mean?"

"Something became clearer. Something that's been hard to see . . ."

Chase was making no sense. He stared at the road

ahead, but he didn't seem to be seeing anything but some distant revelation visible only to him.

"I don't know what you're talking about." Tally turned her head to look at the traffic ahead of them. "The light's turning red."

"What?"

"The light!"

Chase slammed on the brakes, and the car squealed to a stop just past the limit line. A turning car honked at them.

"Sorry," Chase muttered.

Tally cocked her head. "What's going on?"

Chase drummed his fingers on the steering wheel. "I think I'm starting to remember things."

A tiny sliver of unease rippled through her. Chase's voice sounded strange. "What things?"

Chase said nothing. A few seconds later the light turned green. "You want to get something to drink?"

"Now?"

"Yeah. There's a smoothie place up ahead."

"All right."

A moment later they pulled into the parking lot of a strip mall. Chase parked in front of a smoothie shop with purple-and-white-striped awnings and table umbrellas.

"I'll be right back. Get a table outside." Chase got out of the car and disappeared inside the shop. Tally chose a table with a wide umbrella, its fringe wildly applauding the unseen wind.

A few minutes later Chase reappeared with two frosty crimson drinks. He handed one to her. "Cherry mango."

"Thanks." Tally guided the straw into her mouth and drank. The smoothie was sweet and tangy. "It's good."

Chase eased into the chair opposite hers. "Yeah."

Above them the umbrella trembled as a gust lifted it. He took a sip of his drink and then toyed with the straw.

"You gonna tell me why we stopped here?" Tally asked.

Chase took another drink, swallowing slowly. "I want to tell you something I've never told anyone," he said. "I'm expecting you to keep this a secret because you've got one yourself."

Tally waited.

He looked up at her. "This stays between us."

"Okay."

Chase nodded once, as if to reassure himself she could be trusted. "When I was four, my baby-sitter's house caught fire. I don't remember everything about that day, but I do remember some things. Like the sound the fire made when it was burning the room I was in. It . . . it roared like an animal." He looked away and was silent for several seconds.

"I remember other things too," he continued. "They're more like still images, like movie frames. I've never been able to remember everything about the fire, not even the fire itself. And that's always bothered me. It's like my brain has kept it all hidden away somewhere, just out of reach. And the fire, it's like it's still alive somehow and it still wants me. Like it knows I got away."

Tally could think of no words in response. She said nothing.

Chase drew the drink close to him and sipped it, taking a long pull on the straw. He closed his eyes as he swallowed. Then he looked up at her. "I know that sounds a little crazy. That's why I've never told anyone. My parents think I don't remember the fire at all. They never talk about it."

"How did it happen?"

"The baby-sitter's son sneaked a cigarette into his room. I was upstairs in the room next to his, napping. At least that's what I remember. And I think there was another little boy with me. When our room caught fire, I waited for someone to come for me, and when no one did, I crawled out on my hands and knees. The other kid followed me. I remember how the smoke burned my throat."

"Why didn't anyone come?"

"Oh, someone eventually did. I don't remember who. Some lady whose face I can't recall now. There's so much I can't remember." He took another drink and then went on. "But lately, things are shaking up inside my head. I think I'm starting to remember. Like when I saw your dad's lighter.

147

The baby-sitter's son had a lighter just like that. I hadn't remembered that until I saw yours in the laundry room the day you got here. And when Josef described how he rescued those kids, something snapped inside me—or opened. I don't know exactly. It's like the memories are just an inch beyond my reach."

Tally was thoughtful for a moment. "Well, maybe it's because *you* were rescued," she said. "Maybe that's why hearing Josef talk about saving the babies affected you like that."

"Maybe." Chase pulled his straw up and down in his cup. It made a whiny sound. "I used to be so nervous around fire," he continued, his eyes on the movement of the liquid in his cup. "I never said anything to anybody, but I used to hate being around any kind of fire, even candles. But lately, I feel like I want to take it on. It's like it's all coming to a head. After all these years. It's like I'm ready to prove I'm the stronger one."

Tally studied the drops of condensation on her cup. "How do you prove something like that?"

Chase shrugged.

"Are you afraid to remember it all?" she said.

Her cousin hesitated a moment. "Sometimes. And then sometimes I just want the release. I just want to open the closet and finally see what's inside, you know?"

Several seconds of silence ticked by.

"What are you going to do?" Tally asked.

"I'm not sure. It's like everything about that day is finally leaking out, but I'm just not in charge of how fast it comes."

"Don't you want to tell your parents?"

Chase lifted his head to look at her. "What would I tell them? Seriously. They think I don't remember it."

"You could tell them you do remember it."

"What good would that do? They weren't even there. I'm the only one who can tell me what happened that day."

"That doesn't mean it wouldn't do any good to tell them."

Chase pulled his straw out and watched a scarlet drop fall onto the lid of his cup. "I think they prefer to pretend it never happened."

Tally crinkled her forehead in thought. She'd been watching Amanda and Neil the last week, studying the family dynamics of the visibly stable, two-parent home. It was her first experience living the life she knew most people thought of as wonderfully normal. The Janvier home felt . . . constant. Chase couldn't possibly be right.

"I think you're wrong," she said. "I think your parents would want to know that you remember. They . . . they seem like good parents."

Chase smiled and stood. He was ready to go. "That's the thing, Tally. Good parents don't like to be reminded of the times they couldn't protect their children."

eighteen

If she closed her eyes, Amanda could imagine she stood in a forest of conifers where a pristine mountain stream ribboned its way parallel to a woodland path. And the air all around her, thin and sweet, hung like delicate, unseen lace. A carpet of spent needles under her feet whispered that the forest was always renewing itself. Fingers of a saffron sun between the piney boughs reminded her that above the treetops, there is more.

She breathed in the heady aroma of wood and sap and leaned against the garage wall, imagining it to be a sturdy trunk and letting the fragrance of possibilities fill her lungs.

The wheeze of a cutting tool blurred the dream, and she opened her eyes. Neil leaned over his worktable as he shaped the yielding wood into usefulness. The tool whined into silence, and Neil blew out his breath on the length of carved wood in his hands. A burst of tiny shavings settled onto the table. He smoothed the etched wood, stroked it tenderly, then brought the board close to his face and scrutinized the grain. He gave it another loving rub with his thumb and another gentle blow to dispel the last remnants of that which was not needed.

Neil didn't seem to mind her watching him

working in his woodshop, but it was hard to be sure. She didn't do it often, and when she did, he seemed to stiffen just a bit, as if she'd overheard one of his prayers. The only person Neil had ever officially invited to join him in the woodshop was Chase, and that was several years ago. Amanda still winced when she remembered how Neil pretended he was fine with Chase's disinterest.

"He can't help what he's wired to enjoy, Amanda," Neil said, after Chase declined for the third time in a year to take up woodworking. "He's not into this."

Chase, fifteen the last time Neil approached him about it, had just bought his first video-editing software program. Amanda knew how excited Chase was to get the software, and she also knew how Neil longed for his son to show interest in his love affair with wood. But the timing of Neil's final invitation couldn't have been more off. She ached for them both that day. It was obvious to her that Chase took no pleasure in telling his dad no. Her husband put away the set of woodworking tools he'd bought for Chase, and then commenced work on a new project— alone. Sometimes Amanda ran into that second set of tools when she looked for seasonal decorations or canning jars. They were still in their original packaging, price tags still affixed.

Neil looked over at her now with just an upward turn of his neck. He said nothing, but she could read him. If there was something she wanted to say, she should just say it.

"It smells sweet in here," she said.

He lowered his head, eyes back on the length of wood in his hand. "Cedar." A slight smile rested on his lips.

"Is that for a bookcase?" She nodded toward the carved board in his hands.

"A chest. The Loughlins want to give Hannah a cedar chest for her birthday."

She knew in an instant Neil had offered to make Hannah the chest at no cost. The girl had leukemia. Their friends Dick and Julie Loughlin probably hadn't even mentioned to Neil they wanted to give their terminally sick daughter a cedar chest—a place in which to put hopes. Neil found out about it somehow and asked if he could make it for her.

Most of the time she loved that about Neil. "That's really sweet of you," she said. "I'm sure it will be lovely."

"Hope so."

"The Loughlins have already been through so much. Kind of puts our little troubles in perspective, doesn't it?" she murmured.

"What troubles are those?" He set the carved piece down and reached for a plain board about the same size.

Amanda frowned. "Well, wondering how long we're going to have Tally with us, not knowing where my brother is, and this thing with Chase."

Neil lifted his head to look at her. "Chase seems fine to me, and I thought you liked having Tally here."

She moved toward him. "I do like having Tally here, but she misses Bart. It would be nice to know that he's okay. And . . . and I'm not convinced Chase is fine."

Neil picked up a pencil and began jotting down some figures on a scrap of paper. "With your brother, no news is usually good news. As long as we hear nothing, I'm of the mind that Bart is fine and he's just being Bart. The best thing that can happen is that he just shows up here in a week or two. If he calls us from a Polish jail, on the other hand, what are we really going to be able to do for him?"

She waited for him to mention Chase.

"And Chase?" she said, when he did not.

"I already told you what I think about that. I've watched him this week. He seems fine." Neil put the pencil down and reached for a tape measure.

Amanda watched him pull out the tape, hold it close to a plank of honey red cedar, and make a mark with the pencil. He let go of the tape, and it darted like a snake back inside its metal cocoon.

"I talked to Penny Ryder at the school," she said.

Neil looked up at her, expressionless.

"You said I could," she said.

"I remember what I said. What did she tell you?" His voice was controlled, calm.

153

"She said that if Chase has repressed memories of the fire, we owe it to him to help him deal with them now while he's still at home."

Neil made another notation on the paper. "But did you ask her how we would know that he has repressed memories? What symptoms he would show? Did she think it was possible that thirteen years could go by with no indication he's got memories he hasn't dealt with and then—*bam!*—one day at a church barbecue he starts talking to a gas grill?"

"Neil."

"I'm just telling it like it is, Amanda. For his sake. Have you thought about how he'll feel if he gets the impression you think he's crazy?"

Amanda bristled. "I never said I thought he was crazy!"

"And I didn't say you did. I said, have you thought about how he'll feel if he gets the *impression* you think he's crazy. What's he going to assume if you say to him, 'Hey, Chase, I saw you talking to a fire and I just want to make sure you're not losing it'?"

Amanda opened her mouth and then closed it. She had no answer for Neil on that point. She already imagined the look Chase might have if she was completely wrong about all of this.

But what if she wasn't wrong? "Penny said that if Chase has no disturbing memories of the fire, then just asking him if he remembers it won't be his undoing," Amanda said. "If we ask him and he says no, there's no harm done."

Neil put the pencil down. "And if he says he doesn't and he wants to know what happened, what are you going to tell him?"

Amanda looked down at the carved piece of wood for Hannah Loughlin's cedar chest. "The truth." She raised her head to look at her husband.

"The truth."

"Yes."

"All of it? That he could have died? That a baby did die?" Neil's voice faltered, and he looked away from her.

Amanda raised a hand to touch the bridge of her nose as she counted several seconds to stave off a rush of emotion. Behind her closed eyes she could see Alyssa's parents racked with grief at their baby daughter's funeral. She could see the skeleton of the burned house when they drove by it on the way home. She could see Chase in his bed that same night, telling her his pajamas smelled like smoke and waking her later because he heard baby Alyssa crying.

"Amanda, think about it." Neil's voice wasn't much more than a whisper.

She pulled her hand away from her face. It was wet. The tears had started to come anyway. "But it's the truth," she said. "What is it we think we're protecting him from?"

Neil leaned forward on the worktable, resting

the weight of his torso on his arms and crushing the tiny wood shavings under his palms. "He doesn't need to know what happened if he doesn't remember it." He delivered each word with measured force.

"What if he does remember it?" Amanda's voice rose in pitch and volume. It surprised her.

Neil snapped his head up. "If Chase remembered it, we'd know!"

"How? How would we know?"

"Because he wouldn't be able to hide it!" A rare and softly delivered curse fell from Neil's lips, and a vein began to twitch in his neck. Amanda stared at him. In that moment she knew Neil was keeping something from her. Something he knew about the fire. Something she did *not* know . . .

For a moment there were no words between them, and all she could hear were her own words from a moment earlier: *But it's the truth.*

"Neil." Her voice sounded fragile. "What is it?"

Her husband's arms were still stretched out on the edge of his worktable. His chest rose and fell several times before he spoke. "Don't." He did not look at her.

"Don't what? What is it? What do you know?" Amanda sought his gaze, and he turned his face from her.

She reached out for him. "Neil, what do you know?"

For a second there was nothing but silence. Then

he swung around. "It's not what I know; it's what I don't know. Can't you just leave it alone?"

A thin strand of fear worked its way into her chest. "What don't you know? Tell me!" Both arms were on him now.

Neil was silent.

"If it's about Chase, I deserve to know," she said. "I'm his mother."

When he turned his head to look at her, his eyes were rimmed with glassy wetness. "Keith said—"

Her heart thudded in her chest. Keith was the baby-sitter's son. The boy who lit a cigarette in his room. "Keith? What did Keith say? Tell me!"

Again Neil turned his head away. When he opened his mouth, his voice sounded weary. "Keith told the police Chase wandered into his room and saw the lighter before the fire started, that Chase had it in his hands when he came into his bedroom after using the toilet. Keith said he took the lighter away from Chase and told him to go back to his mother's bedroom where he was supposed to be sleeping. Then Keith went out on his balcony to smoke the cigarette. He said he left the lighter on his bed and that he had his back to the sliding door while he smoked, that he didn't turn around until he smelled smoke. He said when he turned around, his room was on fire."

Neil fell silent.

"What are you saying?" she said in a strangely even tone.

Neil turned his head toward her but didn't look at her. "I'm not saying anything."

"You think Chase started the fire? You think Chase killed that baby? Is that what you think?" Heat roiled about inside her, and she felt her chest begin to heave with too much oxygen.

"Stop it, Amanda."

"You think Chase killed that baby?"

"Amanda."

"Keith was lying. He'd say anything. How could you even *think* what you're thinking?"

Neil pivoted. "You're thinking it right now. You are. Listen to the way you're talking to me, and tell me you're not picturing it right now." Neil's voice broke and his face contorted into a mask of pain. "He was only four! He was too young to know what he was doing, and you know it. If that idiot of a boy left his lighter on his bed in a house full of little kids, he most certainly did kill that baby. But you can't tell me you know for certain Chase didn't start that fire. We weren't there."

"No," Amanda whimpered, gazing at nothing. "No. That's impossible. Keith was lying. The police, they would've . . . Surely they didn't . . ." Her voice fell away.

"That's right. They didn't believe Keith."

Amanda snapped her head up. "But you do? You believe him?"

"No! I don't! I don't want to think Keith was telling the truth. But this is not about what I think.

158

This is not about what any of us think. This is about what really happened. You keep telling me, 'What if he remembers? What if we're wrong?' I ask you the same question. What if *we're* wrong, Amanda? What if Keith was telling the truth after all?"

Amanda closed her eyes and forced herself to see the baby-sitter's son carelessly leaving a burning cigarette on his bed, like she'd always imagined he'd done.

"Chase didn't start that fire." She opened her eyes when the image was firmly planted.

Neil stared at her for several seconds. "Still want to ask Chase about it?"

When she said nothing, Neil turned back toward his worktable.

She stood there, unable to answer him.

"Just leave it be." Neil picked up the carved piece for the cedar chest and ran his fingertips across the indentations, caressing the tiny dips and curves.

Amanda turned from him, the richness of the cedar now too pungent for her lungs. She left the garage with the question hanging between them, and jealous of the wood's ability to extract from Neil such intimate consolation.

nineteen

A spill of moonlight fell across Chase's bed-spread, peeking through the plantation shutters. The blue glow of his open laptop provided the only other light in the room.

Chase sat on the floor, knees bent, staring at the stripes of moonlight that fell across his bed like a white picket fence. One hand toyed absently with the frayed edges of a hole in his jeans.

He'd caught Tally looking at him that day, staring at him and then turning abruptly away when she saw that he'd noticed—in the car on the way to school, at lunch while Matt lamented the span of years in between each World Cup soccer championship, and at the dinner table.

He shouldn't have told her anything. But it had felt good to finally tell someone . . . Regret over saying anything at all battled against the relief that talking about the fire had given him.

He was fairly certain he could trust Tally. She had secrets too. And Tally didn't seem to be like the other girls he knew—totally into themselves, into one another, and into guys fawning over them like addicts. She wasn't an older version of Delcey. Tally seemed different. Perhaps it was because she was his cousin and they shared the same blood. Or maybe it was because she was the daughter of Uncle Bart, a man he'd secretly admired for years because legend had it he never took crap from anybody. Or maybe it was because they shared a common desire to keep something secret that would change everything if exposed.

She probably wouldn't tell his parents. But confiding in her had changed her opinion of him. And that bothered him.

Chase moved forward on his knees and reached under his bed. He pushed away video cords, an outdated issue of *Movie-Maker* magazine, and an empty box of Ritz crackers. He felt for an aluminum case blazoned with a graphic of shiny U.S. state quarters. His fingers felt the cool metal, and he withdrew the box, placing it on a wobbly stripe of hushed lunar radiance. He spun the dials on the combination lock. The box opened, revealing not rows of uncirculated state quarters but an assortment of Bic lighters, matchbooks from classy restaurants and sports bars, and a thin stack of two-dollar bills.

Chase eased Tally's antique lighter out of the case and fingered the shiny finish, the etched swirls and flourishes. It was cool to the touch. He placed his thumb on the striking mechanism and kept it there for several seconds. Then in one deft movement, he ran his thumb across the mechanism. In a clicking instant the flame appeared, bowed, and then craned its little head as if to see who had set it free. It seemed to wave. *What have you been up to?*

There was a lighter like Tally's on that day. Silver, like this. Hinged cover, just like this.

He remembered it was Keith, the baby-sitter's son, who had a cigarette in his bedroom, Keith who had a lighter like this one. Chase didn't remember the bedroom catching fire, but he remembered the stink of burning fabric and walls. The audible applause of the flames.

But he could not remember the shape of that fire; he could not remember what it looked like.

The one he did remember was the one he breathed life into two years later in the field behind his house using a thin yellow lighter he'd found in the dirt. But the moment he gave the second fire life, it tried to run away. Tried to hurt him.

Chase had given a name to the fire that wanted loose, that echo of the fire that turned the baby-sitter's house to ashes: *Ghost*.

To his immense relief, he was able to corner Ghost with a garden hose before it clawed its way to his backyard fence and before anyone even knew about it. Afterward, he tried to pretend— year after year—that it didn't exist.

But lately, even before he found the matchbook on the trolley, Chase had begun to imagine how he might master Ghost for good. Silence it, once and for all, and send it back to oblivion. And when he saw Tally's lighter, which was so much like Keith's, the desire intensified.

Chase turned the lighter in his hand, surveying the little flame from every angle. Keith's lighter wasn't exactly like this one. But close. Very close. There had been swirls and flourishes. Tiny etchings. And the striking mechanism made the same popping noise when the fire obeyed the summons to appear.

He closed his eyes, probing the folds of his mind.

Keith had showed him the lighter the day of the fire. No, Keith got after him for touching it.

Keith.

Red hair. No. Not red. More like copper brown. Green T-shirt. Keith came into his bedroom, and behind him was the sound of a toilet finishing a flush cycle. Keith saw him and frowned.

"Hey! What are you doing with that?"

Remember.

"That's not for little kids. Go back to your room. You're not supposed to be in here."

Again, he closed his eyes.

He saw a blue bedspread. No, a floor mat. He had been lying on a blue floor mat.

There were two blue floor mats. And a crib.

The other little boy had blond hair and a striped shirt. And a smudge of reddish orange, probably lunch, on the collar.

Keith had the lighter in his hands now. He stood by his bed, and the door was cracked open. He flicked at the top, and a happy orange flame danced out of the silver lighter. Keith had a cigarette in his mouth. He turned his head to light it. The lighter clicked shut, and the flame skittered away.

There was a break in the memory, and then there was smoke. And the roar of a beast.

No air, no air.

Mommy! Daddy!

Hot.

Someone is crying.

No air.

The carpet is hot. His eyes are stinging. Someone is crying.

Mommy!

Daddy!

A knock at his door startled him, and the lighter fell from Chase's hand. His eyes flew open.

"Chase?"

Tally.

"Can I use your computer? Delcey's using the one downstairs."

Her voice sounded tiny and airy from behind the closed door. A rush of pressure filled his ears.

He grabbed the lighter as the door opened, and a flood of amber light from the hallway spilled into the room. Tally stood framed in the doorway. Her mouth was open.

"I . . . I didn't think you were in here," she said, stumbling over her words. "You didn't answer, and there was no light on."

"I'm busy," Chase said, but the words came out in a whisper. He wasn't sure if she'd heard him.

"Why are you sitting in the dark?"

She was in the room now, staring at him. He was aware that his upper lip was prickled with sweat.

"Are you okay? Do you want me to get your mom?" she said quickly.

"No!" he croaked and started to scramble to his feet. He dropped the lighter, and it landed with a quiet thud on his carpet. For a second both of them just stared at it.

Then Tally knelt down and picked it up. "What are you doing with this?" Her voice was laced with suspicion.

"Nothing," Chase said hastily.

She turned the lighter over in her hands. He could tell she was thinking. But what was she thinking? Of going to his parents?

"I thought holding it would help me remember. And I was right. The baby-sitter's son did have a lighter like this one. He caught me looking at it before he kicked me out of his room."

Tally looked from the lighter to him to the lighter again. She said nothing.

Chase sat heavily upon his bed. He had to convince her to let him have it back. The lighter was like a key to his past, a past that was lost to him and was finally being returned. He couldn't let her have it back. Not yet.

"I remember the room I was in, the other little

kid, what he wore," Chase continued. "I remember the baby-sitter's son lighting the cigarette that started the fire. I remember not being able to breathe. The heat. Someone grabbing me. It's all coming back."

Tally's eyes were on the lighter. "I think you should tell your parents."

The lighter shone in her hands. He would have to make a deal with her if he was going to get it back. He stood, closed his bedroom door, and came back to the bed and sat down. "I think I should wait on that. If I tell them now while everything is still sketchy, it will only make them worry. Worry won't help me. And it won't help them. But I promise I will tell them. When the time is right, I promise I'll tell them."

"But what if your parents could fill in the blanks for you? Then you wouldn't have to guess and you wouldn't have to use this." She lifted the lighter.

"If filling in the blanks was something they wanted to do, they would've done it a long time ago. I think the fire haunts them like it haunts me, but in a different way. They want to forget. I want to remember. If I can just go to them later and tell them, 'Hey, I just want you to know that I'm cool with what happened when I was four; I remember it, but I'm cool with it,' I'll get my wish and they'll get theirs."

Tally walked over to the bed and sat down beside him. Moonlight splashed them both. "But what if you can't remember it all? What if it just stops?"

"I'll cross that bridge when I get to it."

Tally was silent beside him for a moment. "Why can't you just be glad you didn't die? Why do you need to remember?"

The specter of Ghost swirled about him. Chase could smell the ash, the cinders, the fragrance of power—even as he sat in the cool shadows of his moonlit room. "Because it's like the fire remembers me."

Several seconds of dead air hung suspended between them.

"That doesn't make any sense," Tally finally said.

"I don't expect it to make sense to anybody else but me."

Tally appeared unconvinced.

"Every time I remember something new, I feel it lessening its hold on me," Chase said.

"What parts don't you remember?"

Chase envisioned the blue mats. Keith. The lighter. The blond-haired boy. Then smoke. Heat. The deafening blast of power. Fear. "Everything in the middle," he said. "The fire itself."

Tally was silent. When she opened her mouth, she extended the lighter toward him. "I can't let you keep it forever," she said. "When my dad comes, I'll need it back."

Chase felt a twinge of bliss race through him as

he reached for the lighter. "I don't want to keep it." His fingers closed around the smooth metal. "I actually can't wait to give it back to you."

Tally nodded and then stood.

"Still want to use my computer?" he asked.

She walked to the door. "I'll see if Delcey is finished. You shouldn't sit here in the dark. It's creepy."

"You can turn on the light."

Tally flipped on the light switch as she opened the door. She turned back to him. "Don't lose it. My dad would be ticked."

"I won't."

She hesitated a moment longer and then left, shutting the door softly behind her.

He waited until her footfalls down the hall and stairway were no longer audible. Then he turned the lighter in his hands, opened it, and placed his thumb on the striking mechanism.

A tiny flare jumped to attention and began to flicker in a slow swaying motion.

Chase.

Chase.

Chase.

The flame appeared needy. Hungry for affirmation.

Chase frowned.

twenty

Her aunt sat at the dining room table with a long-stemmed wine glass sparkling under the pewter chandelier. A small box of old photos lay open on the table, and a handful of the pictures were spread out over the polished wood. Amanda took a sip from the glass, set it down, and sighed quietly.

Tally had come to the dining room to speak to Amanda, but she didn't know how to break the silence in the room. It seemed a holy moment somehow. She cleared her throat.

Amanda drew back. "Tally. I didn't hear you come in. You startled me."

"Sorry. I just wanted you to know we're going back to the nursing home tomorrow. We're going to drop Chase's car off at home first. Matt's taking us this time."

"Oh. Of course. I'm glad that's going well . . . At least it seems like it's going well. Is it?"

Tally took a step forward and nodded. "I guess. They're interesting guys. Eliasz is blind. He's the Jewish one. Josef is Catholic. Did Chase tell you they smuggled babies out of the Warsaw Ghetto?"

"Actually, no. But I didn't ask much about how your first day went. I try not to hover. I've heard teenagers hate that. So, Chase is doing okay with it? The project, I mean. The filming is going okay?"

The strange conversation Tally had with Chase had occurred less than twenty-four hours earlier. She had no idea what to tell Amanda about Chase's ability to handle school projects at the moment. "I guess so. It's not like Matt and I can help him much with the filming or editing."

"Oh. Right."

Tally looked at the spread of old pictures on the table. The images were colorless. Men and women in dark wool. Stoic, unsmiling faces. Children in buttoned-up suits and loafers. Hair cut short. "Are these from Poland?" she said.

Amanda nodded. "I was hoping there would be information written on the backs of these pictures letting us know where in Warsaw Bart was headed. But my grandmother wasn't a very good record keeper. Half of these don't have anything written on them at all. I don't even know who some of these people are. It's like she didn't want us to know."

Tally studied the men in several sepia-toned photos. One was of a tall man with a handlebar mustache and trimmed beard, wearing a white doctor's coat. He was staring off into space as if gazing into the future instead of posing for a photographer. "Is that my great-grandfather?" she said.

Amanda nodded. "That's Aron Bachmann. It was taken six months before the Germans invaded. I suppose it was the last photo taken of him."

"Are there any here of my great-grandmother?"

"There's one of her standing outside the hospital where she worked. It's in here somewhere. I think it was taken before she was married. And there's this one." Amanda handed her an eight-by-ten photo of a woman in a tea-length creamy white dress, holding a nosegay of teacup roses. Brown curls framed her expressionless face. "I think that was taken the day she remarried here in the States," Amanda said. "I wonder if the majority of the family photos were lost in the ghetto when she and my dad escaped. My grandmother wasn't a very sentimental person, as I remember. I was always kind of afraid of her. I think the war did things to her. Like it does to all people."

"What was her name?"

"Marta."

"How did she and Grandpa get out of the ghetto?" Tally asked.

Amanda shook her head. "She never talked about it. And my dad must've remembered bits and pieces of what happened, but he never wanted to talk about it either. He was six when the Germans invaded and almost twelve when World War II ended. So he must've had a few memories of the ghetto. But he never wanted to talk about it. Ever. I had to respect that."

"What was he like?"

Amanda patted the chair next to her. "So my brother never talked about him much?"

Tally sat down. "No. He never talked bad about him or anything. He told me once he and his dad saw everything differently. Like if my dad saw something blue, Grandpa would say it was red. Like that."

Her aunt fingered a photo of a little boy in short pants and a jacket standing by a fainting couch. She handed it to Tally. "That's him. That's my father, Edward. Looks like he was four or five then."

Amanda took another sip from her wine glass and then set it down. "My dad was older than all my friends' fathers; he'd been married before. He was like Neil in some ways, and not like him at all in others. But I don't know that he and Bart had anything in common except determination."

Tally waited.

"My dad—your grandfather—didn't like surprises, and Bart, well, he was always full of them," Amanda continued. "Our mother, who is kind of a fragile person, couldn't really handle the two of them and their differences. They argued a lot about everything. Things at our house actually improved when Bart left. For a little while, anyway." Amanda turned quickly to face Tally. "I don't mean for that to sound unkind. It's just the way it was."

Tally nodded.

"But I missed Bart, very much," her aunt continued. "Things got quiet, but they also got boring.

My parents had kind of a funny marriage. My dad and his first wife were married seven years and never had any children. And I'm not sure what happened there because he never wanted to talk about that either, but I think he brought some baggage from his first marriage into his second. And then there was the war, of course. He had that lurking in his past at every step. I was actually as happy as Bart was to finally be on my own, but I didn't make the same kind of break he did.

"After my parents divorced, my mother only waited ten months before marrying again. She's living in Australia, you know."

"My dad told me," Tally said.

Amanda studied her for a moment. "Did . . . did your dad ever say anything about Grandpa not giving him any share in his estate?"

"His estate?"

"His will. Grandpa didn't leave anything to Bart in the will. I actually tried to give part of my inheritance to your dad, but he said he didn't want it."

Tally had never heard her father mention a will or an estate.

"It wasn't a whole lot, Tally. I want you to know that. After taxes and the cost of the funeral, there wasn't a whole lot left."

"Okay." Tally didn't understand what her aunt was getting at.

"And of course I don't know what was in the box Dad had me send to Bart."

"The box?"

"With the letter. You said there was a letter in the box that I sent after Dad died." Amanda took a sip of her wine, peering at Tally over the rim of her glass.

Tally didn't know how much her dad wanted kept secret. The contents of the letter, certainly. He asked her not to divulge that. But he'd never mentioned the rest of it. It didn't seem to matter much now. The pocket watch and wedding ring were long gone.

Amanda put the glass down. "I'm not trying to get you to tell me what was in the letter, Tally. I swear it. But if there was anything else in that box that would let us know where Bart is, maybe we should talk about it."

"There was just the letter, your grandmother's wedding ring, a pocket watch, and a cigarette lighter."

Amanda blinked at her. "That's it?"

Tally nodded.

Amanda traced her finger on the stem of her wine glass. A long pause followed. Tally was about to stand up and walk away when her aunt spoke. "So many secrets," Amanda murmured.

"What?"

"We keep so many secrets. And we pretend they're all for the best."

Her aunt seemed to be talking to herself. Tally didn't know if she was expected to respond.

"My grandmother had her secrets. My father had his. You have yours. And I . . ." Amanda's voice drifted away. She wrapped her fingers around the stem and brought the glass to her mouth. When she set the glass down again, she turned to Tally. "What do they really accomplish, anyway? I mean, think about it. What secret did anyone any real good? Can you think of one?"

"I promised," Tally said softly.

"I'm not asking you to tell me your secret. I'm just asking you what good comes from keeping one."

Tally pursed her brows together, wondering if her aunt truly expected her to give her an answer. She could think of one time when a secret did a great deal of good. "Sometimes you can save someone," Tally said.

Amanda blinked at her. "What do you mean?"

"Josef and Eliasz smuggled twenty-five babies out of the ghetto. Those babies probably would've died if they hadn't gotten them out. There was no food, no medicine. Josef told us a hundred thousand people died there."

"Babies . . . ," Amanda echoed.

"Yes. Twenty-five babies. But they had to do it in secret. And when their secret got out, they got sent to the concentration camp. They could've saved more if their secret had stayed safe. But someone told on them."

"So it was a good secret," Amanda said softly.

"Well, yeah."

"I wish I knew if he was okay," Amanda said, after another long pause.

Tally assumed she meant Bart, but her aunt's tone seemed vague.

"You're not worried, though, are you?" Amanda continued. "You wonder but you don't worry."

Tally said nothing. Her father told her once that worrying about something that hadn't happened yet and probably wouldn't was stupid.

The two women sat in silence. Amanda picked up a picture of a dark-haired woman in a long white dress and ran her finger along the edge. "I don't know who this is."

When Tally said nothing, Amanda went on. "You know, I met your mother once," Amanda said languidly. "She and your dad were in Los Angeles to see a friend of theirs or something. Neil and I lived in Orange County then. My parents drove down from Simi Valley." Amanda turned her head toward Tally. "She was pregnant with you. You could just barely tell."

There weren't many people who'd ever met her mother—that she knew of, anyway—so there hadn't been many times in her life when she'd been able to ask what she was like. She would've eventually asked her grandmother if she'd had more time with her.

"Did you like her?" Tally said.

Amanda nodded. "Your mother was so . . . so

176

beautiful. Stunning, really. But not like a model or a movie star. In fact, I didn't think she was beautiful when I first met her. Her eyes and the shape of her mouth were kind of hard . . . I don't know how to describe it. But the more I looked at Janet, the more I realized how striking she was. And Bart was over the moon in love with her."

"Did she love him?"

Amanda shook her head gently. "I really don't know. I don't think she was ready to meet any of us. It was Bart's idea, I think, to come see us. And after we were all together in the same room, even he seemed to wish he'd never told me they were in town . . . He and my dad. You know. They couldn't have a conversation without arguing. Janet and I didn't talk much. I wanted to get to know her better, but she just wasn't a talkative person. Well, not to me, anyway."

Tally closed her eyes, wanting to drink in the image of her mother shaking Amanda's hand, saying, "Nice to meet you," and Amanda holding Chase, who would've been just a baby then.

When she opened them, her aunt was looking at her. "I can see her in your eyes, Tally. But there's more Bart in you than anything else. And my dad too, actually. I can see my dad in you."

Another set of silent seconds ticked by.

Tally reached for the photo of her great-grandfather. "May I borrow this photograph? I'd like to show it to Josef."

Amanda looked down at the photo of Aron Bachmann. "How come?"

"Because Josef and Eliasz told us there were many Jewish doctors in the ghetto helping them smuggle the children out. They gave up their sleeping powders and pretended that the babies who came to see them had died."

Amanda tipped her head. "And you wonder if Aron Bachmann was one of those doctors."

"He could've been."

Amanda again glanced at the picture in Tally's hand. "I suppose he could have. It would be something if they knew him, huh? You'll ask them?"

Tally nodded.

"Take it." Her aunt scooped up the photos scattered on the table and dropped them back in the box. "Let me know what they say."

Amanda rose from her chair, put the lid on the box, and set it on top of the buffet table behind her. "Well, I've papers to grade," she said. She pushed in her chair. As she left the dining room, Amanda asked Tally if she would like a nice cup of hot cocoa.

twenty-one

Amanda leaned against the railing of the indoor tree house Neil had made, looking up at the nine-year-old in the far corner who held a copy of *The Incredible Journey* in his hands. The boy's lips moved as he formed the sentences with his mouth. The afternoon bell had rung. All but one other student had already left the classroom.

From her vantage point she could see Gary huddled in his Thinking Corner with a curly-haired girl and a math book. The girl was frowning. Gary said something that made her smile.

Amanda turned her attention back to the boy in the tree house. "Time to go, James," she said softly. "You don't want to miss your bus."

The boy looked up at her and then snapped the book shut. He clambered halfway down the five-rung ladder and jumped to the floor. "I'm taking it home with me."

"That's great." Amanda watched him as he grabbed his book bag off his desk, shoving the novel inside. He yelled good-bye as he sprinted out of the room.

A few feet away Gary got to his feet. "You'll get this, Madison. You're already getting it. Don't give up, okay?"

"All right," the girl muttered.

"See you tomorrow."

The girl sauntered out, and Gary turned to face Amanda. "Man, the natives were restless today," he quipped.

"Yeah. I guess."

Gary studied her for a moment. "How's it going?"

Amanda lifted and lowered her shoulders. "Good."

Gary began to put workbooks away in the cabinet behind his desk. "You seemed kind of far away today."

She thought she'd put up a fairly good front. Amanda opened her mouth to deliver a witty comeback, but no words came out. She closed her mouth.

He took a step toward her. "What's up? Is it about Chase?"

Amanda opened her mouth again to answer him, but a wave of frustration crested in her chest.

Gary moved in closer and leaned against her desk. "Do you want to talk about this?"

She blinked back hot wetness from her eyes and cleared her throat. "No," she said, and her voice sounded funny in her ears. She slid into her desk chair.

"Sure." Gary pulled a tissue from a box on his desk, and it made a soft sneezing sound as it came away in his hand. He handed it to her and then started to move away. She reached out and stopped him.

"I'm sorry," she mumbled. "I'm really sorry. I can't believe I'm acting this way." Amanda dabbed at her eyes with her other hand.

"Hey, it's not a sign of failure to admit how you really feel. If I learned anything from my divorce, it's that."

She pressed her lips together and shook her head, folding the tissue into a neat square. "I don't know how I really feel," she said.

"About what? Did you guys go see that psychologist? Did he tell you something you weren't ready to hear?"

Amanda leaned forward on her elbows and rested her head in upturned hands. Her arms were just inches from Gary's waist. She could smell his cologne. "No. A psychologist didn't tell me anything. Neil did."

Gary bent to make eye contact with her. A warm flutter coursed through her. "What did Neil tell you?" His voice was as gentle as summer cotton.

Amanda bolted from her chair and began to pace the carpet behind her desk. "I just hate this. I hate guessing. I want to know the truth. Neil says I don't. But I do. I'm not like him. I can't hide behind a pile of lumber and be content to only wonder what really happened!"

"What do you mean, what really happened? Are we still talking about the fire? About Chase?"

Amanda massaged her forehead and continued to walk the patch of carpet. "Yes. It's about the fire."

"What about it?"

"Neil says . . . Neil . . . He said the baby-sitter's son told the police he caught Chase in his room handling the lighter just minutes before he lit the cigarette."

Gary waited a second. "So?"

"So then Keith shooed Chase back to the bedroom next door where he was supposed to be napping."

"Okay."

Amanda sighed and stopped pacing. She stood a foot away from where Gary stood, still leaning on her desk. "Keith told the police he lit the cigarette in his room, but then he tossed the lighter on his bed and went onto his second-story balcony to smoke it so his room wouldn't smell like cigarette smoke."

Gary blinked. His eyes widened just a tad.

"He said he was outside on the balcony when the fire started. He said he had closed the sliding door and had his back to it. When he smelled smoke, he turned around and saw that his curtains on the sliding door were on fire. If he's telling the truth, then . . ." Her voice fell away.

"Then someone else started the fire."

"And killed that little baby." Amanda's voice broke, and ready tears spilled from her eyes. Gary moved away from the desk and closed their class-room door. Then he walked over to her, gently took her arm, and led her back to her chair.

"Let's just think about this for a minute," he said as she sat back down.

"Neil thinks Chase did it," she murmured. "That he went back into Keith's room and saw the lighter on the bed . . . that he started playing with it. The fire marshal said the fire began on the bed. I'd always thought Keith had fallen asleep on the bed with the cigarette burning. Neil never told me what Keith told the police. The cops didn't believe

Keith because he lied to them about so many other things about that day, like where he had been before and during the fire. But Neil does believe him! He says he doesn't, but he wonders if Keith was telling the truth. And that's the same thing!"

"Hold on," Gary soothed. But Amanda continued.

"Neil thinks that's why Chase never talked about the fire after we moved here. He never mentioned the fire again. Not once! Neil thinks it's because his subconscious knew he couldn't handle the memory of it and blocked it out."

"Amanda, you're both making assumptions about things you simply can't know," Gary said softly.

"Neil says if we drag this out into the open and make Chase deal with it, the horror of what really happened will all come back to him. If Chase remembers he started the fire, he'll know that baby died because of what he did!"

Amanda leaned forward on her desk, wishing she had said nothing. Wishing she knew nothing.

"Amanda, listen to me." Gary's soft voice was close. He was leaning over her. "Are you listening?"

She nodded her head.

"Even if your son started the fire, it was an accident. Think of all the things that contributed to his touching that lighter, if he even did it. He was supposed to be napping, but he was awake. Upstairs and unsupervised. Where was the baby-sitter when all this was happening?"

"Outside in the front yard with the other kids."

"And how did Chase get the lighter, assuming— only for a moment—that he did start the fire. How did he get it?"

"Keith left it on his bed."

"And why didn't the smoke alarm go off?"

Amanda swallowed a sob. "Dead battery," she whispered.

Gary reached out and rubbed her shoulder in a gentle caress with his thumb. "So who's really responsible for what happened to that baby girl?" His touch sent a shiver down her spine.

"But . . . but we told Chase never ever to play with matches," she stammered. "He knew fire was dangerous . . ."

"But what did you tell him about lighters? You and Neil don't smoke, right? Do you really think he'd ever seen fire come out of a tiny box before? Amanda, he was only four."

"I don't know, I don't know," Amanda muttered.

Gary caressed her shoulder in consolation. "That's right. You don't know. You don't know what happened. So it doesn't do any good to speculate. You start saying, 'What if?' and you can imagine just about anything."

"What should I do?" Amanda lifted her head. "I don't know what to do."

"Well, if it was me, I'd get professional advice

184

from someone I trust. If you trust Penny, and it seems like you do, you'd probably be wise to do whatever she suggests."

"I don't want Chase to remember it. I want to know what really happened. But I don't want him to."

"And he's the only one who can give you what you want, is that it?"

She nodded.

"Amanda?"

"What?"

"It was an accident. It wasn't his fault that baby died. Even if he held the flame to the bedspread himself, it wasn't his fault. He was a toddler left unsupervised in a house without a working smoke alarm and with access to fire. Your baby-sitter is the one who bears the responsibility for this tragedy. Not your four-year-old child. No matter what really happened."

A second round of tears began to fall. "I just don't want it to be true."

"It wasn't his fault," Gary said, and on her shoulder his hand lingered.

twenty-two

The pink wingback chairs were already in place when Tally, Chase, and Matt arrived at La Vista del Paz to finish interviewing Josef Bliss and Eliasz Abramovicz on Wednesday.

"The guys didn't want to finish the interview without them," one of the nursing staff said, nodding to the chairs.

"In fact, we've ordered a set for our room," Josef replied, as he slowly maneuvered his body from his wheelchair to one of the rosy-hued chairs.

"Yes. And a flat-screen and a minibar." Eliasz winked and settled into his own chair.

"Comedians. Both of you." The nurse's aide turned to the three teenagers. "Okay. Go easy on them. They've been nothing but trouble since the last time you guys were here."

"Hush now, *kochanie.* Go get everything ready for our pedicures." Josef waved a withered hand and smiled.

The woman tousled his wispy silver hair and walked away.

"So you guys are roommates?" Matt took a seat on a straight-back chair across from the older men. "How'd you get to the same nursing home, anyway? And how'd you both get to San Diego, of all places?"

Eliasz's unfocused gaze settled on the top of Matt's head. "You want us to start today backward from San Diego?"

"No." Chase adjusted the tripod. "We want to go back to where you left off. At the ghetto. You had just saved twenty-five babies."

"Yeah, but we only have today to shoot the rest

of this, so you know . . ." Matt's voice trailed off as he looked over at Chase.

"You want us to keep it snappy?" Josef said.

"We want you to keep it authentic." Chase bent his body to peer into the viewfinder.

"Yes, well," Josef said. "It will not be hard to keep it authentic. Where did you say we left off?"

"You had just smuggled out twenty-five babies." Tally sat between Chase and Matt like before. She held the photo of her great-grandfather in her hands.

"Ah, yes." He looked at Chase. "You are ready? You are recording?"

Chase nodded.

"Yes. Twenty-five infants. We would have saved more, of course, but a man who needed medicine for his sick wife turned us in for a handful of *złotych*. That happened five months after we started. Late August 1942. The Nazis took me, Eliasz, and his mother and father, along with five others. We didn't know if the Gestapo knew about Katrine and Sofia, and I prayed that they did not. Sofia told me just before we smuggled out our last two children that we were going to have to choose a new meeting place. So we had—what would you say?—an inkling that something was wrong.

"On our last mission, a young father begged us to take not only his newborn daughter, but also his six-year-old son out of the ghetto. His wife had died giving birth to the infant, and this father

187

feared for his son's life as well. There was a rumor that he and his son were to be in the next group being sent to Treblinka. We resisted at first since we could not use our traditional means of smuggling out a sedated baby in my tool bag. A six-year-old boy obviously wouldn't fit in a tool bag. But Sofia said we should try using the sewers, as other smugglers were doing, and with Katrine's help, we risked an early-morning rescue.

"We actually thought that because we were doing it a different way, we would lay to rest any suspicions about us. But when we first arrived at Treblinka, we heard that the nurse known only as Sofia had been caught smuggling children out of the ghetto and executed. The rumor was that another woman was with Sofia, but she got away. The people at the camp who told us this didn't know Katrine's name, and I was glad they did not. If they did not, perhaps the Gestapo did not. And I was more relieved than I can say that Katrine had escaped. Sofia had all the records of where the children had been placed. I don't know what happened to those records. I doubt any of the surviving parents were reunited with the children we smuggled out for them."

"I certainly never found out what became of my baby sister, Marya," Eliasz said.

"Anyway," Josef continued, "I was inside the apartment with Eliasz and his parents when the Gestapo came for us. This was less than an hour after they had killed Sofia, but I did not know it at the time. I could barely understand what they said. I don't speak very good German. But I knew they were accusing us of criminal acts against the *Führer.* They honestly did not care if it was ammunition or food or children that we had smuggled. All that mattered was that we had defied one of their mandates. And since I was a sympathizer of Jews and had participated in their criminal acts, I was worse than they were. They were not happy with me."

"Josef was unconscious from a beating when they marched us to the transport to Treblinka," Eliasz said. "My father and I held him between us. And actually it was a very good thing he needed to be dragged, because I was able to hide my blindness that way. I just walked wherever my father walked and dragged my half of Josef." Eliasz turned to his old friend. "Have I ever thanked you for having been beaten senseless, Josef?"

Josef smiled. "Can't recall that you have."

Eliasz smiled back. *"Dziękują przyjaciel."*

Josef waved a wrinkled hand. "My pleasure." The man smiled, lowered his hand, and continued. "Now Treblinka was nothing more than a little train station. That's how we knew it. But in the months leading up to this, while the Jews practically starved in the ghetto, the Nazis used slave labor to build the death camp that would have the same name. It was in a beautiful part of Poland. Many trees and woods. Not a place where you would think atrocities could occur.

"There were two parts to the camp, the part where the Germans and Ukrainians lived, and our part, where the gas chambers were. There were a dozen gas chambers. And no crematorium. I cannot tell you how horrifying it was to be in that place. There are no words for it. Many of the people on our transport were killed the same day we got there—Eliasz's parents and many others.

"Eliasz and I were young and strong, however, and as long as we could keep up the ruse that Eliasz could see, we lived. There was a high fence—four meters, I'd say—all around the camp, made of chain link and barbed wire. The Nazis wanted it to be camouflaged with tree boughs woven in the chinks at all times. Eliasz and I did that for months, working around the camp day after day after day, replacing old branches with new ones. Remember how I told you Eliasz made beautiful challah? This was just like that. I told him, 'Weave the branches like the dough, Eliasz. Braid it like bread.' And that is how we survived."

"How did you get out?" Matt said.

"About a year after we arrived at Treblinka, in early August, a handful of brave resisters staged a final revolt. They broke into the munitions warehouse, stole guns, and began to shoot the guards in the watchtowers and set fire to the buildings. They were very brave men. I do not think any of them survived. But their heroism allowed some of us to escape into the woods, including Eliasz and me. The camp was dismantled just a few months later because there was such extensive damage from the fires."

As the word "fires" fell from Josef's lips, Chase had the sensation of heat on his arms. He felt himself being mentally pulled away from the nursing home lounge and its odors of age and ammonia. Instead, the faint scent of smoke filled his lungs. He closed his eyes and saw swaths of flame and shapes in the ashen fog. A bed. A crib. Someone was crying.

Smoke.

Flames.

Fear.

"Chase?"

Tally's voice startled him, and his eyes snapped open.

"What?" The image and its accompanying smells skittered away.

His cousin stared at him. On her other side, Matt seemed not to have noticed the seconds that Chase had mentally checked out. "Wow," Matt said. "So you guys escaped into the woods. Then what?"

Eliasz laughed. "Then we lived like little rabbits, wandering the countryside. Sleeping in burrows, eating lettuce in gardens that did not belong to us, running at the slightest crack of a twig."

Josef grinned. "It was rather comical. Finally, though, we met a woman who gave us shelter in her barn until the war was over. We were seventy miles from Treblinka when she found us. Her husband was very ill. I don't think he even knew we were there.

"When the war ended, we went to Austria because I knew that was where Katrine would have gone to be with her family. This woman helped us get papers to go there. But I never found her. I don't know where she went after she fled the sewers with Sofia. There was nothing to indicate she had been killed or caught, so I assumed she got away. Everyone did. But I never heard from her again. And I was unable to locate her family in Vienna.

"In 1947 Eliasz and I came to America. First to Chicago, then to Texas, then to California. We opened a bakery in every city we lived in. We had many good years after we left Poland. Many. And I met a lovely woman in Chicago named Helen who patiently waited for me to get over losing Katrine."

"She was the definition of patience," Eliasz quipped. "She was a wonder. Helen waited ten years for him to get over Katrine."

"What can I say? I was in love with my Katrine," Josef said. "Not knowing where she was, wondering if she had emigrated to the States too, like so many had. I couldn't just let her go. I couldn't. I still wonder what happened to her."

"Lucky for you Helen didn't let *you* go." Eliasz turned in the direction of the teenagers. "Helen wasn't Katrine, but she let me live with them for forty-five years and never complained once about putting up with me. She was a saint. And that's saying a lot, coming from a Jew."

Josef laughed. "So we had good years. When I entered this nursing facility a few years ago, Eliasz came with me, even though he did not need to at the time. It has been a good life, considering."

Matt stretched back in his chair. "Cool. So you guys have been friends your whole life."

"Yes. We have."

Chase stopped recording and put the lens cap back on his camera. "That was really great. We have some editing to do and we have to record our own comments, but I'll come back and show you the DVD when it's finished, if you want."

"Yes," Josef said. "That would be nice."

"I love to watch a good movie," Eliasz joked.

Matt laughed and stood up. He looked at his watch. "Hey, we should probably get going."

"Well, glad to have been of help to you," Josef said.

Chase began putting away his camera equipment. Matt bent to help him, no doubt to speed things along. Chase, too, was oddly anxious to leave. Out of the corner of his eye, he saw Tally lean forward and extend a photo to Josef. The old man bent toward her and reached for it.

"What is this?" He fumbled for a pair of glasses in his pocket.

"This is Chase's and my great-grandfather. Aron Bachmann. He was a doctor in Warsaw just before the war," Tally said.

Josef peered at the man in the photo and cocked his head.

"He was Jewish," Tally continued. "But he married a Catho-lic woman. He and his wife and son were relocated to the ghetto too. He died at Treblinka. We don't know what happened to my great-grandmother and grandfather after the ghetto, though. Except that they escaped to England."

"So this is him. Aron Bachmann." Josef's voice was contemplative.

"Aron Bachmann?" Eliasz tipped his head toward the conversation. "What does he look like, Josef?"

Josef held the photo close to his eyes. "Medium build, late thirties, I'd say. Handlebar mustache."

Eliasz nodded. "The Aron Bachmann I knew had a mustache like that. At least that is how he was described to me. My mother would tease my father that he should grow one so handsome. And yes, he was a doctor."

Chase stopped packing his camera equipment. "Was he part of your smuggling ring?"

"No. He was the young father who asked us to smuggle out his son and newborn daughter." Eliasz turned to Josef.

Tally looked at Chase. His questioning eyes met hers.

"Ah, yes," Josef said, nodding. "I think you're right."

"You're sure the father's name was Aron Bachmann? And that he was a doctor?" Tally asked.

"Yes. Yes, I think so. His children were the last we rescued. Could that little boy be your grandfather? Is that what this means?"

Again Chase and Tally exchanged glances. It couldn't be the same Aron Bachmann.

"I don't see how," Chase said. "When our grandpa escaped the ghetto, his mother was with him."

"The little boy's and baby's mother died, right? You're sure?" Tally's brow creased in bewilderment.

"Yes. She had a terrible infection. Her husband had no medicine to save her," Josef answered.

Tally quickly directed her attention back to Eliasz as a new thought seemed to occur to her. "Do you know where Aron Bachmann was from? What part of Warsaw?"

Eliasz rubbed his chin. "Can't recall at the moment. People in the ghetto came from all over. I don't know that I ever knew."

Josef handed the photo back to her. "You look puzzled."

"I was hoping you'd remember where in Warsaw the Bachmann family lived. My father is over there somewhere, and we don't know where he is." Tally slipped the photo into her backpack.

"But that's not all?" Josef asked.

"If, in some wild way, this is the same Aron Bachmann, then the woman who escaped with our grandpa wasn't his real mother," Chase said. "But she pretended she was. For the rest of her life she pretended it. And our grandfather just let her."

Josef stroked his chin. "Perhaps it was the best way for them to leave the war and the ghetto behind them. We, each of us, had to find a way. Don't judge her too harshly. Or your grandfather."

For several seconds, no one said anything. An uneasy silence hung in the room.

Matt nodded toward Eliasz. "How come you never married, Eliasz?"

The old man grinned. "I never found anyone as beautiful as Helen."

Matt laughed. "How do you know she was beautiful? You're blind!"

"Ah, well. That doesn't mean I cannot see. What do you see when you close your eyes, my young friend?"

Matt shrugged. "Nothing."

"And you?" Eliasz said toward Tally. When she said nothing, he turned to Chase. "What do you see when you close your eyes? You, the thinker."

"I . . . I don't know what I see," Chase mumbled.

"When you who see close your eyes, you become like me. You see with the eyes of your mind and your dreams, and they never rest. When you have experienced the very worst in man—and the very best—everything becomes very clear. I see my mother in my dreams. I see my sister whom she loved and surrendered. I see Helen, who took me into her home as if I were her brother. And yes, I see the Nazi soldier who shot my parents, and the guards who entertained themselves by urinating on us while we worked at the fence, and the young women from my old neighborhood that they took and raped. I see the perfect, and I see the atrocious. Close your eyes and tell me you cannot see."

The air in the room seemed to freeze in a wordless moment. Chase's voice felt useless in this throat, and he was aware of how very much he suddenly did not want to close his eyes.

"Okay, wow," Matt said. "Well, that was, like, really deep." He turned to Chase. "Too bad you'd already turned off the camera, dude."

Chase grabbed the camera bag and tripod. Time to go.

twenty-three

Matt pulled into the driveway of the Janvier house, and Chase and Tally climbed out of his car and into the fading sunlight. "Hey, thanks for coming to soccer practice," he called out to them. "Sorry it went long."

Chase slung his camera bag over his shoulder. "It's all right. I should've guessed we wouldn't have gotten out of the nursing home in under half an hour. I should've just driven my own car."

"Yeah, but then you wouldn't have gotten to watch those awesome soccer plays."

Chase closed the back door. "No. I would've gotten a paper written for English."

"Sorry, dude."

"It's cool. I've got a Red Bull in the fridge in the garage. I'll get the paper done tonight. See ya." Chase turned and began heading up the flagstone steps to the front door.

Tally was about to follow him when Matt called out to her. "Hey, Tally!"

She turned back around.

Matt leaned his torso toward the open passenger window and cocked his head. "Would you want to go out sometime?"

"Out?"

"Yeah." Matt grinned. "Out."

"Like, just you and me?"

He laughed. "Like."

"But I don't know how long I'm going to be here," she said.

Matt continued to smile at her. "You're going to be here on Saturday, aren't you?"

"Probably."

"Well, you want to go out Saturday?"

Tally turned to see if Chase had already gone

inside the house, but he was waiting for her on the front porch, looking at her with his hand resting lightly on the doorknob. There was no way to guess what he thought of Matt asking her out. And she had no idea what Amanda and Neil would say. Tally swung back around.

"I'll check," she said.

"Cool." But Matt's tone was pensive. "Catch you later."

"Okay."

The tires on Matt's car made a slight squealing sound as he pulled away from the curb. Tally turned to face the front door. Chase was still looking at her. Her face felt warm.

"What are you looking at?" she mumbled as she closed the distance between them.

"What's the point of going out with him if you're only going to be here a few weeks?" Chase's hand was still on the doorknob

"Does there have to be a point?" She didn't wait for him to answer. "Besides, I didn't even say I was going."

"If my parents say you can, will you?"

Tally studied his face. Perhaps Chase thought she would say something to Matt about what Chase had told her in secret. She would never do that. "Will they?" she said.

"If they base their decision on what they think your dad would say, well, knowing Uncle Bart, they'll probably say yes."

She narrowed her eyes. "What do you mean, knowing Uncle Bart?"

"You know what I mean." He turned the door-knob.

"No, I don't." Tally reached for his arm.

"Don't worry about it. You should take it as a compliment. Uncle Bart's always fascinated me." Chase opened the door. She tightened her grip.

"Wait! You don't think I should go out with Matt?"

Chase hesitated for only a moment. "Does it matter to you what I think?"

She stared at him. "Does it matter to you if I go?"

Chase looked at her and did not answer.

"I wouldn't say anything," she said softly, releasing him.

"About what?" Chase replied. But he stepped into the tiled entry and headed for the stairs without giving her a chance to answer.

Plates of sweet and sour chicken sent pungent, tangy odors spiraling around the dinner table. Neil offered a quiet table grace, and they began to eat.

After a few moments of silence, Amanda cleared her throat. "Neil, those men at the nursing home that Chase and Tally have been interviewing knew an Aron Bachmann in the Warsaw Ghetto. He was a doctor."

Neil looked up from his food. "Really? Not your grandfather, though?"

Amanda shook her head and glanced at Chase. "Well, I don't think so. This one had a wife who died right after giving birth to a baby girl. So . . ." Her voice trailed off.

"Interesting, though. That there could be two Aron Bachmanns in the ghetto who were both doctors. I wonder how many people lived there." Neil took a sip of water.

"Four hundred thousand," Chase said without looking up from his plate.

"Really? That many?" Neil set his glass back down. "Well, then maybe it's not so odd that there could be two of them."

"It could've been him." Again Chase spoke without looking up.

"Pardon?" Neil said.

"No, it couldn't," Delcey chimed in.

Chase lifted his head. "It could've been him."

"Well, I don't see how," Amanda began, looking from son to husband. "I mean, the Aron Bachmann your friends knew had a wife who died in the ghetto. So it couldn't be."

"But what do you really know about your grandmother?" Chase replied. "I mean, the woman who said she was your grandmother. You told me she never wanted to talk about the war, the ghetto, her life before the war, not even her dead first husband. And Grandpa didn't either."

"That doesn't mean she wasn't really your grandmother and that there weren't two Aron

Bachmanns in the ghetto, Chase." Neil placed a forkful of food in his mouth. The cashews made a crunching sound.

"Both doctors?" Chase continued. "Both smuggled out a young son? Both sent to Treblinka? Both died there? That sounds a little too coincidental."

"But . . . but who would that woman be, then? The woman I knew as my grandmother?" Amanda frowned.

"I don't know. A neighbor, one of your grandmother's friends, or a cousin, or a sister. There were probably lots of people who would've taken your father in. He was just a little kid. Six or seven years old, right?"

Neil leaned forward on his elbows. His fork dangled. "And so you think your grandpa didn't remember his real mother? And that this other woman just let him think he hadn't lost both his parents?"

Chase shook his head and lifted a piece of pineapple to his mouth. "No. I don't think that at all. I think he remembered who his mother was. That wouldn't be something he'd likely forget. Just because he was a little kid doesn't mean he wouldn't remember."

Next to Tally, Amanda coughed. She reached for her water glass and nearly knocked it over. Chase didn't seem to notice.

"He probably had to go along with it because of

the war and the danger of being labeled Jewish," Tally said.

"Okay, but what about after the war?" Neil said. "Why keep it a secret after the war ended? It wouldn't have mattered then."

"It obviously mattered to them," Chase said.

Neil took a drink from his glass but kept his eyes on Chase. Tally couldn't read the expression on his face.

"But what's the purpose of the secrecy after the war, or even years later, when they were both here in the States and this woman, Marta Bachmann, remarried?" Neil asked as he set his glass down. "I don't see the need for secrecy then."

Chase shrugged. "It wasn't your secret."

Amanda coughed again. "Well, I don't think we'll ever know for sure, and I, for one, am quite happy to believe what I've always believed, that the woman I knew as my grandmother was my biological grandmother."

"Of course you are," Chase whispered to no one. But Tally heard him.

"What?" Amanda asked.

"Nothing."

Tally chanced a glance at Amanda. Her aunt's face was slightly ashen.

"Well, it's not like it makes a difference now." Neil wiped his mouth with his napkin.

"Okay, so do I or do I not know who my great-grandma was?" Delcey asked pointedly. Her cell phone vibrated, and she pulled it out of her pocket.

"I think it's safe to say you do, and put that phone away, please." Neil looked over at his daughter. "You know how your mom and I feel about your phone at the table."

Delcey huffed and stuck her phone back in her pocket. The stretch of silence that followed made Tally uncomfortable. She looked over at Amanda, the only one not chewing. Her aunt stared at the plate in front of her, raised her head to look at Uncle Neil, and then lowered it again. She looked lost.

Tally decided to change the subject. "Eliasz, the blind man at the nursing home, says he can see in his dreams."

Four heads looked up. A tiny grin appeared on Chase's face.

"He can see in his dreams?" Neil asked.

"Uh-huh. And when he closes his eyes."

Neil finished chewing the food in his mouth and swallowed. "I think this man was teasing you, Tally."

Tally looked at Chase. He cocked his head slightly. *You going to let him get away with that?* his look said.

"No, he wasn't," she countered.

"Is he blind from birth?" Neil asked.

"Yes."

"Then he was just teasing you. I'm sure it's

impossible for someone blind from birth to conjure images in his head of things he's never seen."

Delcey dropped her angry frown over missing her phone call and turned to her father. "How do you know that?"

"Well, let's think about it." Neil sat back in his chair. "How could his brain assemble an image of, say, a red apple if he's never seen the color red and he's never seen an apple? He has no raw materials to work with. He would have to have the real image in his mind already to imagine it or dream it."

Tally opened her mouth to say that Eliasz certainly didn't sound like he was teasing, but Chase's voice next to her filled the quiet space after Neil finished.

"But what if it's not uncomplicated things like red apples that he sees but deeply complicated images?" Chase said. "Images that shaped him, changed him, nearly killed him?"

Tally felt Amanda flinch in her chair on her other side.

Neil stared at his son across the table. "I don't doubt Eliasz's memories of the war are very powerful, but they can't have any true visual shape in his mind. You have to have vision to create a visual memory of something. I'm sure that what Eliasz remembers is what he felt, heard, and smelled."

Chase stared back at his father. "He said his best friend's wife was beautiful."

Neil blinked. "I'm sure he remembers, say, her perfume or perhaps the shape of her face beneath his fingers. The sound of her voice. But he can't know what she really looked like."

"What if he can?" Amanda's voice sounded thin.

Neil turned to his wife. "It's not possible, dear. Look it up if you don't believe me. I'll bet any one of you that I'm right. People born blind don't see in their dreams. They don't see when they close their eyes. That would be creating something from nothing. Only God can create something from nothing."

A moment of awkward silence followed.

"I'm finished." Chase stood up, grabbed his plate, and walked into the kitchen.

"I'm going to look it up on the Internet." Delcey jumped out of her chair and headed for the den. "But I'm not betting you, Dad," she called over her shoulder.

Neil stood and wordlessly took his plate into the kitchen. He and Chase were side by side for only a moment by the sink. Then Chase turned and headed for the stairs.

"Homework?" Neil called after him.

"Yep," Chase answered from the third step.

A moment later Tally heard the kitchen door to the garage open and shut. Tally looked at Amanda. Her aunt offered her a weak smile and said Tally didn't have to help with the dishes since no one else was doing it. Tally decided to stay and help.

They didn't talk. Not about Matt wanting to ask her out. That could wait until morning.

And not about what a blind man sees when he dreams.

twenty-four

A manda stood in front of Neil's open closet with five hangers in her hands; freshly pressed button-down shirts hung from them. She studied the length of the wooden rung in front of her and the long row of business shirts that ended where a row of dress slacks on a lower rung began. Amanda leaned into the shirts that were already hanging there and breathed in deeply, snagging a whiff of Dior Homme—Neil's preferred fragrance—mixed with faint traces of coffee and leather. The aroma was calming.

When she'd met Neil in college, she'd been impressed by his taste in clothes and cologne. It surprised her actually, since Neil wasn't particularly mindful of his appearance. He wore his hair unremarkably short and chose neutral colors for his expensive clothes, never buying anything with a logo bigger than a dime. His polished looks were accidental, unplanned. Neil didn't know his physical appearance was impressive and didn't count on it mattering much.

The only child of two college professors, Neil lived and breathed academia in his growing-up years. He was knowledgeable in so many things, yet somehow he never made her feel uninformed. She loved that about him. She spent the better part of their early dates listening to him expound on deep philosophical issues like the problem of evil, whether or not the mind can exist outside the body, and how the atheist lives a life of faith—he cannot prove that God does not exist. But what she found most amazing was his kindness to strangers. Neil opened doors for men and women alike, gave up his seat on buses and taxis, tipped twenty-five percent, chased down people who'd dropped their wallets or car keys, and went out of his way to return a lost dog. It was Superman kindness, the kind of benevolence a comic book hero shows when he doggedly rescues a complete stranger as if saving his own soul. This quality was one of the things that first attracted her to Neil, his kind attention to people he didn't even know.

Neil was a good man. He had given her a good life. They had a beautiful home in an upscale neighborhood. Financial security. Two healthy children. Nice cars. They'd taken vacations to Hawaii, Vail, and Orlando. Neil didn't drink excessively, wasn't abusive, and didn't smoke or gamble or cheat on her. He was active in their church, made beautiful things in his woodshop that he gave away, encouraged her to pursue her own career, didn't berate his kids, didn't annoy the neighbors, didn't stay out late, and wasn't addicted to the office.

He was a good man.

A queer sensation ran through her as nagging snippets of the moments she spent confiding in Gary mingled—tangled—with the scent of her husband.

Gary had been the kindest of listeners the last few days—calm, objective, and ultimately the voice of reason. But his compassionate touch left her confused. When he left the classroom after she reassured him she would be fine, the echo of his hand on her shoulder stayed with her. Things seemed a bit strained as he said good-bye, as if he knew something indefinable had passed between them as he consoled her.

She closed her eyes and buried her face farther into the shoulders and sleeves of Neil's shirts, inhaling, inhaling, inhaling. The floppy fabric gave way, though, and she found herself starting to fall forward. She lifted her head and reached out with her free hand to steady her footing.

After a moment, she parted the shirts, creating room for the hangers she held in her hands, and hung up the freshly laundered Van Heusens that didn't smell like anyone. Amanda leaned against the door frame of the closet, crossing her arms in front of her chest.

The conversation at dinner had replayed itself in her mind all evening. She didn't know why Chase had made such a big deal about her grandmother's possibly not being her blood relative. It was like he wanted her grandmother to have been an imposter. Like he was glad there were secrets in the family's past. Like it was all a part of something bigger, something that had nothing to do with her grandmother or blind men. And Neil didn't seem to get it at all.

She'd willed Neil to catch her eye from across the table with a look that said, *Don't worry, Amanda. I'll talk to him later.* She'd wanted him to sense what she had sensed: Chase was trying to communicate something to them. But that's not what Neil had done. He'd taken his plate to the sink and then disappeared into the woodshop. Where he still was two hours later.

Amanda closed her eyes and pictured Neil knocking on Chase's door and stepping into his room. She pictured him sitting on Chase's bed and asking their son if he really thought the blind man at the nursing home could see in his dreams. And when she imagined Chase saying yes, she pictured Neil saying, "Tell me why."

In the next instant, it was Gary she saw on Chase's bed asking those questions, risking the answers.

Amanda's eyes snapped open. "Stop it," she whispered.

She pulled away from the door frame and slid the closet door shut. She numbly moved to the granite-topped bathroom counter with its matching porcelain sinks and leaned on it, supporting her weight with both arms and inhaling slowly, willing herself to be reasonable.

Gary was an acquaintance she'd known for a mere three weeks. He could be objective about this situation because he wasn't emotionally involved. Gary had nothing to gain or lose by being honest, and she wanted to believe there was nothing wrong with unloading on him. She wanted to believe he was just a dispassionate colleague. An objective bystander.

But it had been awkward today in the classroom. And the day before, since he'd comforted her. She'd had a hard time concentrating on the children. And Gary seemed to always be looking at her. He sensed it too. An awkwardness that hadn't been there before.

Finally, between classes he approached her desk while she recorded test scores on her computer. "Everything all right?" He wore a *Monsters, Inc.* tie.

"Yes. Fine." She knew she didn't sound convincing.

"Look, I don't want you to worry that you told me too much the other day. Or that I think of you differently. Or Neil. I'm sure he's a great father."

"N-no . . . ," she stammered. "I just . . . had a lot on my mind. You know."

"Of course."

"And . . . I'm a little embarrassed. I don't usually have a meltdown like I did the other day."

"You probably just needed to vent. That's normal. I'm sure any psychologist would agree."

The memory of his hand on her shoulder filled her mind, and she squirmed slightly in her chair. "I should've dumped on Penny, then."

He cracked a smile. "Oh great. So I totally bombed as your listening ear?"

"Hardly. You were wonderful." The moment she'd said it, she wished she hadn't. Her face grew warm, and she couldn't look at him.

A press of students spilled into the room at that moment, chattering and laughing. She'd risen quickly to her feet and moved to greet them. When the noise of their arrival faded, Amanda stole a glance at Gary. He was talking to a trio of fourth graders, but he must've felt her gaze on him. He raised his head to look at her while he continued to speak to the children. A tiny smile rested on his lips, but it was a questioning smile.

When the school day ended, Gary seemed to be in a rush to leave. Maybe it was just her imagination, but he was out of the classroom in less than five minutes. And he gave her a long glance as he said good-bye for the day.

"See you tomorrow?" she'd said.

"Yes," he answered.

She'd watched him leave the room and walk down the long hallway toward the double doors

212

that led to the rest of their lives. As she'd gathered her things, she kept hearing Gary say yes, yes, yes.

Amanda could still hear his response as she leaned on her bathroom counter. She slowly looked up to stare at herself in the mirror above the sinks.

"What do you think you're doing?" she said, but only her lips moved. No sound came out.

It wasn't right that she kept reliving those moments with Gary. Not right. Neil was a good man. A good husband. A good father. He loved Chase. He didn't want Chase to suffer. They didn't agree on much about their current predicament, but they certainly agreed on that. They both loved Chase and wanted what was best for him.

If only Neil saw it the way Gary did . . .

No. No, no, no! This is ridiculous. I am not in love with anyone but Neil. I am in love with Neil. She lowered her head. *This is not happening. This is not happening.*

Two tears escaped her closed eyes and splashed side by side on the granite countertop.

"I am in love with Neil," she whispered.

She looked at her reflection again. "I am in love with Neil."

Amanda swiped away the fallen tears, rubbing her wet fingertips onto her jeans as she walked away from the mirror.

twenty-five

Chase knelt in a tiled room. He held a brick in one hand and the stub of a pencil in the other. Someone was kneeling next to him. He turned his head and saw Eliasz.

Eliasz took the brick and pencil out of his hands. "Hurry!" Eliasz still had his old man's face and gnarled hands, but his voice sounded young. And he looked straight at Chase.

"You can see," Chase said.

Eliasz seemed not to hear Chase or didn't care to comment on the obvious. He thrust a canvas tool bag into Chase's empty hands. "Hurry, before it's too late!"

"Too late for what?"

A window broke and he heard a woman screaming. Feathery shards rained down on him and on the bag. A *whoosh* replaced the screaming, and a ribbon of flame fell into the room.

Ghost.

Chase looked up at Eliasz, but the old man was gone. The tiled room was gone.

His knees felt hot carpet, and his hands held the canvas tool bag. Smoke and ash swirled around him. In the corner of the room, Ghost twirled about like a dancer.

Chase watched the dance, mesmerized. Someone was crying. He couldn't breathe.

Mommy! Daddy! The words stung his throat.

He had to get out. Chase started to crawl away from the dancing flame. Was the door over here? He bumped into something. Arms and legs.

Another little boy. The boy was crying. This was the boy with the stain on his shirt. He was banging on the closed door with his fist.

Move away! Chase yelled. *Move away!*

But the boy didn't move away. Chase pushed him. Hard. The boy screamed and toppled over. But Chase opened the door. There was another loud whooshing sound.

The other boy scrambled ahead of him, on top of him. Chase felt a sharp sting as the boy's foot smacked him above his ear.

Dancing Ghost yelled his name as he began to crawl away. And someone was crying.

Chase looked up and through the smoke he saw Eliasz, staring at him. "You forgot the bag."

Chase turned back toward the smoky darkness where Ghost roared like a jubilant dragon. The bag lay where he dropped it, almost in the embrace of the happy, hungry flames. He tried to crawl back but his legs wouldn't move. He fell forward on the carpet. He tasted the fibers on his tongue. He could see the bag in the shadows ahead of him. He could see Ghost reach down for it.

"No!" Chase yelled.

Arms reached out for him, to pull him back. He

swung around to resist, his head crashed against something hard, and the dream—the smoke, the flames—vanished.

Chase opened his eyes.

Tally knelt over him. Fear shimmered in her eyes. The fuchsia streaks in her hair shone pink in the amber glow of the hall nightlight.

He lay in the hallway.

"Chase," she said.

He bolted upright, nearly knocking her over. "What's going on?" he rasped.

"I think you were sleepwalking," she said softly. "And having a nightmare."

"What are you doing here?" He was aware at once at how unkind his hushed voice sounded, even though strands of sleep still permeated his thoughts.

"I . . . You . . . I got up to use the bathroom, and when I came out you were in the hallway. Crawling on the carpet. And groaning. You're not in your room. Did you know that?"

Her voice had risen in pitch from a whisper to a soft but agitated tone. Chase slid his back up against the wall and looked down to the end of the hallway, toward the door to the master bedroom. He waited several seconds to see if a stripe of light would appear under his parents' bedroom door. When it did not, he rose to his feet. Next to him, Tally did the same.

"Go back to bed," he said softly. "I'm fine."

His cousin hesitated. "You scared me," she finally said.

"Sorry." He turned, moved past her, and headed for the stairs.

"Where are you going?"

He turned. "Is it okay with you if I get a drink of water?" He didn't wait for her to respond to his sarcasm. Tally followed him down the stairs and into the kitchen. The clock above the stove glared an emerald 3:10 a.m.

"I told you to go back to bed." He wrenched open the fridge, pulled out a blue-capped bottle of water, and twisted off the top.

"I don't have to do what you say."

He took a long drink, never taking his eyes off of her. He pulled the bottle away from his mouth. "What do you want?"

"I want to make sure you're okay."

"I told you I was fine."

She took a step toward him. "You're covered in sweat. You were having a nightmare about the fire, weren't you? I heard you."

He took another drink, a shorter one this time. "Heard what?"

"You were saying you couldn't breathe. You were, like, crying. You were saying, 'Hot, hot, hot.'"

"So?"

"You were in the hallway! You weren't even in your own bedroom!"

Chase shrugged. "I'm not the first person to walk in his sleep."

"You were calling for your parents."

Chase looked away as his face grew warm. He heard the voice in his dream, his voice. *Mommy! Daddy!*

She took another step toward him. "I think you should tell your parents how much you're starting to remember."

"I don't have to do what you say," he said, mimicking her tone from seconds before.

"I didn't say you had to; I said I think you should."

He took another drink and wiped his mouth with his hand. It was shaking slightly. "I already told you. They don't want to know about this."

"I think you're wrong about that."

Annoyance began to fill the spot left by retreating alarm. "When did you become such an expert on parents?" he said. "Where are *your* parents? Huh?"

Tally drew back as if dodging a slap.

"Let's get something straight, okay?" Chase went on. "I live in the real world. *This* is the real world, and you don't know anything about it. You've been here a couple lousy weeks. And, I might add, you're not staying. After you leave, I'll still be here. I have to be here. So I'm the only person who gets to decide what part of my personal life I share with my parents and what part I don't. I don't have the luxury of a single parent who treats me like a college roommate."

"Like a *what?*" Tally challenged.

"You heard what I said. You don't even know where your dad is. He doesn't know where you are. Apparently, that's no big deal to either one of you. You haven't heard from your dad in a month. That is *not* the real world, sister."

Several seconds passed before Tally responded, "I'm *not* your sister."

Chase nodded. "My point exactly."

The two of them stood silent in the lustrous moonlight that washed in from the expansive window over the kitchen sink. Sammy the dog had wandered in from Delcey's room and now sat between them, wagging her tail.

"I want my lighter back," Tally finally said.

For a split second, Chase regretted having been so harsh. He was about to lose the lighter. But the dream had opened a door, and he had seen a shape. He had seen the fire's writhing body. Finally, after all these years, he had seen Ghost *face to face.* Maybe he didn't need the lighter anymore.

"Fine." He placed the water bottle on the counter and swept past Tally. He took the stairs two at a time and headed for his bedroom. He could hear Tally behind him.

His room smelled of the sweat and tension of his nightmare, and he hesitated before he stepped in.

219

Behind him, Tally hesitated too, as if she could also sense the nightmare's peculiar odor. He clicked on his desk lamp and knelt by his bed, noting that his sheet and blanket were a jumbled tangle. Chase reached under the bed for the state quarter box and placed it on top of the chaos that was his bedcovers. He spun the combination lock and opened it. The lighter was on top. He grabbed it and extended it toward Tally, who stood several feet away.

She took a few steps toward him and closed her hand around her father's lighter. She lifted it slowly from his open palm. When Tally had it in her hands, he snapped the lid on the box shut and stood.

"There. Happy now?" he said.

Tally slowly raised her head to look at him. "No. Are you?"

"You wanted it back. You have it."

His cousin looked down at the lighter in her hands. He expected her to turn around, leave his room, and go back to Delcey's.

"What happened at the nursing home today?" she said instead.

"What do you mean?" he asked. But he knew.

"When Josef was talking about the escape from the concentration camp. You . . . you went pale. I thought you might pass out."

"You thought wrong."

She looked up at him. "So what happened?"

He didn't think he could explain it to anyone. He didn't think there was a way to describe what it felt like when a memory returned to you in jigsaw pieces. "Nothing happened. A little more returned to me, that's all."

She turned to go, and Chase reached out and gently grabbed her arm. "Tally."

Tally turned her head back around. Her eyes looked sad. He let go of her arm.

"Look, I'm sorry about what I said in the kitchen," Chase said softly. "About your dad. I'm really sorry about that. I was angry. I shouldn't have said it."

She looked down at the lighter in her hands and was silent for several long seconds. Then she extended the hand that held the lighter.

"I don't want Delcey to find it." Her voice was expressionless.

Chase hesitated and then reached for the lighter. "I won't let anything happen to it."

She turned and walked silently out of his dimly lit room, into the hall where she'd found him minutes before, and finally back to Delcey's room where his sister's soft snores whistled like a spring breeze.

twenty-six

Morning sunlight fell around her as Tally entered the kitchen. Uncle Neil stood at the counter, perusing the newspaper as he sipped coffee. He turned a page, carefully avoiding the half-full bottle of drinking water Chase had left there the night before. Behind him Amanda stirred eggs in a pan on the stove. Delcey was still upstairs. Chase apparently hadn't come downstairs yet either.

Tally yawned silently and wondered if Chase had had as much trouble falling back asleep as she did. She couldn't get the image out of her mind of him crumpled in the hallway and whimpering like a lost child. That was no typical nightmare.

"Good morning, Tally," Neil said, not looking up from the paper. Her aunt turned and smiled at her. Amanda looked tired.

"Morning," Tally said. She didn't know if it was a good time to ask about Matt's request to take her out on Saturday, but she knew he'd ask her about it at school. And she certainly didn't want to ask with Delcey and Chase as spectators. Best to ask about it now before anyone else joined them. "Matt asked if he could take me out on Saturday night."

Neil and Amanda both turned to face her.

"On a date?" Amanda asked.

"Just the two of you?" Neil tipped his chin.

They both looked a little shocked.

"Yeah."

Neil cast a glance at Amanda and then motioned Tally toward the table. He sat down next to her. "Do you want to go?"

Tally hadn't really given that much thought. "I don't know. Maybe."

"I don't think . . . ," Amanda began.

"What do you think your dad would say if he were here?" Neil interjected.

Tally's eyes fell on the half-full bottle on the counter. "I don't know what he'd say," she said. "Maybe he'd think it wasn't that big of a deal."

"And how do you feel about that?"

Tally shrugged. "Are you saying no?"

"Did you think we would?" Neil sipped his coffee.

Tally pulled in her lower lip. She did think they'd say no. She nodded.

"How come?"

Tally thought for a moment. "Because I'm only visiting here. And my dad doesn't know Matt."

"Good reasons?" Neil asked.

She nodded. They were good enough. Besides, she really had no burning desire to be alone with Matt.

"Probably best to just stay friends for now, don't you think?"

Again she nodded.

"I think you're being very wise." Neil sipped his coffee and picked up the newspaper. Amanda set a plate of eggs in front of her.

"I think so too," her aunt said. But Amanda barely looked at her. Delcey entered the kitchen and asked what her parents were talking about.

"Nothing," Amanda said as she handed her daughter a plate.

Tally ate her breakfast and waited for Chase to enter the kitchen. Seconds before it was time to leave, he appeared in the kitchen, tossing out a "hey" to the room in general. His backpack rested on one shoulder and his camera bag on the other. He said nothing as he grabbed an apple off the counter and the water bottle from the night before. He headed for the garage and called to Tally to follow.

"We're going to shoot the cemetery shots today," he yelled as his hand turned the doorknob to the garage.

"Chase! That's not enough to eat," Amanda said. "And I don't know whose water that is!"

"Watch the cedar chest as you back out," Neil called.

Chase disappeared into the garage without a verbal reply to either parent.

Tally reached for her book bag by her feet.

"What cemetery shots is he talking about?" Amanda asked her.

"The opening intro to our sociology project.

We're going to have Matt walking through a cemetery like he's looking for the headstones of relatives he lost in the Holocaust."

"Matt *so* doesn't look Jewish," Delcey said.

Tally turned to her. "Just his feet will show."

From the garage a car honked. "Gotta go," Tally said.

She walked quickly into the garage, closing the door behind her. She stepped carefully around the woodworking projects in progress and got inside Chase's car. She'd barely closed the door when he threw the car into reverse and sailed out of the garage. "Nice looking out for the cedar chest," she said.

Chase reached up to the visor above his head where the garage door remote was clipped. He pressed the button and the door closed. "I knew where it was," he said. He pressed his foot to the gas and punched his way out of the driveway and into the street.

"Are we in a hurry or something?" she asked.

"I overslept." Chase shoved the gearshift into first and took off.

"Yeah, well, I didn't sleep that great either." Tally stared out the window at the quiet houses on the street. Several sprinkler systems were fully engaged, dousing the already-green lawns and landscaping with diamond droplets of water.

"We're not talking about it." Chase didn't look at her.

She turned to him. "What?"

"We're not talking about what happened last night."

She shook her head. "You act like such a little kid sometimes. Can't you just say, 'Hey, I'd rather not discuss what happened last night'?"

"I'd rather not discuss what happened last night." His tone was clipped.

Tally turned her head to face the road ahead of them. "I don't even know why I'm nice to you."

Several seconds went by before he opened his mouth. "I don't know why you are either."

Tally turned to look at her cousin. "Why don't you want to talk about it?"

Another long pause. "Because I don't understand it yet." Chase slowed for a turn and took a swig of the tepid water. He made a face. "I'm missing some minutes."

"What do you mean? What minutes?"

Chase hesitated before answering. "I can remember being in Keith's room before the fire started. I remember escaping the master bedroom after it had filled with smoke . . . And now I finally remember seeing the fire in the corners of the room. But I don't remember the time in between."

"Maybe you were asleep. You were supposed to be asleep."

Chase shook his head. "I wasn't asleep."

"How do you know?"

He looked at her. "I just do." He turned back to

face the road. "And there was someone else in the room. I could hear crying."

"The other little boy."

Chase paused. "Besides him. Maybe. I don't know. That's why I don't want to talk about it right now. It frustrates me." He took another drink of the water and then capped it. "This water's disgusting."

Tally thought for a moment. "Do you know when the fire was?"

"I told you that already. When I was four."

"I mean the date."

Chase shrugged. "A few weeks before Delcey was born. May or June, maybe."

"And where was it?"

"What?"

"Where? What city?"

"Where I was born, I guess. Laguna Hills. What are you getting at?"

"If you know the date and the city, you can probably look it up on some kind of online archive. Wouldn't a major house fire, especially one at a day-care provider's house, get in the newspaper?"

Chase studied the road ahead, but he appeared deep in thought. "Yeah. Yeah, it probably would."

"Maybe you could look around on the Internet. Maybe there's a news story out there or a public record that would help you fill in the missing minutes."

Chase tapped on the steering wheel with his thumbs. "I'm surprised I didn't think of that myself."

They rode for a few minutes in silence.

"You'll tell me if you find out anything?" she asked.

"Yeah. I'll tell you."

"Chase?"

"What?"

"I'm not going on that date with Matt."

"Why not?"

" 'Cause that's how I want it."

They rode the rest of the way in silence.

twenty-seven

Amanda rinsed the breakfast dishes and watched the remnants of scrambled eggs slither down the drain. Next to her Neil filled a travel mug with coffee, the business section of the newspaper under his arm. Dior Homme wafted in subtle waves toward her.

From across the open kitchen Delcey yelled good-bye as she sailed out the front door. Neil screwed the lid onto his cup as the front door slammed shut. Amanda turned to him. "That was really good how you handled that with Tally," she said.

"You mean about the date?"

She nodded. "You got her to make a smart decision about it without telling her what we would or wouldn't allow her to do."

Neil pounded the lid to make sure it was on tight and shrugged. "Oh, I don't know if it was that brilliant."

Amanda folded her arms and leaned against the edge of the sink. "Yes, it was."

Neil opened the cupboard above him and shrugged.

"I was all ready to tell her flat-out no," Amanda said.

Neil smiled as he moved boxes of cookies and crackers. "I know you were."

"I don't care what Bart would've done."

"Yeah, I know. Are we out of granola bars?"

Amanda reached up to the second shelf and handed Neil a box of fruit and oatmeal bars. "I just wish . . ."

Neil took the box. He waited for a second before saying, "You wish what?"

Amanda couldn't tell him what she wished. She didn't know where to begin. She just knew she wished things were different between Neil and Chase. Between Neil and her.

"Nothing." She closed the cupboard.

"We'd better go or we'll both be late." Neil slipped the granola bar into his briefcase.

"Neil." Amanda took a step away from the counter.

"Hmm?"

"Did you . . . Was Chase trying to tell us something last night?"

Neil blinked at her. "Last night?"

"When he kept insisting that my grandmother and father might've had secrets they felt they couldn't tell anyone about."

Neil zipped his briefcase closed. He didn't look at her. "Like what?"

"Like maybe . . . I don't know. Sometimes things aren't what they seem."

"I'm not sure what you're getting at."

"Well, when he said that Eliasz could see in his dreams, and when Chase challenged that a blind man could see things that tried to kill him . . ."

"Amanda."

"Neil, I think he was trying to let us in on something. Haven't you noticed how distant Chase has been the last few weeks?"

Neil stared at her. "You mean since the barbecue, don't you?"

"Yes. Yes, I do."

Neil picked up his briefcase. "Chase is who he's always been. That's how all young men his age are. It's how I was."

"Yes, but . . ."

"Amanda, we agreed we'd drop this."

Amanda ran her hand across the chair back next to her. "I didn't agree."

When she looked up at him, she saw pain in Neil's eyes. "Have you forgotten what I told you?" he asked. "What Keith told the police?"

"I haven't forgotten."

For a moment, Neil said nothing. When he

spoke, his voice sounded tired. "What is it you want, Amanda?"

She swallowed hard. "I don't want to make a mistake."

"And you think I do?" He stood still in front of her as if standing his ground, waiting, it seemed, for her to challenge his motives. When she said nothing, he reached for his coffee mug. "I can't be late this morning." He moved past her.

Neil was out the front door the next moment and walking down the stone path to his car. From the window above the sink, Amanda saw him open the driver's door of his Nissan. A man she did not know walked by with a dog, and Neil bid him a cheerful good morning.

The day passed quickly, but Amanda's thoughts were a jumble. Everything in her life seemed to be mixed up.

Gary's questioning stares from across the room did not help. At a five-minute lull in the day, he had asked her if anything was wrong, and she had only minutes to tell him about the tense conversation around the dinner table the night before. About what Chase had said and what Neil had said.

A new set of students had come into the room before she could find out if she was right about what Gary would've said, had he been there.

When the last bell rang at a little after three and Amanda sent the last child off to catch the bus, she sank into her desk chair. Gary wasn't in the room. She leaned back and closed her eyes.

There was something odd about how Neil had handled the situation with Tally this morning. Something that grated on her.

Despite his deft handling, it made her mad. No, not mad. Envious.

She wanted Chase to experience those moments of parental brilliance Neil had granted to his niece. A girl he barely knew. His own son should command that kind of attention.

Why couldn't Neil be that way with Chase? Why couldn't he sit down with his son, his own flesh and blood, and counsel him like he had counseled Tally?

She wasn't being unreasonable. He was. She wasn't the one distancing herself from their children. He was.

All those hours he spent in the woodshop, making beautiful things for people he barely knew or didn't know at all. Those were hours he stole from her. From their kids.

They were drifting apart. And this thing with Chase was just fanning the sails, furthering the distance. She was becoming a stranger to Neil.

The moment this thought entered her mind, a feeble laugh seeped out from deep within her. Amanda felt tears spilling down her cheeks. It was too funny.

She was becoming a stranger to Neil.

"Just the sort of person he likes," she whispered aloud as she wiped the tears from her cheek.

"Hey."

Her wet eyes snapped open, and a jolt of embarrassment and fear coursed through her. Gary had come back into the room. She didn't know when. He was standing right beside her. "Do you want me to call someone? Penny?"

She shook her head and laughed. "I don't think a child psychologist is what I need right now."

"I know it's none of my business, but this thing with your son . . ."

Amanda interrupted him. "It's not just about Chase." She leaned forward onto her desk, resting her forehead in an up-turned palm.

"Okay, so if it's not . . ."

She turned her head to look at him. "I think you know it's not."

Gary looked away. Then he stood, walked a few paces, and came back. He leaned against her desk, his left hand just inches from hers. A moment of silence passed.

"You need to talk to somebody," Gary said. "Trust me on this."

"I don't know what to do," she murmured, but she did not look at him.

"Amanda."

She slowly turned her head toward him.

"You and Neil need to see a counselor." Gary's eyes shined with unspoken thoughts.

"Neil won't go," she said, never taking her eyes off him. "He thinks everything will be fine if I just let this go."

"Then go alone."

"Go alone," she echoed.

"Yes, if you have to."

His closeness, his confidence, even his compassion taunted her. Reminded her of what she longed for from Neil.

"Is that what you did when your marriage was in trouble?" she said. "Did you go to a counselor? Did your wife go with you?" The unkind edge in her voice surprised her. It seemed to surprise Gary too.

He paused a moment before answering. "It's what we should've done."

"Would she have gone?"

Again he paused. "I waited too long to ask her."

"I see. So it's your fault she left you. Is that it?" It was out of her mouth before she could stop it.

Gary stiffened. She felt heat on her cheeks.

"Wait. I'm sorry," she said quickly. "I don't know why I said that."

Gary looked away, nodding.

"Gary, please. I'm sorry!"

"It's okay."

"No, it's not. I shouldn't have said that."

Gary lifted his head to look at her. "There were some things I could've done differently. Should've done differently. You don't want to be the one to give up on your marriage, Amanda. Don't be the one to give up."

She studied his face, and her eyes traveled to his Superman tie. Superman. The hero who saves strangers.

"Do you hear what I'm saying?" he said.

Her eyes locked onto Superman's outrageously big torso, the muscles practically bursting from his royal blue cartoon leotard. "Neil would rather spend time in the woodshop than with me. Or our kids."

"If that's true, then he's telling you something," Gary said gently. "I'm not excusing what he's doing or not doing; I'm just telling you he's trying to tell you something."

"What am I supposed to do?" she exclaimed. "I'm not a mind reader!"

Gary waited until she looked up at him. "If you want this thing to work, you're going to have to find a way to hear each other."

He stood up, picked up his briefcase, and left the room.

Amanda sat for several long moments, lost in conflicting thoughts and vaguely aware of Gary's footfalls down the long hallway of the school building. In the silence that followed, she heard her cell phone beep from inside her purse. She withdrew it automatically, hardly caring who was calling.

"Hello?"

"Hey, Amanda. This is Nancy Fuentes at Pima County Human Services in Tucson."

"Oh. Yes. Hello, Nancy."

"Look. The post office received a letter addressed to Tally in care of Virginia Kolander. There's no return address, but the postmark is from Ukraine. I had it overnighted to Tally. You should get it today. If there's anything in there about Bart Bachmann's whereabouts, can you call me?"

"Oh! Of course."

"Right. I gotta run. I've got court in two minutes."

"All right. Bye."

Amanda stood up and reached for her book bag and purse, vaguely wondering what in the world Bart was doing in Ukraine.

twenty-eight

The computer lab hummed with the sounds of clicking keys and cooling fans. Chase chose a work station far from the door and the rest of his study hall classmates. None of the other students would be interested in what he planned to research, and the school's higher-ups only cared if the visited sites were pornographic, violent, or anarchist. Still, it was no one's business but his own what he wanted to look up. He wanted privacy.

Chase had spent the better part of the morning

mulling over why he hadn't thought to scour the Internet for details of the fire. But the fact was, it wasn't until the last few weeks that his fear was being replaced by a desire to master it. He wouldn't have thought to research the details of the fire before. It would've brought him too close to an entity whose power and form he couldn't grasp. But that was changing.

Ghost was no longer a shapeless monster from his past. Ghost was becoming his opponent. Something to be beaten. A foe to vanquish. His dream had showed him that much—that he and Ghost had unfinished business.

He would do what the men at Treblinka had done, those men who decided one August day to steal their enemy's weapons and wage war upon them.

His recollection of the day Ghost got its name was far more complete than his memory of the day the baby-sitter's house burned down. The day had been warm, the air still. His mother was in the garage—back then it was still a garage—sorting boxes. Delcey was napping. He was in the back-yard playing with the garden hose, painting his name on the back fence with a fan-shaped sprinkler while he waited for Delcey to wake up. His mother said she'd take them to the beach after Delcey's nap. He was bored in the house, and it was too hot to be in the garage.

A verdant, sloping lawn sprawled across the backyard, edged with dirt peninsulas of sago palms, birds of paradise, and several swaying jacarandas that tossed purple confetti-like blossoms onto the flagstone patio every June. A tiered wooden play structure with a curling yellow slide and monkey bars occupied one corner of the yard. In the other, a vegetable garden that would one day be replaced by a swimming pool. The back gate that opened to undeveloped land beyond was usually latched. Chase wasn't allowed in the field: it was home to rattlesnakes, coyotes, and wild cactus. And the mere thought of tangling with any one of those things was typically sufficient motivation to obey his parents. But on that afternoon he'd heard the mewling of a cat on the other side of the wooden fence while he painted a fat, loopy *s*. And when that sound caused him to look up, he saw that the metal catch was merely resting atop the locking slot. Then he heard the cat again.

Chase dropped the hose on the grass, walked to the gate, and slowly pulled the door open. Coyotes ate cats. Everyone knew that. He didn't want a cat to be eaten by a coyote just inches from his gate. He stepped out onto dirt and a greenish brown sea of coastal sage, wild mustard, and cactus. He thought he saw a flash of black and white at the base of a young pepper tree a few feet away.

"Kitty?"

Another momentary glimpse.

The neighbor's cat, Ozzie. That's who it had to be.

Chase looked back over his shoulder to the safety of his yard. He saw the hose happily gushing water on the grass. The concrete path that led to the garage was quiet and empty. His mother was nowhere to be seen. He knew if he went to her she would help him get the cat, but he also knew she'd be mad that he'd opened the gate when he wasn't supposed to.

The cat meowed.

"Ozzie?"

Meow.

Chase walked toward the pepper tree, his heart thumping in his chest. A rustling made him jump, and he saw a cat he did not recognize dash away farther into the brush. Not Ozzie.

Stickers poked at his toes through his open flip-flops. Chase looked down and saw a little pile of dingy cigarette butts, several chocolate-brown beer bottles, and a slim cigarette lighter the color of lemon Jell-O. He crouched down, yanked a sticker away with a wince, and studied the evidence of disobedience. He knew teenagers went back there sometimes. Mr. Barrett next door had once yelled at them to go home or he'd call the police.

None of that mattered to Chase in that moment, though. His eyes were drawn to the lighter. He knew fire slept inside the hard plastic. He had seen people flick the metal wheel at the top with their thumbs to wake the fire from its nap. He was in awe of the power that people with lighters had. The fire had to do whatever they commanded. When they wanted it, it had to appear. When they didn't, it vanished.

Chase knew in an instant that he wanted that kind of power. But he didn't like fire. He didn't like it when his mother burned candles or his dad lit a fire in the fireplace because in his head were dream pictures of a fire that towered over him like a man. He didn't like that dream. He wanted to flick it away.

Still on his haunches, he reached for the lighter and curled his small fingers around it. It was warm and light and reminded him of a PEZ dispenser without the cartoon-image head. He held it upright like he'd seen others do and rubbed his thumb on the striking mechanism. Nothing happened. He tried again. And again. On the fourth try, a tiny flame appeared like a genie out of a lamp. Chase toppled over in surprise, the lighter fell from his fingers, and the flame skittered away.

The jolt of surprise lasted only a second. Chase picked the lighter back up and again ran his thumb across the striking mechanism. The tiny flame obeyed the summons and hovered, bending and bowing like a dancer.

As Chase watched he slowly became aware that what he thought was a dream was real. The dream where there was just him and no Delcey, because Delcey was inside his mommy's big tummy. The dream where there had been smoke and power and heat. The dream that came to him in pieces.

The baby-sitter's house. A little boy like him with an orange stain on his shirt.

Blue mats. A crib. Nap time.

There had been a lighter too, but different than this one.

And a tall boy with red hair. Keith.

"You're not supposed to be in here."

"That's not for little kids."

"Get back in the other bedroom where you belong."

Smoke. Heat. Power.

Someone is crying.

Mommy! Daddy!

Then there were black boots and water and ashes, and everything became colorless and heavy.

The dream wasn't a dream. It was real.

He turned the lighter, looking at it from every angle. "I remember you," Chase said. And the little flame waved. *I remember you,* it seemed to whisper.

Chase felt powerful talking to the little flame that was but a tiny ghost of the dream fire. The flickering sliver of orange and yellow and blue was beautiful, graceful. Why had he been afraid of it? The fire had to obey him.

His next move was impulsive, spontaneous. Chase would remember it as being the moment he wanted the little ghost to know he knew how to make it happy. Chase knelt down and made a tiny pyre of sticks and dried grass, a miniature altar where he would show the little ghost that he was not afraid.

He touched the lighter to the pile of brush, and the flame fell on it like a hungry dog. Snapping noises like the clicking of teeth rose from the burning sticks, and wisps of gray smoke curled upward. It was astounding how grateful the little ghost was. Chase smiled and tugged a handful of brown weeds from a few inches away and tossed it to his pet. A tiny whooshing of the fire swirled upward. Chase grabbed another handful to feed the happy flame. The little ghost stretched to grab the gift, and Chase felt its heat on his face. A thin arm of flame reached past the pile to a clump of brown grass.

Yes! the little ghost seemed to say.

Chase felt a flicker of fear. The little ghost was not paying attention to him anymore. It stretched higher and then opened its little arms, the clicking sounds now sounding like applause. A fist of fire reached for him, and Chase stood up.

The little ghost was crawling away from him now, touching everything in its path. It was getting bigger, spreading like a spill of milk across the brush.

"Hey!" Chase said.

But the little ghost ignored him. Instead it turned toward the fence and his house.

"No!" Chase yelled.

Mine, the little ghost seemed to say.

Chase looked toward the house, to where his mother worked in the garage and where Delcey lay sleeping in her crib. He saw the hose spouting a frothy rush of water onto the grass. Chase dropped the lighter and ran to the gate. He grabbed the hose and ran back as far as the length of rubber would allow him. The fan-shaped sprinkler head sent a sweeping arc of sparkling water over the little ghost's crackling form. Smoke rose as the water rained down, and the little ghost fought against it.

"Stop it!" Chase shook the hose, willing the water to work faster. Dull black began to replace the glowing yellow and orange. The water was winning. Chase could feel his heart madly beating under his shirt.

The little ghost hissed his name as it faded: *Chase.* And then it was gone.

For many long minutes Chase stood motionless as the water fell on charred, muddy dirt, unable to turn back to his house.

The little ghost was not little. Ghost was big. Ghost was powerful. Ghost could not be trusted.

Streams of mud began to cover his flip-flops, and he turned around and walked back to his yard. He tossed the hose onto the grass and then turned back toward the gate and pushed it shut. The latch wouldn't catch. He shook the door. Metal thumped against metal, but the latch wouldn't catch.

He banged on the door over and over, hot tears streaming down his face. It wouldn't catch.

His mother found him that way, many minutes later, pounding on the gate and crying.

"Chase! What's wrong?" she'd said as she ran toward him.

"I can't lock it! I can't lock it! Someone left it open, and I can't lock it!"

His mother reached up, lifted the catch, and slid the metal in easily. She knelt down.

"It's okay now. See? I fixed it."

Chase just stood there, staring at the locked gate, his chest heaving as relief swelled within him. Then his mother lifted her head and sniffed the air. Her eyebrows crinkled. Chase couldn't breathe as he waited for her to say something.

But after a moment she stopped sniffing. The curious angles of her eyebrows dissolved. She looked back down at him. "Delcey's awake. Want to go to the beach now?" Her voice was gentle.

Chase nodded slowly. His mother took his hand, which stung from beating against the fence, and led him away.

"Did you have fun playing with the hose?" she said as she turned off the spigot.

He could not answer her.

There were only a few details Chase wanted to know. He wanted this question answered: what happened between the moment Keith shooed him away and the moment Chase and the stained-shirt boy realized their room had caught fire and they had to get out? If there was a news article or a county record archived on the Web, it was entirely possible someone knew those answers and could fill in the gaps. He typed a series of words into the Google search engine: *House fire. Day-care provider. Laguna Hills 1995.* The year Delcey was born.

He pressed the Google Search button.

Fifty thousand hits were delivered to his screen. Frowning, Chase scrolled down the first page. Then the next. On page five he found the link to a law journal that cited a suit brought by a couple named Brent and Michelle Tagg against Laguna Hills day-care provider Carol June White. The Taggs had sued Ms. White for the wrongful death of their baby girl, Alyssa Rose Tagg, who died unattended in the upstairs bedroom of Ms. White's home when Ms. White's house caught fire. The house's two smoke alarms had dead batteries inside them. The fire was believed to have started in Ms. White's son's room. The son had admitted to lighting a cigarette in his bedroom shortly before the house caught fire.

The fire had occurred in May 1995. Two other

unnamed children had also been left unattended in the house but were safely rescued.

The Taggs won their lawsuit.

The article went on to cite other cases involving wrongful deaths, but by then Chase had stopped reading.

A hot weariness fell over him as his brain at last acquiesced, turning over the memory of the crib, the cries, the name of the baby who had been napping in the room with the blue mats. He saw the crib in the smoke. Saw Ghost swaying in the corner of the room. Heard the cries of a baby who struggled to breathe. Alyssa.

And in that same moment he remembered another detail that had eluded him. He'd been in Keith's room a second time. When Keith wasn't there.

Chase didn't hear the bell ring.

twenty-nine

Tally stepped out of Chase's car, and a breeze swept past her, welcoming her with a caress, it seemed, to the garden of remembrance.

The cemetery, a montage of grass and stone and pastel dashes of petals, lay quiet and somnolent in the late-afternoon sun.

Matt climbed out of the backseat holding a Dr Pepper. His eyes scanned the sloping lawns and the silent rows of marble and granite interruptions. "Wow." His voice broke the quiet. "Creepy and cool at the same time. I don't think I've ever been to a cemetery."

Tally sniffed the air, catching the fragrance of oaks, fresh-cut grass, and wilting roses. "Me neither." Chase didn't appear to drink in the landscape or hear the comments. She turned to her cousin. "Have you?"

Chase slung his camera over his shoulder and shut the car door. "When my grandpa died."

"The one who was a little boy in the ghetto?" Matt asked.

Chase started to walk away, toward the oldest part of the cemetery. "Him too."

Her cousin's stride was quick and purposeful. Chase didn't look back to see if Tally and Matt were following him, and for several moments, they didn't.

Matt turned to her. "What's his problem? He hasn't said a word since we left school. Did you take the last Twinkie at home?"

Tally stared after Chase, watching him stroll past monuments to former lives. She was sure of one thing: Chase had learned something about the fire he hadn't known before. "I don't know. Maybe he has a lot on his mind."

"Like what?" Matt's tone was dubious.

Tally shut the passenger door. "Just stuff." She began to walk away.

Matt fell in step with her. "What stuff?"

A fraternal wave of loyalty swelled within her. Matt didn't know about the fire. The only people in Chase's life who did were his parents. And they acted as if it had never happened. She was the only one he had ever trusted with his scattered memories of the fire.

No one else. Not even his best friend.

"I just got here. How would I know?" Her tone was unconvincing and she knew it.

Matt touched her arm and stopped walking. "You do know. You know what's eating him. I can tell you do. Is it a girl?"

"We shouldn't be talking about this." Tally took a step.

But Matt's hand was on her arm, pulling her to a stop. "About what?"

When she didn't answer, he looked away in disgust and then turned his head back to her. "I think I have a right to know. I'm, like, his best friend."

"Well, maybe he can tell he's not yours," she said.

"Not my what?" Matt made a face.

"Not your best friend."

"I just said, I'm his best friend."

"But is he yours? You're friends with everyone, Matt."

He nodded, but it was clear he didn't agree with her. "You're saying I'm a bad friend."

"No. You're a great friend. You probably are Chase's best friend. But maybe he can tell he's not your best friend."

Matt stared at her, no doubt assessing the difference between being a best friend and having one. "What the hell is going on here?"

Tally started to walk away again. "A best friend would ask."

He caught up with her. "I *am* asking."

"You're asking the wrong person." Tally's eyes were on her cousin. He had stopped far ahead at a row of gray knee-high markers. Matt grew quiet as they walked.

When they reached Chase, he pointed to the gravestone closest to him. "Matt, start here. Crouch down. Run your fingers across the name on the stone, slow, like you're deciding if you really want to touch it. But don't lean in. It has to be just your hands and your legs that we see. You can talk if you need to. I'm editing out the audio anyway."

Matt tried to make eye contact with Chase, but when it didn't happen, he squatted and reached for the headstone. "Like this?"

Chase knelt on the grass and held the camera at a side angle. "Do it again. Slower this time. And don't get your head in the shot."

"What do you want me to do?" Tally knelt beside her cousin.

Chase turned to face her. "Just stay close by me." His eyes lingered a second. Something lurked behind them. She nodded slowly.

Matt stretched out his arm again. "Like this?"

"Again. Slower. Cover the date she died with your fingers. It doesn't match our story. Her birth date does."

Matt inched his arm forward and slowly extended his fingers to the inscription on the stone: *Ingrid Friedman. Beloved daughter and sister. Born July 12, 1932.* Then he exhaled slowly, as if swallowing one question and preparing to ask something completely different. "How's that?"

"That's the shot. Now get up slowly and move past the next two headstones. Walk slowly. Stop, turn your feet, and look at the name on the third one."

Matt obeyed.

"Now move on to the fourth one," Chase said. "Hesitate before you crouch."

Again, Matt obeyed.

"Now, slowly drop from a crouch to your knees, folding them under you. Drop your hands in front of you, like they're useless. Slouch but don't relax your neck or head. Good. Just stay that way."

As if on cue, a gust of wind sent a swirl of toast-colored oak leaves tumbling around the headstone and Matt's hands and knees.

"Don't touch the leaves," Chase commanded. "Just let them do whatever they want. You don't care about the leaves."

The breeze settled for a moment and then picked back up. A second later the dead leaves were gone from the shot as if they had never been there.

"Good. Okay, now stand up and slowly walk all the way down this row of gravestones. Don't stop. Just keep walking all the way to the end. And don't turn around. The farther away you get, the more of your body we'll see. And we don't want your face in the shot."

Matt exhaled and stood. "Right." He sounded resigned. He began to walk away.

Chase slowly stood as he trailed Matt's retreating form. When Matt was five headstones away, Chase spoke. "What were you two talking about?" He sounded a little annoyed.

"What?" Tally had heard what he said. It just surprised her.

"What were you two talking about?"

"I . . . Nothing."

"Nothing." He didn't believe her. That was obvious. She could tell by his tone he knew they'd been talking about him.

"He knows something's bothering you, Chase."

"What did you tell him?"

"I told him nothing."

"What did you tell him?"

Tally tried to get Chase to look at her, but he kept his eyes trained on the LCD screen on his camera. "I told him I thought you had a lot on your mind and that if he was concerned about you, he should ask you himself. That's what friends do."

"You told him I had a lot on my mind?"

Tally huffed. "I said I *thought* you had a lot on your mind. He just cares about you, Chase. I think he's a little hurt I know something about you that he doesn't."

Chase turned his head slightly and looked at her. "How does he know you know something? You said you told him nothing."

"He guessed! Besides, I don't see why you don't just tell him. He's your closest friend. It's stupid how you hide this from everybody."

"Yeah? Well, it's my stupid business and no one else's. I don't have to tell anybody anything." He swung his head back to face the little screen on his camera.

Tally studied him silently. A vein in his neck seemed to quiver just below the skin. "What did you find out today?" She spoke softly.

Chase was silent.

"You found out something today, didn't you? You found an article on the Internet."

Chase swallowed, wordless.

Far ahead of them Matt reached the end of the row of gravestones. He paused and slowly turned around. "That good enough?" he yelled.

"Turn back around! Stand with your hands at your side. Count to thirty and then you can walk back," Chase called back.

"Chase?" Tally inclined her head toward her cousin.

Chase kept the camera trained on Matt's unmoving body. "He likes you, you know."

"You said you would tell me what you found out."

"He's only had one girlfriend. He comes across as the confident jock, but inside Matt's as fragile as the rest of us."

"What did you find out?"

He didn't answer.

"Chase!" she responded in an intense whisper.

"Not enough." His voice was heavy.

Tally blinked. "What do you mean, not enough?"

"I still can't remember what happened between the time Keith chased me out of his room and when that other kid and I crawled through the smoke out of the master bedroom."

"So you found an article or something?"

But Chase seemed not to have heard her.

"I have to find a way to get those minutes back," he said, but not to her. "They're right there in my head. When I close my eyes, I can tell I'm on the verge of seeing them. So close. They're right there. Just out of reach."

"Chase, what did you find out?"

He still seemed not to have heard her. "I need to go talk to Eliasz. He can see what isn't there. I don't know how he can, but he can. I want to know how he does it."

"What are you going to do?"

253

"I'm going back to the nursing home to talk to Eliasz."

"I just don't see why you have to know. What difference does it make?"

Chase turned his head slowly to look at her. He hesitated a second before answering her. "Because a baby died in that fire. Right in the room I was in. Her crib was just inches from the mat I was lying on. Her name was Alyssa. It's her cries I keep hearing in my head." He turned back to face the long row of stones and Matt, who was now turning around.

Tally sucked in her breath. "A baby?"

"That's right. A baby."

Matt started walking toward them. Chase flicked off the Record button.

"But, Chase," Tally said, "don't you think that's why you can't remember? Deep down you probably don't want to."

"I need those minutes." Chase placed the cover on the lens and grabbed his camera bag.

Tally sighed quietly. It didn't make any sense that Chase would want to remember the last tragic details of the fire. No sense at all. "Why? Why do you have to remember? Why do you want to remember what happened to that baby? You should be glad you can't remember it."

He pivoted quickly to face her. "Well, I'm not glad. And don't tell me what I should or shouldn't do."

"I just don't get it. Why are you dwelling on this?"

254

Chase turned his head and eyed Matt, still several yards away. "Because I have this bad feeling it's my fault."

"What? What's your fault?"

Chase turned his head toward her, but he did not look at her. He gazed at the hundreds of lost lives that stretched behind her like a prairie of grass and stone. "The fire."

She froze. "What?"

Now his eyes zeroed in on hers, his voice a whisper. "What if it's my fault that baby died? What if I can't remember those minutes because it's my fault? I held the lighter in my hands. I remember how it fascinated me. I remember going back into Keith's room. Do you hear me? I remember going *back* into his room. What if that second time I did more than just hold the lighter? What if I was the one who started the fire?"

"But you didn't . . ." Tally's voice fell away.

"What if I did?"

She stared at Chase, unable to comment. She didn't know what to say. What if he had started the fire?

A moment later Matt rejoined them. He looked from one to the other. "Are we done?"

Chase slowly looked away from Tally. "Almost." He began to walk back to the car.

Her heart pounding, Tally rushed to keep up with him. She didn't want Matt to ask what Chase had been telling her. She had no answer for him.

thirty

The Federal Express envelope leaned against the front door, creating a vibe of expectancy on the shaded porch. Delcey, sitting in the front seat as Amanda pulled into the driveway, was quick to notice it.

"Hey! There's a FedEx envelope!" The girl dashed out of the vehicle before it came to a complete stop and before Amanda could tell her the envelope was most likely for Tally.

Amanda turned off the ignition, grabbed her book bag from the backseat, and stepped out into the waning five o'clock sunshine. She saw Delcey read the recipient's name on the envelope.

"It's for Tally." Surprise and curious envy blanketed her daughter's words. "It's from Arizona."

Amanda came around the car and walked up the wide steps to the porch. "It's a letter for Tally from Uncle Bart." She reached for the envelope, and Delcey handed it to her. Amanda slipped it under her arm as she fiddled with her key ring.

"Really?" Delcey said. "Is he coming home? No offense, but I'd like my room back." The keys slipped from Amanda's fingers, and Delcey reached down for them, huffing. "And when are we going to have our garage back? It's stupid that you and Dad have to park your cars in the driveway and use the front door. No one else on our street does that."

Delcey shoved the house key into the lock and turned it. An electronic chirping and the clicking of Sammy's nails greeted them. Delcey crossed the threshold and punched a security code into the alarm system. The cocker spaniel danced around her feet as she passed through the entry and tossed the keys onto the granite counter of the open kitchen.

"You know I can't answer either question, Delcey," Amanda said as she followed her daughter inside. "I don't know what Uncle Bart has written in this letter."

"What if he says it's going to be another month?" Delcey bent down to stroke Sammy's golden head.

Amanda placed the envelope and her own book bag on the counter. "I told you I'd clean out the sewing room if I had to." She stepped into the kitchen, opened a cupboard, and grabbed a bottle of Tylenol.

"Well, when will you know if you have to?"

"Delcey, please."

"Please what?" The girl stood up straight.

Amanda took a glass from another cabinet and filled it with water from the dispenser on the outside of the refrigerator. "Let's just wait and see what Bart says in the letter." She tossed two capsules in her mouth and drank.

"What if he says it's going to be another month?"

The water stung as it slid down her throat, too cold. She set the glass down with more force than she intended, and the sound of granite meeting glass made her wince. "You heard what I said."

"Why don't you try hearing what *I* say?" Her daughter headed for the stairs, and the dog trailed happily after her.

"What is so awful about sharing your room with Tally?" Amanda called after her.

"You *so* don't get it," Delcey muttered as she sprinted up the steps. "It's my room. My private space. *Was* my private space."

Her daughter disappeared into the upstairs hallway. "Well, we don't always get what we want just because we want it!" Amanda said to no one. She heard Delcey's bedroom door close.

Amanda picked up her glass and turned back toward the kitchen's interior, placing the cup in the sink next to the breakfast dishes. For a moment, a tiny wedge of seconds, she envied Bart—not his life, but his ability to happily squander responsibility. She reached down and touched Neil's fork, remembering the last words he'd said to her before he left for work that morning. She had just told him she didn't want to make a mistake when it came to Chase. *"And you think I do?"* he'd asked. Without warmth.

She fingered the cold tines. Despite the curt tone, he was reminding her they shared a common hope. Neither one of them wanted to mess with

Chase's happiness. They both wanted to protect Chase from a past they knew too little about.

Wait a minute . . . That wasn't quite right. Neil wanted more.

Neil didn't just want to protect Chase from remembering too much about the fire; he wanted to protect himself too. He didn't want to tangle with the notion that his son had caused Alyssa Tagg's death.

It wasn't just Chase's happiness at stake. It was Neil's too. And hers.

Neil didn't want Chase to remember the fire. And he didn't want to know if Chase did. It was easier for him to pretend everything was fine.

Chase was fine.

Their marriage was fine.

It was all fine.

Amanda walked to the door that led to the garage and opened it. She breathed in the minty scent of pine and cedar and then stepped in, closing her eyes for a moment. The aroma let her believe for a second or two that she was somewhere besides a garage. She opened her eyes and took in the stretch of the concrete floor and automatic doors.

The place her car used to occupy was now a sea of boards of all shapes and sizes. Some leaning against the wall, some resting on the concrete, some leaning against sawhorses and utility tables. Odd-shaped remnants lay in an amber-hued pile like rocks at the beach. "A woodworker never throws anything away," Neil had told her once.

A pile of wood curls and shavings lay on the floor under a silent table saw, marking the spot where Neil's car used to be parked. Behind her, on long white shelves, cans of polish, stain, and mineral spirits sat in neat rows, their heady, danger-scented fluids hidden inside. Amanda turned back to the table closest to her, and her gaze fell on a shiny claw hammer. She reached for it and stroked its smooth handle, surprised at its weight in her hand.

Amanda wondered why Neil needed a hammer this large; it seemed out of place. Unnecessarily big. Offensive, even, to the audience of silent, aromatic boards at her feet. She looked around the garage. Near the door to the third stall, where Chase parked his car, sat the cedar chest. Amanda reached behind her and flipped on the light switch. Fluorescent bulbs sputtered overhead.

The chest glistened under the silvery white shop lights. Amanda walked toward it. The sides and top were embellished with carved blossoms and leaves. Honey brown swirls and twists decorated the trim and top like pulled taffy.

It was beautiful.

Amanda reached hesitantly with her free hand and touched a shimmering petal, expecting to feel sticky lacquer. But the sparkling bloom was dry and smooth. And as she did so, she realized she still held the hammer in her other hand.

A crazed thought skittered across her brain. With one blow she could smash the flowered trim. With several she could pound right through the top, especially if she put everything she had into it. If she just started hammering, she could destroy its beauty in mere seconds. That's all it would take, the hammer and a few moments of raw determination. What had taken one person a hundred hours to create, another could obliterate in minutes. It was that easy . . .

The door for the third stall squealed and began to shimmy upward with a jolt. Amanda jumped and the hammer fell from her hand, landing inches from her toes. A burst of sunlight flooded her vision. Chase's car came into view and moved forward into the garage. She stepped back, out of the deluge of light. She could see Tally in the front seat, looking at her quizzically. Chase too.

As the car moved slowly past her, Amanda knelt, grabbed the hammer, and walked back to the table where she had found it. Chase cut the engine, and the two teens got out.

"What are you doing?" Chase was reaching into the backseat for his camera bag, but his eyes were on his mother. He looked angry, as if he had read her thoughts.

"Just looking at the cedar chest." Amanda turned to Tally, eager to change the subject. "Tally, you've got an envelope inside from your social worker. A letter came to your grandmother's house from your dad."

"Really?" Hope colored Tally's voice and nearly filled the room.

"It's in the kitchen." Amanda turned away from the worktable and Chase's questioning eyes. She opened the door to the kitchen, and Tally and Chase followed close behind her.

Inside, Amanda handed the Federal Express envelope to her niece. The girl set her book bag down and tore open the envelope. She reached inside and drew out a single sheet of paper—a note from Nancy Fuentes that Tally barely glanced at—and a thin envelope stamped with unrecognizable postage. Tally studied the return address, which Amanda couldn't see. But she saw her niece mouth the word *Ukraine* and felt her unease. It was obvious Tally had no idea what her father was doing in Ukraine. Tally opened the envelope and withdrew a single sheet of paper folded once. As she read, the hope that had filled Tally's eyes began to dissipate and then disappeared altogether.

"He doesn't know when he's coming for me." Disappointment was etched in every word.

Amanda took a step toward her niece, her motherly instinct pushing her forward. "May I see it?" Amanda held out her hand, and Tally silently dropped the letter into her palm. Chase leaned in to read it over her shoulder. Bart's script was messy and hurried, as if he'd written it on the back of a bouncing rickshaw.

Hey, Tally-ho,

I've run into a bit of a problem in Warsaw. Things haven't quite worked out like I had hoped. I haven't given up, but it wouldn't be too smart for me to go back there just yet. I tried to call you last week at your grandma's, but I must have written her number down wrong. The call didn't go through.

Now I don't want you to worry, Tal. Everything I've promised I am going to do. Just not sure when. In the meantime, I've met someone who needs my help. Don't have time to go into it, but I know you'll understand. You'd even be proud of me.

I'll come back for you as soon as I can, Tally-ho. Until then, you enjoy your time with your grandma. Be good to her, Tal. She's deserved more of you than I've given her.

Love ya,
Dad

Amanda looked up from her brother's letter, and her eyes met Tally's frustrated stare. Whatever it was Bart was mixed up in, it had to be illegal. No matter what Tally had been told. She was simply going to have to convince Tally to tell her what

Bart was after. The time for keeping her father's secrets was over. Perhaps tomorrow she'd be able to get the truth out of her niece—after giving her some time to get used to the idea that Bart wasn't coming home yet.

Anger at her brother's cavalier approach to parenting and life in general rose within her. Amanda reached for Tally, stretching her arm across the girl's shoulders. "If he knew what had happened, he would've been on the first plane back. I'm sure of it. He thinks you're with your grandma and that all is well."

Tally barely nodded. She held out her hand, and Amanda returned the letter.

"I'm sure you'll hear from him soon."

Her niece said nothing.

"And we love having you here with us. We really do."

Tally slowly folded the letter and put it back in its envelope. She looked toward the staircase, then the open door to the garage, a glance toward the family room, and another long look at the staircase.

"Just go up to my room," Chase said.

Tally hesitated.

"I can hang downstairs for a while. Just go."

Tally moved to the stairs and jogged up. A door opened and closed, gentle and slow.

Amanda turned to her son, amazed he knew without a word that Tally needed a few minutes alone. But his face startled her. He looked like he carried a burden on his shoulders that far outweighed the camera bag he'd slung over one arm. The unspoken compliment froze on her lips.

"Uncle Bart is an ass," Chase said, moving past her and heading for the family room.

"Chase!"

"He is, and you know it."

Her son disappeared into the family room. A moment later audio from the television floated into the kitchen.

Amanda stood unmoving as too many thoughts somersaulted in her head. Gary's nearness. Delcey's annoyance. Tally's disappointment. Chase's pain. And Neil. She had always thought Neil and Bart were polar opposites. But that wasn't true at all. They didn't have the same attitude toward duty, but they sure shared the same approach to trouble—if you don't see any, don't ask if it's there. They both liked to assume everything was fine at home and had no inclination to find out if they were wrong.

If Neil only knew how alike he and Bart were in that respect. He would never admit it, of course. Never.

As if on cue, Neil's car pulled into the driveway. He was early. Probably came home to deliver the cedar chest to the Loughlins and their dying daughter. Amanda watched him walk up the steps to the front door, losing sight of him for only a moment as he crossed the threshold in the entry. She heard the front door close. Neil rounded the corner and their eyes met.

"Hey." He seemed surprised to find her in the kitchen doing nothing.

"Hello." Amanda watched him put down his briefcase and travel mug.

Neil glanced at her before his eyes traveled past her. "Is there a reason that the door to the garage is open? You bringing in groceries or something?"

"I haven't brought groceries in from the garage in four years, Neil."

Neil swallowed. She could tell it was on the tip of his tongue to ask if something was wrong. But she knew he wouldn't ask.

"Well, it needs to be kept closed, remember?" Neil walked past her and grabbed the handle of the door, pulling it shut. Amanda turned to the hall that led to the laundry area and the sewing room.

"Did you hear me?" Neil called after her.

"I did." She kept walking.

"Where are you going?"

"To empty out the sewing room."

"What for? What's going on?"

Finally he asked. Kind of.

"Tally might be here for a while."

thirty-one

Chase's room was bathed in quiet, the only light coming from his laptop screen, which displayed a news archive from the *Orange County Register,* dated 1995. The headline: "Baby Dies in Fire at Day-Care Provider's Home."

It was the only other hit on his Internet search, other than the legal brief, that offered him a glimpse of what Ghost had done with a little bit of freedom. He hadn't had time to read the news article at school. The final bell had rung as Alyssa's name clanged in his head. The computer lab supervisor had to touch his shoulder to tell him study hall was over. It wasn't until after a silent meal with his family that he'd been able to resume the search in his bedroom.

The article named the baby-sitter's son as Ghost's unwitting partner. The fire began in the son's room after he'd lit a cigarette. The teenager claimed innocence, saying he and his cigarette were outside on a balcony when Ghost embraced the house like a jealous lover. But the teen had lied about everything. First he said he wasn't even home when the fire started. He said he never lit a cigarette or even had a lighter to light one. No one believed him when he said he was finally telling the truth.

The article went on to say that smoke alarms in

the house were nonfunctioning and that two young boys napping upstairs had been rescued by a next-door neighbor who'd seen the flames from her own upstairs bedroom window. But neither the neighbor nor the panicked day-care provider could rescue five-month-old Alyssa Tagg, who was also napping upstairs. By the time firefighters arrived and could enter the room, the baby was dead. Two older children, who had been outside and across the street with the day-care provider, were unharmed. Charges of negligence were pending. Parents of the dead child were already hinting at a wrongful-death suit.

Another hit was a short archived obituary for Alyssa Rose Tagg. Just a dozen or so lines. The child had been alive for less than half a year.

Chase leaned back in his desk chair. The puzzle was nearly complete. The cast of characters was fully assembled. Keith, Miss Carol, the stained-shirt boy, the neighbor in pink who grabbed him off the hot carpet as he fought for air, the firemen with the black boots, his father at the ER, the doctor with the green cap and green shirt with no buttons. And Alyssa.

The scene was set. He could see the two bedrooms. Keith's and Miss Carol's. He could see Keith's annoyed face. Pimples all over it. He could hear Keith yelling at him to get back to the other room where he belonged. Taking the lighter from him. He could see the blue mats and the crib.

He could see Ghost swaying in the corner of the room, its long tail snaking out of the vent high on the wall above the crib.

He could see the smoke, feel it burning his lungs.

He could hear the stained-shirt boy crying and could see him banging on the door while Chase lay in the way . . . could see himself trying to get out the door and the other boy pushing ahead of him, knocking him down.

He could hear Alyssa's choked cries as the air in the room became a smothering blanket of heated fog and doom.

And he could also see himself back in Keith's room. A second time. Before the smoke. But the memory was a mere snippet of time. A blink. He couldn't remember how long he'd been there the second time, when he went back to his blue mat, or what he had done. One piece was still missing.

The one piece that mattered. The one piece that would explain everything and would surely reveal to him how to silence Ghost for good.

The truth would silence Ghost.

He ran his fingers through his hair. Eliasz showing up in his dream had needled him. As did the image of the tool bag in the burning room, the tool bag that Eliasz had used to smuggle babies out of the Warsaw Ghetto. In his dream, Eliasz told Chase not to forget the bag, as if Alyssa were inside it, waiting for deliverance.

Chase couldn't rid himself of the notion that Eliasz was in his dream for a reason. He had to go back and talk to him.

He ran his hands over his face as he imagined what he would say. *Okay, so there was this fire at the baby-sitter's house when I was four, and a baby died. The baby-sitter's son was blamed for it, but he said he didn't start it, and I remember holding his cigarette lighter and him telling me to get back to the room I was supposed to be napping in. I remember being back in his room a second time, but then I don't remember going back to the room where the blue mats were. I just remember being on my blue mat and the room filling with smoke and the baby crying and not being able to breathe and calling for my parents and Ghost sliding down the wall and reaching for me.*

"Who is Ghost?" Eliasz would say, and Chase would realize he'd said the name out loud.

Ghost is the fire.

"Why do you call it by that name?"

Because it haunts me.

A soft knocking at his door startled him, and Chase's eyes snapped open. The imaginary conversation vanished.

"Chase?" His mother's voice. She sounded worried.

For a moment he said nothing. Had he said anything out loud? "What?"

"Can I talk to you for a minute?"

He hesitated. "I guess."

His mother opened the door and stepped into the darkness of his room. "Is it okay if I turn on a light?" Her tone was even more anxious now.

"I don't care."

She flipped on the light switch by the door, and the recessed ceiling lights around the perimeter doused the room in a soft glow. His mother wore a weak smile. He looked down at his computer screen as she walked toward him and quickly leaned forward to minimize the Internet browser.

"Am I interrupting anything?" She sat down on his bed, just inches from him. Her eyes were on his laptop, which now offered a view of Chase's wallpaper: the Coronado Bay Bridge at twilight.

"Just some homework." He waited.

His mother inhaled, as if drawing strength to speak. "I just wanted to tell you that I appreciate how you've befriended Tally and made her feel welcome and wanted here. I thought it was amazing how you knew she needed a place to be alone with her thoughts this afternoon. It was a very kind thing you did, offering your room to her. I . . . I wish I had thought of it first."

Chase shrugged. "It was no big deal."

His mother shook her head. "No. You're wrong. It is a big deal. And I really do appreciate how you've bonded with her. That's a big deal too. She's had to deal with so much in her life. I can tell she thinks a lot of you. I've been surprised, really. I thought Delcey would be the one to step in, but Delcey . . . I don't know. I just . . . I'm glad you're here for Tally. Really."

Chase felt an awkward heat steal over him. "Okay."

Again his mother breathed in, like preparing for an incoming volley. "But you won't tell her that you think Bart is . . . is . . ."

"An ass," he finished for her. "No. I won't."

"He's not a great father, but she loves him. In spite of all his flaws, she really does love him."

"Mom."

"I just had to say it, Chase."

He nodded.

A third intake of air. "I know your dad has his flaws too, Chase. So do I. But we love you. I hope you know that." Her voice hinted of pained emotion.

Chase couldn't look at her. "Yeah," he said.

"You seem tired, Chase. Are you feeling all right?"

"I'm fine." His answer was quick.

"Everything going okay at school?"

"Yep."

"And here at home? Everything okay?"

For a split second Chase considered turning to her and telling her he knew about Alyssa Tagg, that he remembered the fire, that Ghost was closing in on him, and that he was desperate to find the lost minutes of that day. But then he would have to tell her he might've been the one that set Ghost free, didn't try to stop it, killed an innocent child.

He didn't want to see the look of horror on her face. Or feel her fear. Or hear her agonized voice ask him how he could've done something like that.

"I'm good." He kept his tone casual. Light. He did not look at her.

"Because if there was anything, I want you to know you can tell me. Tell us."

"Yep." Chase nodded once. She suspected something.

"No matter what it is. You can tell me."

He slowly swiveled his head to look at her. The unspoken seemed to float between them. She didn't know it had a name: Ghost. But she knew it existed. He waited, but she said nothing else. "I'll keep that in mind," he said.

She nodded, brows furrowed, and slowly stood. "Want to help me move Tally's bed into the sewing room? Dad's taking the cedar chest over to the Loughlins'."

He rose. "Yeah. Sure."

They moved silently from one room to the next. Delcey was pulling Tally's clothes out of the little dresser. Tally had an armload of bedding in her hands.

"Tally and I can get the mattress downstairs," Chase said to his mother. "You can take the bedding down."

"All right."

Tally wordlessly handed the bedding to Amanda. A moment later, Amanda and Delcey were out of the room, taking their armloads to the sewing room.

Chase lifted one end of the mattress and Tally grabbed the other. "You all right?" he said to her.

His cousin lifted and lowered her shoulders.

"Not that it's any of my business, but maybe it's time to let someone know what your dad is really doing over there."

"Yeah."

Surprised, Chase hoisted his end of the mattress. "You agree?"

She lifted her side. "I want to go with you when you talk to Eliasz."

Outside, from several miles away, a fire engine's wailing wafted in through Delcey's open window. Chase stared at the window for a moment, hearing for the first time an invitation instead of a warning.

"All right," he said.

thirty-two

The shining halls of the La Vista del Paz Assisted Living Facility smelled of pine and overdone macaroni. A third aroma mingled with them, but Tally couldn't name it.

"I really don't like this place," Chase muttered

as they walked past the reception desk. A gray-haired volunteer smiled at them as they walked away.

"It's so nice when young people come here," she said to the nursing assistant next to her.

A man in a bathrobe grabbed at Chase as they made their way down the main hallway to the B wing, to Josef and Eliasz's room. "Tell me where to go!" he said.

Chase and Tally stopped.

"Tell me where to go!" His worn-out voice was urgent.

"I'm sure the lady at the desk can help you," Tally pointed to the gray-haired woman now many yards away.

"Please, tell me where to go."

Tally looked wide eyed at Chase.

"Go have a cup of coffee and a smoke," Chase said.

The man nodded. "Okay." He walked away from them.

Tally blinked at Chase as they resumed walking toward room B-34. "Why'd you tell him that?"

"He needed to have a place to go. I gave him one."

They walked a few seconds in silence.

"And where's he supposed to get a cup of coffee?" Tally continued.

"Hey, in a place like this, when everything else has been taken from you, you should be able to get a pathetic cup of coffee if you want one."

Seconds later they were at the room. Chase knocked softly on the door. When no one answered right away, he opened the door slowly. "Mr. Bliss? Mr. Abramovicz?"

"Yes? Who is it?" The voice that greeted them was library soft and heavily accented.

"It's Chase and Tally. Can we come in?"

"Yes, yes. Of course."

The two teens opened the door fully and saw that Josef and Eliasz were sitting across from their beds in black fake-leather recliners. The television was on and *Jeopardy!* played on the screen, but the sound was muted. Josef held a folded newspaper and a pencil in his hand. Eliasz, his head bent in sleep, snored softly.

"Did we have a meeting today? Did we forget?" Josef leaned forward in his chair.

"No," Chase answered quickly. "We just . . . I mean, I just wanted to talk with Eliasz about something."

"Oh." Josef pointed to his friend with his pencil. "Well. He was out on the town last night. Partying late, you would say."

Chase and Tally smiled.

"Grab those two folding chairs behind you there," Josef continued. "We start talking about him and he's bound to wake up."

Two metal chairs leaned against the wall behind the door. Chase reached for them. He and Tally opened the chairs and sat down facing the two men.

"So. You have another question about the ghetto?" Josef began. "Treblinka? Is it something I can answer for you?"

Josef looked from one to the other. Chase didn't speak right away. "You can probably help me," Tally replied. "I mean, maybe you can. I think only Eliasz can help Chase."

"What is it?" Josef set his paper down on a table covered with magazines, books, and butterscotch wrappers.

"My father left for Poland more than a month ago. He . . ." Tally hesitated, glancing at Chase. She could either ask Chase to leave the room while she told Josef told the truth, or she could choose to trust him. Her cousin nodded as if he knew she needed his confidence. She turned to face Josef again. "My dad was given a letter written by my grandpa just before he died—we told you about our grandfather last time. Remember?"

"Yes," Josef said. "He escaped the ghetto as a child with a woman you thought was your great-grandmother."

"Right. Well, Grandpa died a couple years ago, but my dad never read the letter. He thought it was an apology or maybe a hate letter." She paused. "My dad and his dad didn't get along very well."

"Ah," Josef said.

"But he kept it. It came to him in a little box with a few things that had belonged to his dad.

Chase's mom, my dad's sister, sent it to him. There was a pocket watch, our great-grandmother's wedding ring, and a cigarette lighter. My dad kept this little box in the trunk of our car. But then a few weeks ago, I came home from school and he was reading the letter. He had just quit his job, and he was planning to sell the ring and the watch because . . . because it was a bad job he'd left and we had to get out of Texas."

Josef's wiry eyebrows rose slightly. He said nothing.

"That's when he told me he was going to Poland."

"The letter was an apology?" Josef said.

Tally shrugged. "I don't think it was an apology or a hate letter. It was more like . . . a map. Like a treasure map."

Chase turned his head to stare at her.

"A map?" Josef asked. "To what kind of treasure?"

"Money, jewelry, gold. Things my grandpa buried in his backyard before the Nazis came for them. Aron Bachmann was wealthy before the war. In the letter Grandpa said he'd buried the jewelry and gold on the property before the family was sent to the ghetto. But he never went back for them."

"Too dangerous," Josef murmured. "It would've been too dangerous, you know."

"Even after the war?" Chase asked.

Josef turned to him. "After the war, Poland was a different place. You know this. You know what became of the Eastern Bloc countries. Besides, perhaps it was too painful for him to return. He lost his father, his mother, perhaps a baby sister. There could be many reasons why he never went back." Josef redirected his gaze at Tally. "The letter told him where this money and jewelry was hidden?"

"I think so. I didn't actually read the letter. He just told me."

"And he went all the way to Warsaw to dig them up?" Josef half laughed as he said this.

Tally felt her face redden. "Yes."

"Would he have any claim to that stuff?" Chase asked.

Josef shrugged. "Who can say? If the land no longer belongs to your family, well, a Polish court might say whatever is buried in the land belongs to the people who now own the land."

"Even if that land originally belonged to an innocent victim of the Holocaust?" Chase asked.

"Yes, well, that is muddy water. Has your father found this treasure?"

"No," Tally answered. "I mean, I don't think so. He hasn't kept in touch with me very well. I just got a letter from him yesterday. The first one. He said he ran into trouble in Warsaw and that it wouldn't be smart for him to go back yet and try again."

"So he is coming home?"

Again Tally shook her head. "He's in Ukraine right now. He didn't say why. Do you know why he would go there?"

"I couldn't begin to guess. I do not have good memories of Ukrainians. I cannot tell you why he is there. Does he think Ukrainian soldiers took the treasure from his property during the war?"

"I . . . No, I don't think he does. He said he met someone who needed his help. That's all he said."

"Did your father petition a court or speak to a lawyer when he arrived in Warsaw?"

Tally opened her mouth, but Chase spoke first. "He most likely went to the property at three o'clock in the morning the day he landed with a flashlight and a shovel."

Tally glared at him.

"That's what I would've done." Chase met her gaze.

"Ah, well. He might've been seen or chased off the property by dogs or the owners. Not the best way to go about it, I'm afraid." Josef sat back in his chair.

"Doesn't sound like there is a best way," Chase countered.

"No." The old man nodded. "Except, of course, to let it stay buried."

"That's just the easy way," Chase replied. "Not the best."

"It only looks easy, my friend. Think of all the

years your grandfather let this treasure sleep. And the secret he kept about his mother, if indeed we are talking about the same family. And the memories of the ghetto he never shared with anyone. Some might say he took the easy way of bearing all that he'd experienced during the war and after. To never talk about it at all looks simple. It looks like the coward's way."

"Isn't it?"

"Like I told you a moment ago, unless you have been through the fire, you cannot understand how it can change you. How it can change the way you think. The way you survive."

"You think I don't know about fire?" Chase's tone was terse.

"Well, you are young."

Her cousin leaned forward in his chair, his gaze boring into the old man's watery eyes. Tally could see Chase's chest rising and falling—hinting of composure about to burst. "Hey, I've *been* through the fire," he said to Josef. "Don't tell me what I can understand and what I can't."

Josef sat wordless in his chair, and Tally sucked in her breath. The air in the room felt thick. "Chase?" She said his name softly.

"What are you talking about?" Josef's words were edged with equal parts astonishment and annoyance.

Chase continued, his voice charged with emotion. "You don't know what I know. What I'm able to understand about choices and survival and buried secrets."

"Chase." Tally touched his arm. He seemed not to feel it.

"I never presumed to know *your* life story, Chase." Josef attempted to sit up straighter. "If there's something you're trying to tell me, then just say it."

For a moment, Chase seemed about to explode in anger. Then he relaxed and sat back in his chair. The room stilled. Chase finally spoke, his tone tight but even. "I've been through the fire too. I've got memories that haunt me just like you do. And I'm alone with them just like my grandfather was with his. But just because something is buried doesn't mean you don't know it exists. Just because you can't see it, doesn't mean it isn't there."

As Chase said the word "see," he nodded toward Eliasz, who still slept soundly.

Josef slowly looked at his friend and then turned back to face Chase. "What is it you've come to ask Eliasz about?" His voice sounded protective, unsure.

Chase hesitated before answering. "I . . . I don't know. I'm not sure how to explain it."

"What? You don't know why you came here to see him?"

Chase answered, his voice low. "I had a dream. About the fire."

Josef shook his head, confusion setting his wrinkles at odd angles. "I don't understand what you are saying. What fire?"

Chase seemed to be struggling to keep his voice steady. "When I was four, I survived a fire at my baby-sitter's house. Another child in the same room as me did not. My parents think I don't remember the fire, but I do. I remember a lot about it."

Josef was silent for a moment. "What does this have to do with Eliasz?"

"The other night I dreamed about the fire." Chase's voice was soft and entreating, all hint of anger gone. "Eliasz was there. And in my dream, Eliasz could see."

"What do you mean, he could see?"

"He could see! He was looking at me. Talking to me. He was in the room with me and the fire, and there was a tool bag like the one you used to smuggle babies out of the ghetto. He told me to get it. And when I tried, I couldn't."

"But it was just a dream," Josef said.

"Maybe it wasn't."

"I don't understand."

Chase pointed to Eliasz sleeping in his chair. "That blind man can see when he dreams. Do you know that's considered impossible? Did you know that?"

"What do you want me to say? I am not in his head when he sleeps. What is impossible for men is not impossible for God. If God lets Eliasz see when he dreams, so be it."

Chase leaned back in his chair. "That's why I want to talk to him. If not today, then I'll come back. I need to talk to him. I need to see in my dreams."

"But you already can," Tally said tentatively.

"Not like he can."

Across from them Eliasz began to snore.

thirty-three

Amanda walked slowly back to her classroom after an hour-long faculty meeting, rubbing her neck as she went. Her head ached and her thoughts flew in every direction. Gary had sat next to her in the meeting, as he had for the past three staff meetings. But this time, having him near her made her restless. Her eyes kept straying to the emptiness on his left ring finger and the strong hands that had no familiarity with wood. He'd caught her staring at his hands at one point, and she'd quickly looked away. It wasn't the first time he'd caught her staring at him in the last few days. She found herself overly aware of his presence in their classroom, drawn to him in a way that eluded explanation. His glances back to her were questioning. He sensed something too.

Gary had stayed after the meeting to talk to one of the fifth-grade teachers, and she hoped he'd be at it for a while. She needed time alone to think before heading home.

Amanda entered the darkened classroom and sat down at her desk. She tipped her head back and closed her eyes. Her unspoken thoughts were a whispered prayer.

God, help me . . .

She could not put words to the rest of the thoughts that tumbled in her head, thoughts that frightened her. They hinted—whispered—of an attraction to Gary that warmed her with both fascination and shame. She remembered this feeling from years ago—with Neil. There was a time when just his presence in a room distracted her, mesmerized her. Nothing good could come from having those same thoughts about Gary. Nothing.

"Make them go away," she breathed. "Go away."

Her cell phone trilled in the book bag at her feet, startling her. Amanda reached inside for it and saw that the incoming call had an Arizona prefix. Nancy Fuentes. She had forgotten to call Tally's social worker after reading Bart's letter. Amanda flipped open the phone. "Hello?"

"Mrs. Janvier, this is Nancy Fuentes. Did you get the letter?"

"We did. I'm sorry I forgot to call you back. I . . . I just forgot."

"Okay. So did your brother say when he was coming back?"

Amanda sensed anticipation in Nancy's voice— not so much a desire for a father and his daughter to be reunited, but for a sticky problem to be solved. For everything to go back to normal.

To being fine.

"No, I'm afraid he didn't."

"He said nothing about when he's coming back for Tally?" Nancy asked.

"He said he had run into a problem in Warsaw and that it wasn't a good idea to go back there yet. So now he's in Ukraine. But he still plans to go back."

"What do you mean, a problem? I thought you said he was in Poland looking up family."

Amanda could almost hear Nancy's inaudible thoughts: Bart was either running from the law or running from trouble. "He was . . . um, he is," Amanda answered.

"Do we need to contact the Polish authorities? Or perhaps the Ukrainian police? Do you even know why your brother left Poland?"

"No. I . . . I'm not sure."

"Not sure if we should contact the police or not sure why he left Poland?" Nancy's voice took on a new tone: displeasure.

"Look, I promise you I am not keeping anything from you, and I am not protecting Bart," Amanda said. "I have no idea what kind of problem my brother ran into in Poland."

"But Tally does? Tally knows?"

"No, she doesn't. I read the letter. My brother didn't say anything about what happened."

"But Tally knows why he went in the first place, right? She knows and you don't."

Amanda leaned forward and kneaded her forehead with her free hand. "I haven't wanted to push her on that. She made a promise to her father."

"Well, let me just remind you of a couple of things you and I talked about when you brought Tally home with you. There are statutes on permanency for minor children who have no home or have been removed from their home. We don't have the freedom or the inclination to let a kid hover in limbo for months on end. And there are laws about child abandonment too. Your brother did not give Virginia Kolander legal custody of his daughter. He just left her here in Tucson with no way of reaching him. That means this county is responsible for Tally right now, and we've temporarily given custody to you and your husband. The key word is *temporary*. The clock is ticking, Mrs. Janvier. We can't deposit a kid in temporary custody and then tell a judge there's no end in sight."

"I know, I know . . ."

"I think you're going to have to push Tally on this. We need to know why your brother went to Poland. We've done a background check on Bart, Mrs. Janvier. His record isn't exactly spotless."

Amanda grimaced. "Yeah, a few bad checks and unpaid traffic tickets . . ."

"And driving uninsured with an open bottle. And trespassing. And shoplifting." Amanda didn't know about the shoplifting, but she didn't say so.

"I think it's time we all stopped keeping secrets, Mrs. Janvier. You need to find out from Tally why your brother was in Poland. And I am going to get in touch with the authorities in Warsaw. We can't keep pretending this will all just go away on its own. I know you're new to all this, but I'm not. That's just not how it works."

Amanda heard a noise behind her and turned. Gary walked back into the room. He glanced at her and then flipped the light switch. Fluorescent tubes doused the room in fake white light. He closed the door.

"I think it's time we all stopped keeping secrets . . ." Nancy's comment echoed in Amanda's head.

"Mrs. Janvier? Did you hear what I said?"

Amanda nodded, only half aware that Nancy couldn't see her. "Yes."

"Is Tally with you right now? Can you ask her?"

"No. I'm still at work, and Tally and my son are at a nursing home, working on a school project."

"Then I want you to promise me you two will talk about this tonight. And I want you to call me tomorrow."

"Tomorrow's Saturday," Amanda murmured.

"I don't care. I want to know why your brother

went there. If he's in trouble, it won't help him to sit on this."

"All right. I'll talk to her."

"And you'll call me."

"Yes. Yes, I'll call you."

"All right. Good-bye."

Amanda closed her phone and set it on her desk. Slowly she raised her head. Gary sat at his own desk across from her. His elbow rested on the desk with his chin hammocked in a folded hand. The tie at Gary's neck featured spinning planets zipping around the sun. *Zipping out of control.*

He looked at her but said nothing.

"Tally's social worker in Tucson." Amanda nodded toward her phone. "We got a letter from Bart yesterday. But he didn't tell us where he was or when he's coming back."

Gary sat wordless. His eyes on hers were steeled, unblinking. Searching.

"She wants me to find out why Bart went to Poland." Amanda couldn't control the quaver in her voice.

"Amanda."

She looked away from him. "I told her Tally had promised Bart not to say anything, but Nancy thinks Bart's in some kind of trouble."

"I think it's time we all stopped keeping secrets . . ."

She shook her head to shoo away Nancy's words. "I don't know how I'm going to convince Tally to tell me."

"Amanda."

"She promised Bart . . ."

"Amanda, look at me."

Slowly Amanda turned her head to face Gary. She could feel her pulse racing inside her body, warning one second and dancing the next.

"Is there something *we* need to talk about?" Gary asked.

A trembling mix of humiliation and caution swept across her. "Like what?"

"Like how . . . tense it's been in this classroom the last few days. Do we need to talk about that?"

She shook her head.

"So it's just my imagination?"

Amanda inhaled heavily. Her breath shimmied inside her lungs. Her eyes drifted to the family photo she kept by her computer monitor. Taken last summer, it showed her family of four posed against a sun-swept background of sea cliffs and Torrey pines. Neil had his left hand resting on her shoulder. She remembered how the photographer told him to do that so his wedding ring glistened there. She could almost hear the sound of the surf far below them. She shrugged.

"You don't think there's something we need to talk about?" he asked.

She closed her eyes. "No, I don't."

"Look." Gary's voice was gentle. Tender. Honest. "You've been staring at me. Watching me. I know you have because I've been watching you.

If I overstepped my bounds the other day, I apologize. I didn't mean to make things more complicated for you. But I'd really rather we just get this out in the open."

"Gary, please. Don't." Her voice surprised her. She sounded like she was on the edge of tears. When no sound came from him, she looked up.

"I just . . . I need to know what's going on," he said. "If we're going to be working together for the next three months, I need to know what's going on."

Talking about the pull she felt toward Gary would knock her off balance. Talking about it would shatter the illusion that at least her marriage was under control.

Talking about it would make it real.

She saw Neil in the photograph, and she suddenly realized why he escaped to the woodshop every night, why he refused to talk about the fire with Chase or with anyone. Because talking about it would make it real. And life was easier pretending that something didn't exist, especially if that something could send your world spinning off its axis.

"If we talk about it, everything will change," she whispered.

"Don't you think everything has changed already?"

Amanda wanted strong arms to pull her away, push her back from the edge, but she felt nothing but strange air.

God, help me . . .

She fumbled for words, for equilibrium. "I . . . I can't. I have to pick up Delcey from dance team. I have to get home."

Amanda stood quickly and grabbed her book bag and purse. She reached for her cell phone and knocked it off her desk. It landed at Gary's feet. He bent down, picked it up, and held it out to her.

"I'm really sorry." His voice was laced with hints of sadness. "I think I stepped in where I don't belong. I apologize."

Her phone still lay in his outstretched hand. She slowly reached out to take it, afraid to brush his skin with her fingers.

"You don't need to apologize." She gingerly took the phone. "You . . . you've been such a good friend, and in such a short time. I've never had the freedom to share with anyone what I shared with you. I didn't expect you to understand so much, to put into words what I've known for years. For years I've known what we should've done. And you knew right away. You . . ." Her voice broke and she struggled to regain it. "You saw Chase for what he was. You saw him like I should have. He was just a little boy. Just a little boy. It wasn't his fault. He was just a little boy."

A guttural sob erupted from her. Gary quickly stood and pulled her into his arms. For several seconds he held her while she cried. In her mind she saw her young son, struggling to breathe, flames licking the walls of his room. She heard him calling out her name. Over and over.

Just a little boy!

The arms around her were strong yet tentative. She pulled away.

Gary opened his mouth but no words came out. Surprise shone in his eyes.

"What's happening?" she said.

"I don't want to come between you and your husband," he murmured. "That's not what I want to do."

Amanda stared at him, unable to move. "I have to go," she finally said. She turned and left, unsure of what it was she wished he was trying to do.

thirty-four

Josef Bliss sat motionless in his pseudoleather recliner, his cotton-white eyebrows stitched together with unseen thread. His eyes were on Chase. "I don't see how Eliasz can help you, Chase. He did not know you when you were a child."

"I know he didn't. But in my dream it was like he was trying to show me the truth. He was trying to get me to see something."

"The truth about what?"

"Maybe about how the fire started."

Josef looked at his sleeping friend and back at Chase. "You don't know how the fire started?"

Chase sat forward. "I know where it started. And I think I know what started it. There was a lighter. It belonged to the baby-sitter's son, Keith. The fire began in his room while he was outside on his balcony smoking a cigarette."

"So?"

"I touched the lighter before Keith lit that cigarette. I was in his room. I held it in my hand. In fact, he caught me with it and sent me back to the room next door where I was supposed to be napping. But I went back."

The old man shook his head. "I still don't understand what this has to do with Eliasz."

"I can't remember why I went back to Keith's room or what I did there. I can only remember escaping. Another boy and I crawled to safety after the fire spread to our room. But a baby girl died."

Josef waited for Chase to continue.

"I dreamed of the fire the other night, and Eliasz was in my dream. And he could see. He told me I was forgetting something. He kept telling me to remember."

"Remember what?" Josef said.

Chase sat back in his chair and ran a hand through his wavy hair. "I don't know." A couple of seconds ticked by. "I don't know why I'm here. I don't know anything."

"You think Eliasz can tell you what you cannot remember?"

It sounded ridiculous as soon as the words left Josef's mouth. Ludicrous. "I don't know what Eliasz can tell me. It's just . . . Eliasz can see in his dreams."

"But that does not mean he can see in yours."

Chase felt a wash of warm humiliation enveloping him. It had been a stupid idea to come. Absurd. What had he been thinking? That an eighty-four-year-old blind Jew he barely knew could tell him what really happened thirteen years ago? This had to be one of the more lame things he had ever done. He'd been a fool.

"I don't know what I'm doing here," he mumbled. Next to him, he saw Tally begin to raise her hand to touch him. But she changed her mind.

"You want to know the truth. About who started the fire, yes?" Josef's voice was soft.

Chase winced. He hated those words. *Started the fire. Started the fire.* "Nobody can tell me that. No one else was there."

"That is incorrect."

Chase lifted his head. "What?"

"God knows what happened. God was there. He saw it. He knows who started the fire."

"God."

"Yes. God. Ask him to tell you. You ask Eliasz this, and he will wonder what brand of vodka you've been drinking. God will not."

Chase sat back in his chair. "Ask God to tell me."

"*Tak.* He was there. Ask him."

A weak laugh escaped from within Chase. "Sure. I'll just ask God."

Josef smiled back at him. "Haven't you ever asked God a question before?"

Chase couldn't mask the mocking tone in his voice. "Oh yeah. I've asked God lots of questions."

"No, you haven't." The answer was brusque and gentle at the same time.

"Excuse me?"

"I can tell in your voice you have not asked God many questions. You have not asked him to reveal to you what he knows about this fire. Eliasz cannot tell you what happened. Only God can tell you. Ask him."

"Is that what you did?" Chase challenged. "Did you ask God where Katrine was? Did he tell you? Did he tell you what happened to her? Haven't you wanted to know?"

Josef hesitated only a second. "All my life I've wanted to know. If I had been able to handle the answer, I am sure he would have told me."

Chase suddenly felt young and small. Like a child. For several long seconds he said nothing; he was too afraid a little boy's voice would spring from his vocal cords and whimper that he didn't think he could handle the blistering light of God revealing to him what had happened in that house.

"I don't think it's that simple," Chase said, when

he trusted his voice to sound like his own again.

Josef stared at Chase for a moment. "I don't think there is anything simple about this. Are you sure you want to know?"

Chase saw the lighter in his small hand, could feel the warmth seeping through the smooth silver finish. Saw the smoke. The flames. Ghost. Alyssa's crib. "Yes."

"What if you don't like the truth?" Josef's wrinkles were knitted into a mask of concern and doubt.

"Isn't it worse to wonder? Isn't knowing the truth better than not knowing it?"

Josef tipped his chin. "You confuse knowing the truth with telling the truth. We are meant to be truthful in what we say and do. But there are some things we are not meant to know."

"I need to know if it's my fault."

"But you were just a small child."

Chase nodded. "I need to know."

Several seconds ticked by.

"So would I," Josef said. "I would need to know too." The old man leaned forward in his chair. "I will pray for you. I will ask God to give you what you want. He and I go way back."

Chase felt his lips easing into a smirk. "Okay, sure."

Josef eased back in his chair, and the fake leather squealed in protest. "Eliasz did not bring you here today, Chase. I think God did."

A short stretch of silence fell between them as Chase attempted to digest Josef's proposition. At that moment Eliasz stirred in his sleep.

"Do you think he's dreaming?" Tally said to Josef.

Josef eyed his friend. "No doubt."

"Do you believe that he sees when he dreams?"

"I do."

Chase turned back to Josef. "My dad says that people born blind don't have the images stored in their brain for their unconscious mind to draw from."

Josef shrugged. "That sounds like a scientific answer to a scientific question."

"Isn't that what it is?"

Again Josef lifted and lowered his shoulders. "I am not a scientist. I am just a man who has seen both absolute horror and absolute beauty. Seen it, felt it, heard it, lived it. Who of us can really say what the mind can accomplish with things that are absolute? They have no equal."

Josef stifled a yawn. Chase looked at Tally, and they both stood. "We should go."

"I hope now that you are done filming, you and Tally and Matthew will find other reasons to come visit Eliasz and me. I must say, I've enjoyed our talks. You've reminded me of many things I'd nearly forgotten."

"I'll come back," Chase said. "I think you deserve to know what happens next."

Josef nodded. "That would also be my pleasure. And privilege."

The two teens started to fold the chairs, but Josef told them to stop. "Leave them. I am going to tell Eliasz when he wakes that two show girls came and played gin rummy with me."

Chase and Tally left the room and walked silently down the long hallway. He was glad she said nothing. He didn't want to talk about what had happened in Josef's room. Not yet.

In the lobby, the man in the bathrobe sat near a window in one of the pink wingback chairs Chase had used in the video shot. He held a cup of coffee in one hand and a tubular Pirouline cookie in another. The man smiled at Chase and Tally and toasted them with his mug as they walked through the automatic doors.

thirty-five

They had almost reached the house before Tally spoke. She'd replayed the details of Chase's conversation with Josef in her mind as they drove the few miles from La Vista to home. Pondering them. Wondering if God would do for Chase what Josef said he would.

When they turned onto their street, she looked at her cousin. "I really didn't you think you'd be the one leaving the nursing home today with an answer. I thought it would be me. I really thought

Josef could tell me why my dad left Poland but decided to stay on in Ukraine. I thought he could somehow tell me why he hasn't come home for me. Seems stupid now. How could anybody know that?"

Chase breathed in deeply but said nothing.

"You don't want to talk about it," she continued. "And you don't have to talk about it. I just felt invisible in there."

"You're not invisible." Chase's voice was soft but toneless. "And I didn't leave with an answer."

"But you didn't leave the same way you came in."

Chase turned into their driveway but didn't press the remote to open the single garage door. Tally turned to face him. "You're not coming in?"

He looked straight ahead. "I need time to think." His voice sounded airless and vacant.

"Well, what am I supposed to tell your mom if she asks where you went?"

"Tell her the truth. You don't know."

"What if she asks why you're not home?"

Chase turned to her. "Tell her whatever you want."

She could not read his face, could not tell if he was releasing her from her promise to guard his secret or daring her to keep it. Her own uncertainty troubled her.

He moved the gearshift into reverse, a tacit message for her to get out.

Tally grabbed her book bag from the backseat. She opened the door, got out, and closed it.

Chase was out of the driveway and pointed toward the street before she'd taken more than a couple of steps. She watched him drive away and then headed for the front door.

The interior of the house was quiet except for the muffled sounds of Delcey's stereo upstairs from behind her closed door. Tally moved from the entryway to the kitchen, which was bathed in late-afternoon sunlight. There was nothing simmering on the stove, nothing fragrant roasting in the oven. She wondered if Amanda had dropped Delcey off and then left again to run errands.

She moved through the kitchen to the sewing room, which was now her bedroom. A figure in the laundry room startled her as she walked past it.

Amanda was leaning forward against the front-loading washer, arms splayed as if she might drop to her knees, crawl inside the thing, and go for a spin. Hearing her, Amanda spun around, and Tally could see Amanda's cheeks were wet with tears.

Tally stepped back. "Oh!"

Amanda's hand flew up to her face to wipe away the wetness. Her aunt's face was flooded with fear.

"Are you okay?" Tally took one step forward, unsure.

"I didn't hear you come in." Amanda faked a smile and blinked back tears poised to fall. "You and Chase had a good meeting at the nursing home?"

"I . . . We . . . ," Tally stammered. "Um, yeah."

Amanda nodded and the fake smile widened. She closed her eyes and pursed her lips together. Her aunt was desperate to pretend all was well.

"Is something wrong?" Tally asked.

Amanda brought her hands to her face and gently ran her fingertips under her eyelids, flicking away what rested there. "I'll be okay, Tally. I'm sorry you had to see me like this. I forgot you'd be coming to this part of the house when you got home."

Tally took another tentative step forward. "Are you hurt?"

Amanda smiled. It wasn't fake, but it lacked warmth. "I'm not bleeding. You don't need to call 911 or anything."

The two of them stood wordless for several seconds. "Um. Okay." Tally took a step toward the sewing room, her eyes still on her aunt.

Amanda began to move away from the washer. "Tally, there is something I need to ask you."

"There is?"

"Want to go into your room?"

Tally opened the door to the sewing room. A twin bed ran the length of one wall, flanked on either side by a three-drawer dresser and a night-stand. The remaining walls were covered with shelves, boxes, an ironing board, and a sewing table. Amanda sat on the bed, and Tally slowly sat down next to her.

For a moment Tally feared something terrible had happened to her father. But Amanda's pain didn't seem to spring from anything having to do with Bart. At least she didn't think it did.

"Did something bad happen?"

Amanda's wet eyes widened. "No. No, honey. I just . . . Your social worker is a little worried that your dad . . . might need help. And I want him to have it. Don't you?"

Amanda was hinting at something.

"I know you promised not to tell why your dad went to Poland, and I know I told you I wouldn't ask you to break that promise. But, Tally, something has gone wrong. Your dad even said it in his letter. He might be in trouble. We need to know how we can help him."

"But he didn't ask for help. He didn't say he was in trouble."

"But maybe he didn't ask because he didn't want you to worry. And, Tally, there are legal reasons why we need to know what's going on. Bart didn't give your grandmother legal custody. We can't just leave everything indefinite."

"What do you mean, legal reasons?" Tally knew what legal custody meant. She'd been around the court system enough to know. Bart had been threatened a time or two by government people who didn't like the way he was raising her. But

303

he'd never lost custody. Never gave up custody. He'd always done whatever they asked or moved to a different state.

"The county people where your grandmother lived, they're the ones who have custody of you right now. And that's because no one knows where your dad is. No one can reach him."

"But you said I can stay here!"

"And you can. For as long as you want. But it's complicated, Tally. All of this involves a judge and the courts and statutes. Nancy says it's not good for all of us to continue like everything is just fine."

When she said this, her aunt flinched slightly as if poked.

"What difference does it make if I tell you why he went? He's not even in Warsaw anymore."

"But if he's involved in something illegal . . ."

"I already told you he's not!"

"I know that's what he told you, but . . ."

"He's looking for money and jewelry Grandpa buried in his yard before the Nazis came!" It was out of her mouth in a flash. A rush of relief moved across her. There. It was out.

"What?" Amanda's mouth hung open.

"When Grandpa died, you sent my dad a box with some stuff and a letter."

"Yes."

"Well, the letter told my dad the location of money and jewelry and stuff that Grandpa buried at their house in Warsaw when he was a little

304

boy. He buried it in the backyard. Your grandpa told him to. Your grandparents knew the Nazis were coming for them and that they'd be shipped off to the ghetto, and your grandparents were wealthy. So your dad did what he was told and buried it all. But your grandparents died, and he never went back for it."

"I don't believe it," Amanda breathed.

"It's true. I saw the letter. I didn't read it, but I saw it."

"But that was more than seventy years ago! Those things wouldn't still be there."

"Why wouldn't they? No one knew about it except Grandpa, and he never told anyone."

Amanda sat silent on the bed, processing. "So Bart went there to find this stuff? To dig it up?"

Tally nodded.

"Without telling anyone? That property doesn't belong to the family anymore! How was he going to do it?"

Tally pictured her father as Chase had described—wee morning hours, a flashlight and a shovel—and knew her cousin was right. She didn't answer her aunt. But she didn't have to.

"But you can't just walk onto property that doesn't belong to you and start digging!" Amanda exclaimed.

"Why not? Your grandparents were forced out of that house. It belonged to them. And the jewelry and gold he buried were theirs."

"It's not that simple, Tally. It's never that simple. He's probably running from the Polish police . . ."

"Don't you even care that that stuff was your grandparents'? Do you know what happened to them in the ghetto? Do you know what it was like for them?"

Amanda sighed. "I do care, Tally. I do. But you can't change everything by just wanting it to change."

"Yeah? Well, my dad says you won't change anything by just sitting around and doing nothing."

After a moment, Amanda stood. "I need to call Nancy. If your dad goes back there and gets caught, he'll be arrested."

"What if he doesn't get caught?"

"Look, I'll tell your dad I forced this out of you. I'll make sure he knows I made you tell me. Though I really don't know why he made you promise."

Tally looked at her. "Because you would've told him it was a dumb idea. You might've wanted half."

Amanda drew back. "Did Bart really think that? Did he really think I'd want half if I knew about it?" Her aunt looked hurt.

"He thought maybe Neil would make you ask for half."

Amanda shook her head and stood up. "I got my inheritance from my father already. Remember?"

"I'm just telling you what he told me. He thought Neil might want you to insist on half."

When Amanda took a step toward the door, Tally stood. "Are you going to tell him? Are you going to tell Neil?"

"No."

"But what if he asks?"

Amanda lifted and lowered her shoulders. "I don't think he will." She crossed the threshold to leave and then turned back. "I didn't hear the garage door open when you came home. Chase didn't come home with you?"

Tally shook her head.

"He had somewhere to go?"

"I guess so."

"He didn't say where he was going?"

"No."

Amanda nodded. "Thanks for telling me the truth about your dad. I think I understand now."

Her aunt left the room.

thirty-six

A manda sat across from her husband in the family room with a mug of tea in her hands that she didn't drink. She stared at the cell phone on the coffee table in front of her as her foot tapped a subtle but nervous beat.

Neil, sitting on the opposite couch, had one leg loosely crossed over the other and his elbow propped on the armrest. His chin sat in his palm and his eyes took in the television screen in front of him, but she wondered if he knew what he was watching. The hands on the clock above his head slowly shifted.

Nine thirty. Six hours since anyone had heard from Chase.

Her son had texted her that afternoon, shortly after she had left Tally's room, but that was the last time anyone had heard from him. The message was frustratingly short: *B home 18r.*

She'd heard nothing since then. He didn't answer his phone, and he hadn't returned her calls or text messages.

"Maybe I should ask Tally again if she knows anything," she said softly to Neil.

"You already did. She doesn't know where he is, Amanda. You'll make her feel like it's her fault he's not home." He did not look at her.

"But she said he wanted to be alone to think. That means he's got something on his mind."

"Then it makes sense to give him some room to think."

She set the mug down and stood. "But I don't like sitting here doing nothing! I feel like we should be doing something."

"We're waiting for him. We're doing something."

Amanda began to pace the carpeted space between the two couches. "But what if something happened?"

"If something happened, he'd call."

"But what if he can't call?"

"He said he'd be home later. Look at the clock, hon. He hasn't missed his curfew yet. You're jumping to conclusions."

"And you're just sitting there."

Neil turned his head to look at her. "Because you asked me to. I have things I could be doing. So do you." He uncrossed his leg. "We don't have to be sitting here worrying about something that hasn't happened."

Neil made a move as if to stand.

"Don't you dare." Her voice was a harsh whisper.

"What was that?" Neil said, eyes wide.

"Don't you dare disappear into the garage. Not today. Not tonight."

Her husband sat back against the cushions. "Disappear?" He sounded astonished.

"Please don't go to the garage." She screwed her eyes shut and then opened them slowly, half expecting him to have vanished.

But Neil was still on the couch, looking at her, his head slightly cocked. "I'm sure Chase is fine. I don't like it that he hasn't returned our phone calls, but that doesn't mean something terrible has happened. He's going to be eighteen in a few months. You need to start letting go. If he's not home at ten, if he misses his curfew, we'll call Matt's house and see if he knows where Chase is.

All right?" He looked at her and spoke gently. "Come on." He patted the cushion next to him. "Sit back down. Drink your tea."

Amanda hesitated and then eased herself onto the couch next to her husband. He slid one arm across her shoulder and picked up the remote with his other hand. He switched to the History Channel and settled back against the pillows.

Across from her on the table, her mug rested just inches from the phone. Her tea was growing cold. But she couldn't reach it without loosening herself from Neil's lazy, one-armed embrace. And she was afraid to move.

She closed her eyes. *God, please let him be all right. Please let him be okay.*

After those unspoken words tumbled across her brain for the tenth time, she finally heard the kitchen door to the garage open. The sound made her jump in her seat.

"Steady," Neil said softly. "Let him come in. Let him be the one to talk first."

She listened to the sound of keys hitting the kitchen counter. Of a tripod and camera bag being set down next to them. The refrigerator door opened and closed. The cap to a water bottle twisted off. She heard her son take a drink and then pick up his camera and tripod. He moved through the kitchen and entered their line of vision.

Chase looked at her and then at Neil. "I'm sorry

I didn't return your calls. I was . . . kind of busy, and I wasn't always where I could hear my phone."

"Where were you?" Amanda asked, and next to her Neil said her name and rubbed her shoulder with his thumb.

"Six hours is a long time not to know where you are, Chase," Neil spoke softly, but with implied authority.

"Yeah. I know. I'm sorry."

"Want to tell us where you were?"

Chase hesitated. Amanda could see that he was formulating an answer. "I had to work through some things. And I just needed to be alone."

"What things?" Amanda murmured, and again Neil rubbed her shoulder with his thumb.

"Chase, you know that if something is troubling you, we're here for you," Neil said. "I hope you know you can come to us."

"Sure," he said, but his tone hinted of indifference. Amanda could feel Neil stiffen beside her. Chase had hurt him. She was certain he had not meant to.

An uneasy silence fell across the open space.

"So, do you want to tell us where you were?" This time there was an unmistakable parental tenor to Neil's voice.

Chase continued to study his father's face. He nodded as if he'd come to a decision. Or maybe she just imagined it. "I was out shooting some video."

"At night?"

"Yeah."

"For school?"

"Maybe. Maybe I can use it for an assignment. I think I probably can."

"And you couldn't call to tell us you were out shooting this video?"

Chase took a drink from his water bottle, but his gaze never left his father's eyes. "It didn't occur to me to call until afterward. By then I was already on my way home. Couldn't call you from the car. Didn't have my Bluetooth."

"Didn't occur to you?"

"No. Sorry. It didn't."

"Was this video shoot before or after you needed time alone to think?"

Amanda sensed a layer of challenge in Neil's voice. He was not happy with what he assumed were hints of disrespect. But she didn't think Chase was taunting his father. She thought he was doing something else: inviting Neil to be transparent. But Neil wasn't getting it. She flashed a warning to her son with her eyes. But he wasn't looking at her.

"In between, I guess you could say." Chase took another drink.

"So, in between this time you needed to be alone, you decided to shoot some video that you may or may not use for school."

Another long drink. "Yep."

"Must be some good footage for you to let it intrude on your thinking time."

Amanda shifted in her seat. She breathed Neil's name but he ignored her.

"Really good footage, actually," Chase said. "Maybe you'd like to see it sometime. You know, in between woodworking projects."

Neil flinched as the wound deepened. "That's enough, Chase."

Chase blinked at him. "Is it? I'm just saying I'll show it to you, if you want. But you're usually pretty busy in the garage."

"Chase, don't." Amanda's voice sounded weak in her ears.

"Don't what? I'm just saying I'd be happy to show him this video when he's not busy in his woodshop."

"I'm not in the woodshop right now." Neil's voice was cold.

"Please. Don't do this." Amanda looked from one to the other. "This isn't getting us anywhere."

"You want to see it right now?" Chase patted his camera bag, ignoring her. "You want to?"

Neil sat forward on the couch, and Amanda could feel resentment rippling across the cushions. "What I want," he said smoothly, "is some respect."

Chase looked around the room as if searching for his father's lost reverence. "How have I disrespected you? I'm merely pointing out the obvious.

When have you ever asked to see one of my videos, Dad? When? You never have. But hey, I get it. You're a busy guy. A lot of projects. A lot of wood to cut. I totally get it."

"I think we're done here." Neil looked away from his son.

"Neil, don't. Don't!" Amanda murmured.

Chase hesitated only a moment. "Sure. No prob. You can see it some other time. It's really good stuff. I was downtown tonight, and a warehouse at the Embarcadero caught fire. I followed the fire engines. Got the whole thing on video. One hell of a fire." Chase turned and headed for the stairs.

"Chase!" Amanda jumped to her feet. But Chase sprinted up the stairs two at a time. His bedroom door closed with a thud.

Neil sat silent and inert, a thin line of movement under his jaw the only indication that he'd heard what Chase said.

"Neil, go up to him! You have to go up to him. You two can't just leave it like this!"

"Like what?" His chest rose and fell in quick succession.

"You can't leave it like this!"

Neil stood and looked at the staircase for only a second before pivoting and then heading to the kitchen and the garage beyond. "He has no right to talk to me that way." He put his hand on the door-knob.

"Neil!"

The door to the garage opened and slammed shut.

Amanda turned toward the stairs, to the room above her head, where Chase was. What could she say to him? What should she say to him?

She stood that way, alone in her family room, for several long moments. Then she grabbed her cell phone from the coffee table. She fumbled for her purse and her car keys on the table by the front door, opened the door wide, then stepped out into the chilly night air. She sprinted for her car while pressing buttons on her phone, scrolling through her contacts until she landed on the one she wanted.

Amanda opened the car door, slid inside, and pressed the Call button as she slammed the door shut. She pounded the steering wheel as she waited for the call to go through. When it did she could barely speak.

"Gary. It's Amanda. I don't know what to do."

thirty-seven

Chase stood in his bedroom in darkness. Clouds hid the moon outside his window and smothered any hint of light.

Anger, fear, and longing tugged at him, but he refused to acknowledge even the racing rhythm of his heart. He reached for his desk lamp, and a thin wedge of light chased a mere scrap of darkness away.

He had no idea why he'd said what he did to his parents. The words had just erupted like lava and spilled from his mouth, tumbling out of him when his father made it clear without words that he had no desire to see the video of what he saw at the Embarcadero.

Not even when he told them the video was of a fire. Fire. Ghost feasting on a warehouse as four engine houses battled it. Not even then.

He heard the faraway sound of the door to the garage opening and closing. Then he heard the front door opening and closing.

Chase tossed the camera bag onto his desk and let the tripod thump to the floor. He knew why they could not speak of the fire—why they could never speak of the fire, even with the invitation from him to do so.

Standing on the pier an hour earlier, filming Ghost as it raged against metal and wood, knowing Ghost would happily consume a human with equal indiscriminate gusto, he suddenly understood why.

His parents were sure of what he only wondered: he had started the fire that killed Alyssa Tagg.

Chase closed his eyes as a dull ache fell over him. He slumped onto his bed and dropped his head into his hands.

How did they know? Had he told them? Had he confessed to them the day it happened that he had

316

done it? Why didn't the law journal article say anything about it? Had his parents kept this information from the police? Had they purposely buried the truth, moved away, let Keith the idiot take the blame?

He almost didn't hear the knock at his door. Anger flooded his brain and filled the empty spaces in his head with hot remorse.

When he heard the soft rapping, he looked up, wanting his parents to open the door. Wanting them to step into his room and his pain, to wrap their arms around him and tell him over and over that he didn't mean to do it.

The door opened and Chase realized he had nearly put out his arms. But there was only one figure silhouetted in the light of the hallway.

Just his mother.

No, Tally.

His cousin stepped into the room and shut the door softly behind her.

She didn't look at him. "Look, I didn't try to, but I heard the whole thing. The vent from the family room leads right into the sewing room." Then she raised her eyes. She saw his distress and walked to the side of his bed. She sat down next to him.

"Just tell them you remember, Chase," Tally said. "They don't know what to do. I think that's why they're afraid to talk about it. They don't know how to bring it up."

He was grateful for her presence in the room, but

it offered no peace. "That's not why they're afraid."

She hesitated a moment. "How do you know that?"

"It's not because of what they don't know. It's because of what they do know. What they *think* they know."

Tally shook her head. "What do you mean?"

In the mix of light from the desk lamp and hushed moonlight, his cousin was wrapped in shadow. He was glad he couldn't focus on her eyes when he looked at her. "They think I did it. They think I'm the one who started the fire. They might even know that I actually did."

He felt her take a quick breath. "You don't know that," she said.

"It explains everything. If they *think* I did it, it explains it. If they *know* I did it, well, there's no point in even wondering anymore."

"Chase, just go talk to them."

He rose angrily to his feet. "What? Go to the woodshop and beg? Go comb the streets to see where my mom went and beg her? They don't want to talk about this! Don't you get it? And you know what? I don't want them talking to me about it. I don't want them telling me what happened. They don't owe me anything."

"Chase."

"This isn't their problem; it's mine. I'll figure it out. Without them."

"Chase!"

"Without you too."

He expected her to get up in disgust and stomp out of his room. He wanted her to. But she just sat there.

"Did you really follow fire engines to a fire?"

"Yeah, I really did." He hoped she heard the exasperation in his voice. It annoyed him that this was the question he'd foolishly hoped his parents would ask.

"Were you afraid?"

That one too.

"I'm not afraid of Ghost anymore." It was out of his mouth before he knew it.

"What?"

Embarrassment quickly worked its warm way across his face. He'd never said that name aloud before. Never.

"Nothing," he said.

"Did you say ghost?"

Chase stared out the window. The moon was struggling to break through the clouds. It wasn't making any headway. "It doesn't matter what I said."

But he knew at once that Tally understood. That she knew without his saying another word that he'd been haunted the last thirteen years by a demon that held his memories in its hot, tight fist. And that the demon had a name.

"Did you go to the fire tonight because you . . . because you . . ." But his cousin didn't finish.

"I went to the fire because I was hoping God would show up," Chase said plainly. "Josef got to me, I guess. I don't know what I was thinking."

"So . . ."

"God wasn't at the fire tonight. Not this one."

For several seconds Tally said nothing. When she stood a moment later, she touched him on his shoulder as he stood with his back to her, looking out his window.

"Maybe he was but you just didn't see him," she said.

Chase envisioned the flames, the heat, the shouts, the water cannons, the roar, the men in turnout coats bellowing at him to get back, the audacity of Ghost's corrupt appetite. "He wasn't there," Chase said.

"Do you want me to stay with you for a while?" she said a moment later.

Exhaustion swept over him. He was too tired to think anymore. "I'm all right. I'm tired." He turned to face her. "Thanks anyway."

"Sure." She left the room, closing his door quietly behind her.

He kicked off his shoes, switched off the desk lamp, and stretched out on his bed, his head spinning with scattered thoughts. *Were you there?* he said to the ceiling and the vast beyond above him. *Were you?*

A hard silence filled his room.

Chase lay in the darkness, waiting for an answer.

When it didn't come, he turned over, drew up his bedspread, and begged sleep to bear him away.

Chaotic dreams that had no meaning assailed him during the night, and he awoke well before dawn, half on and half off his bed. He was bathed in sweat, and the smell of smoke and ashes filled his mind. For a moment he didn't know where he was. Didn't know that he was safe in his bed.

He slowly opened his eyes, reorienting himself to his room and the coolness of the pre-morning air that slid in through his open window.

Chase exhaled deeply. *Just a dream.*

He closed his eyes, pulled his dangling legs back onto his mattress, and reached for the bedspread tangled at his feet. His fingers met something hard and cool to the touch.

Chase opened his eyes again. His fingers rested on Tally's lighter.

He sat up quickly. The state quarters box was open at the foot of his bed, and two-dollar bills were strewn about. And all around him, tossed about like confetti, were lighters and matchbooks.

thirty-eight

For the past few Saturdays, Tally had awakened to the aroma of waffles. But when she opened her eyes the following morning at a little after eight, she smelled nothing. She sat up and noticed that her throat felt scratchy and her head ached.

Throwing on a pair of sweats and a T-shirt, Tally made her way into the kitchen to get something to chase away her sore throat, certain she was the first one up.

Her aunt stood fully dressed at the kitchen sink with a little sack of ground coffee in her hands, staring out the window. Amanda seemed frozen there, as if a wand had passed over her and a spell now held her suspended between this moment and the next.

"Hey," Tally said cautiously.

Amanda didn't jump or flinch. She slowly turned her head. "Good morning, Tally. Did you sleep well?" Her aunt's voice sounded like an automaton's.

"Yeah. I think I might be getting a cold, though."

"Oh. That's too bad." Her aunt's voice was bland. "There's vitamin C in the cabinet above the dishwasher. And cold medicine." The spell broken, Amanda turned to the coffee maker and began to slowly spoon grounds into a cone-shaped filter.

As Tally opened the fridge to get orange juice, Delcey popped into the kitchen and dropped a gym bag in the middle of the floor. The dog followed her, nibbling at the handles of the gym bag, and Delcey gently shooed her away.

"So who's taking me to Sara's?" Delcey said as she grabbed a container of yogurt out of the open fridge.

"I can take you," Amanda said tonelessly.

Delcey turned to Tally. "I've got a dance competition today. You can come if you want."

"Oh. Okay. Thanks," Tally stammered. "But I think I'll just . . ."

Delcey swung around to face her mother. "You and Dad are coming, right? You guys said you would. And you need to be there by one or you'll miss the prelims. And I'm going home with Sara. So don't forget."

Amanda poured water into the coffee maker. "I'm coming, Dels."

"Dad too. You said Dad would come too."

Amanda's brow furrowed. "Yes. He said he would."

"That means you're both coming, right? And Dad knows the finals don't start until four?"

"Yes." Amanda flipped the switch to start the coffee brewing. "Yes, we're coming." She didn't turn away from the coffee maker as it began to sputter. She stood in front of it, watching the first drops hit the bottom of the clear glass pot.

Delcey grabbed the gym bag and for a split second stared at her mother. "Mom! I told her I'd be there by eight thirty!"

Amanda followed her daughter to the front door, reaching for her car keys and purse on the entry table. She turned back toward the kitchen. "Tally, I've got some errands to run. So if . . . if anyone asks, I'll be home a little later. Can you remind

Neil we have to leave around noon for Delcey's dance competition?"

"Sure. Okay."

Amanda and Delcey were out the door the next moment. From the window above the sink, Tally watched them get into Amanda's car and drive away.

They'd been gone less than ten minutes when Neil came downstairs and strode hesitantly into the kitchen. "Where is everyone?" He patted the dog and then reached for a coffee cup.

"Amanda took Delcey somewhere."

"Oh." He poured himself a cup.

"She asked me to remind you that you guys have to leave at noon for the dance thing."

"Dance thing?"

"Delcey's dance competition."

"Oh. Well, that's hours away. Don't see why she couldn't tell me that herself."

Tally cleared her throat and winced. "She said she had errands to run after she dropped Delcey off. And that she'd be back later."

Neil blinked at her. "How much later?"

Tally shrugged.

Neil took a sip of his coffee, and his eyes traveled to the open stairway. "Chase up yet?"

"I don't know. Do you want me to go see?"

"No, no. If he's asleep, I don't want to wake him up. I was just . . . just wondering."

He took another sip of his coffee, and Tally

fought to keep from saying something that Chase wouldn't want her to.

"I, uh, I've got some things to take care of too," he said. "But I'll be back in time to leave at twelve. Do you mind telling Amanda that for me?"

"No. I don't mind."

"Thanks." Again, Neil's eyes swept past her to the staircase.

"Do you want me to tell Chase something too?" she asked.

"No. I . . . Well, actually, yes. You can tell him I . . ."

Tally waited. Waited for Neil to perhaps say he was ready to watch that video of the fire at the Embarcadero. But he didn't say it.

"Never mind. I can just . . . I'll just talk to him later." Neil turned to a cupboard, fished out a travel mug, and poured the contents of his mug into it. He grabbed a granola bar and nodded a good-bye to her. Then he was out the front door.

Tally ate a bowl of Cheerios, drank some juice, and waited for Chase to come downstairs. The house was deathly quiet. When she was done she tiptoed upstairs. At Chase's door she listened for the sound of even breathing. She heard instead the sound of a dog barking in the backyard of the house next door. Chase had his window open.

"Chase?" she said softly. No answer. She tapped quietly at his door. "Chase?" Nothing. She opened the door.

Chase wasn't in his bed. His blankets were askew, and the quarters box sat on the top sheet, its cover unlatched. A few stray two-dollar bills peeked out of his rumpled bedspread.

She scanned his room. He wasn't there.

Tally walked over to the bed and opened the box, afraid it would be empty, her heart already beating faster. Her father's lighter was there. The rest of the two-dollar bills were there. But the other lighters and matchbooks were gone.

Tally turned and walked quickly out of the room. In the kitchen, she threw open the door to the garage. Chase's car wasn't there. He had already gone. Apparently before anyone else.

She was alone.

The morning slogged by. Tally curled up on the family-room sofa with copies of *People* magazine and the television remote. She dozed for a little while.

When Neil returned at noon, Tally said nothing about the missing lighters and matchbooks. When Amanda arrived a few minutes later, she still said nothing.

Amanda asked her if she'd seen Chase, and she said no. Both of them asked her to please tell him to stick around the house when he got home. And to please turn on his cell phone. Amanda told her to take some Tylenol and rest. She didn't look well. And then she said that she and Neil would be back by eight. Then her aunt and uncle left, walking to Amanda's car in the driveway in silence.

A few minutes before three, just as Tally was about to hunt for Matt's telephone number to see if he knew where Chase was, the door to the garage opened. Chase walked into the kitchen and barely acknowledged her. He hadn't shaved, and circles rimmed his eyes.

"Where were you all this time?" she said.

"Chill, Tally," he mumbled. "My parents aren't here, are they?"

"No."

He walked past her and headed up the stairs. She followed him. Chase opened his bedroom door and reached under his bed for a collapsed gym bag. He yanked open a dresser drawer and pulled out a handful of clothes, stuffing them into the bag.

"What's going on? What are you doing?" she asked.

He opened his sock drawer and began to rifle through it. "Don't go maternal on me, Tally. I really don't need that from you."

"Where are you going?"

"Depends on how much money I can find." He looked up from the drawer. "You got any money? I'll pay you back, I swear."

"I don't have any money."

"Nothing?"

"I don't have any money, Chase. Where are you going?"

"Somewhere I can think. Where I can remember. That place isn't here." He tossed a pair of socks into the bag.

"How long will you be gone?"

Chase shrugged and grabbed his laptop.

"What about school?"

He turned to his bed, opened the quarters box, and reached for the messy pile of two-dollar bills, counting them quickly. "This will last all of one hour," he mumbled, stuffing the bills into his back pocket. Then he reached into the box for her lighter. Chase turned to her. "Here. You can have this back."

She didn't reach for it. He said nothing for a moment, just stared at her. Then he tossed Tally's lighter onto his unmade bed. "You don't look very good, Tally. You should take something and sleep it off."

Chase grabbed the gym bag and was out of the room, taking the stairs two at a time. Tally ran to keep up with him. "Chase, please wait a minute."

He ignored her, walking briskly to the laundry room. He reached up to a bookshelf of cookbooks and how-to manuals above the washer and dryer and closed his hand around a decorative tin.

"What are you doing?" she asked.

He pried open the lid. "Mom's secret stash of

cash. She thinks no one knows about it, but I do."

The lid came away in his hands, and Chase turned the tin upside down. A small wad of bills and a folded piece of paper spilled out. Chase frowned at the note. "Great. She probably knows I know. Probably a note telling me not to take what doesn't belong to me." He reached for the note and opened it.

The moment he began reading, Tally could tell the note wasn't what he thought it was. Chase's expression began to change, to twist in anger as he read.

"Chase?"

He finished reading, his face a mask of troubled thoughts.

"Chase, what is it?"

But he said nothing. Chase tossed the letter toward her with one hand and grabbed the gym bag with the other. He spun around to leave, stuffing the money into his pocket.

"Chase!"

He stopped and turned, and for a moment she thought he might change his mind. "I have to know what happened that day." A quick pivot and then Chase was in the kitchen. Tally grabbed the letter and followed him. Chase opened the door to the garage.

"What am I supposed to tell your parents?" Tally yelled from the threshold.

Chase was at his car, opening the door to the

backseat. He threw in the gym bag. "Tell them whatever you want."

"I'm going to tell them the truth!"

He opened the driver's door. "Fine. Do it."

"I will!"

Chase slammed the door shut and started the engine. Tally watched him back out. She stepped into the garage and walked to the spot where his car had been. He glanced at her as he swung the car around to face the street. Then he reached up to the remote, and the door began to shimmy down in front of her as he drove away.

In the semidarkness of the garage, which smelled like the deep woods, Tally stood, unsure of what to do. She was aware of the letter in her hands. Chase had expected her to read it. He wouldn't have thrown it to her if he hadn't. As she walked back into the kitchen, she opened the note and read.

Neil,

I never dreamed I would write a letter like this one. I would rather tell you this face to face, but we don't talk anymore.

I can't live like this. I can't keep pretending that everything is fine. It's not fine. It's far from fine. And we're becoming strangers to each other while pretending that it's fine.

I didn't realize how far we'd drifted apart until this thing with Chase. When he told us last night about the fire at the warehouse, I knew he was trying to tell us he remembers the fire. He remembers it, Neil. I know it and you know it. And you walked away from him. You'd rather let our son suffer in silence than admit he may have started that fire. You say you're keeping silent for him, but you're really doing it for you.

All these years you've gotten exactly what you wanted. What about what other people want? What about what Chase wants? What about what I want?

What about

Tally stepped back inside the kitchen, pacing the tiles, the unfinished letter hanging from her fingers. She stopped pacing, pulled open the drawer below the kitchen phone, and fished out Amanda's phone book. Matt's phone number was listed. Tally punched in the numbers on the cordless phone. Matt might mistake her call for a sudden change of heart. But only for a moment. When she explained the situation to him, he'd help her find Chase, date or no date. But Matt's phone went to voice mail almost immediately. Then she remembered that he had a soccer tournament that day. She didn't leave a message.

There was nothing else she could do but call Amanda. She picked up the phone again and dialed Amanda's cell phone. The number rang five times.

"C'mon," Tally whispered. But she knew if

Delcey was in the middle of her dance competition, Amanda had probably set her phone to silent. That call went to voice mail too.

"Aunt Amanda, it's Tally. Can you call home when you get this? I . . . I need to talk to you about Chase. It's important. Okay. Bye."

She hung up. Her head pounded with fever and troubled thoughts. Tally opened the cabinet above the dishwasher and found the vitamin C and an assortment of cold and flu remedies. She popped two capsules in her mouth and swallowed them with a full glass of water.

Amanda's letter lay on the granite counter where Tally had set it down to make the phone calls. She didn't know what else to do but put it back. Tally reached for it and walked into the laundry room. She folded the note, placed it into the empty tin, and screwed the lid back on. She put it back on the shelf, already imagining her aunt asking her if she knew where the money was that had been in that tin . . . and if she'd read the letter that was hidden there.

Tally crossed the hall into her room and collapsed onto her bed. The minute they came home, she would tell her aunt everything. Everything.

That Chase had read the letter.

That Chase remembered the fire.

That Chase remembered that a baby girl died in it and that he was haunted by that fire and what it had done.

332

Haunted by its ghost.

She drifted off to sleep with heavy thoughts of a fiery devil swirling above her head. She dreamed of Chase's ghost, felt it saunter into her room and spread its ashen cloak over her body. In her dream Ghost was a man, and when he spoke his breath came out in smoky blasts of fire and ash. She couldn't make out the words, even though Ghost shouted them. Then Ghost put his hot hand over her nose and mouth, and she couldn't breathe. She tried to call out for help, but there was no air.

A screaming staccato whine filled her ears, and she awoke. A sea of smoke. Alarms punched the thick air with warning.

She staggered out of the sewing room and felt a rush of heat and danger. Her back against the wall, she stumbled to the kitchen. She had left the door to the garage open. Through its rectangular opening, she could see that the garage was an inferno. Fire was spilling into the kitchen and grabbing at cabinets, curtains, and light fixtures. Something exploded in the garage, and flames shot into the kitchen, as if reaching for her.

Ghost.

thirty-nine

The dancers, in a mirage of blue and yellow and bright green, moved like wheat in the wind—bending, twisting, undulating to the sounds of synthesized strings. Then, with a burst of synchronized movement, they sprang forward with kicks and punches and heads thrown back. Ribbons erupted from within their sleeves, swirling about them as they danced across the gym floor to music that had risen to a fever pitch.

Delcey moved among the flashes of color. As Amanda watched she sometimes found it hard to distinguish her daughter from the other dancers. They looked alike and danced in unison, having practiced these moves for weeks.

If she wanted to believe they were all her daughter, she could. It was that easy. And that hard.

The music came to a crashing end, and the dancers arranged themselves across the floor on one another's shoulders and backs, arms stretched to the heavens as if in supplication. Next to her, Neil began to clap lightly.

He turned to Amanda as applause echoed off the high walls of the gym. "Which one is Delcey?"

Amanda searched the arrangement of girls below. All of them? None of them? She didn't answer.

The girls raced off the floor to await their scores and make way for the next team of dancers.

"They did well, right?" Neil asked.

She nodded. For hours she and Neil had sat on the bleachers, watching routine after routine as Delcey's dance team advanced. But she and Neil barely spoke to each other.

Neil looked at his watch. "How many more teams go before we know if Delcey's team has won? It's after six."

She didn't answer him.

"Quite a few?"

Amanda would never be able to explain what happened next. Something sharp and hard inside her snapped, and she felt the shards splinter in a thousand directions. She turned suddenly toward Neil, raising her hand and placing it flat across his mouth to silence him.

"Stop," she said.

Neil slowly reached up with his own hand and took hers, folding his fingers around her hand as he glanced about to see if anyone had noticed what she'd done. Anger and shock shone in his eyes. He pulled her hand away from his mouth and let go.

Amanda sprang to her feet and began to climb down the bleachers. She had to get out.

Out.

She heard Neil say her name, but she kept climbing down, a few stray tears now beginning to distort her vision. If she stayed she really would explode, and there'd be fragments of her everywhere. A few parents she knew from the school looked up at her as she passed them, first smiling, then looking at her with wide, concerned eyes.

"Amanda!"

Amanda hopped down the last two bleacher steps and began to race for the long row of double doors that led to the gymnasium parking lot. She could sense Neil right behind her, rushing to catch up with her. She ran from him.

She hit the crash bar and emerged into the spreading twilight, infant sobs of despair, shame, and disgust spilling out of her. She wiped at her mouth, wiping, wiping, to rid herself of the memory of Gary's kiss.

He had kissed her. And she had let him.

When she had fled to his house last night and told him what Chase had done and said and how Neil had vanished into the garage afterward and how useless she felt as a wife and mother, Gary had done exactly what she knew he would. Embraced her, soothed her. Made her feel important. Wanted.

A cry of frustration escaped her as she remembered Gary's arms around her, his soft voice telling her he'd help her talk to Chase if she wanted him to.

And then the kiss . . . Gary had apologized. Over and over. But she knew he wasn't truly sorry he had kissed her. His distress didn't spring from kissing her but from the realization that he had morphed into what his ex-wife had been, married but powerfully attracted to someone else. He had wanted to kiss her. And she had wanted him to.

She had fled from Gary's house like she'd fled from her own.

Everything was not fine.

Everything was disintegrating.

A stifled cry of anger boiled up within her. A man smoking a cigarette on a bench outside stared at her as she stomped past him.

The words she had written that morning in a coffee shop convened in her head, taunting her. She'd started the note with every intention of giving it to Neil, but she hid it in the laundry room that afternoon to wait for the courage to finish it and tell him she was leaving him.

But she didn't want a new life with Gary. She wanted her old life restored to her, the one that was slipping away like water through her fingers.

Amanda reached her car and realized she didn't have the keys. Neil did. She pounded on the roof of the car and then spun away from it, greedy for escape. A way out.

Neil wasn't running, but he was closing in on her, still calling after her. Anger no longer echoed in his voice. Fear crouched in the three syllables of her name as he shouted it.

"Amanda!"

She moved away, and her purse fell off her arm. She let it hit the pavement and kept sprinting down the rows of parked cars. He was right behind her. She heard him stop for her purse, and then he was at her side, pulling at her, turning her toward him.

"Amanda! What is it? What?"

"I can't do this anymore!" Her voice took on a strange and frantic pitch she didn't recognize. She broke away from him, and a second or two passed before he had her in his grasp again. He dropped her purse at his feet.

"Stop it!" he yelled, shaking her.

Amanda raised her hand and slapped his face. Her fingers stung. "You stop it!" she screamed. "You. Stop it. Stop it!"

As soon as she said it, she knew she wanted nothing more than for all of it to stop. The pretending. The distance. The silence. The shattering.

She let her head fall against Neil's chest, her voice now a whisper. "Stop it. Stop it."

His arms went around her, and she could feel his heart pounding beneath his shirt. But he did not embrace her; he kept her from dashing away again.

"Stop it," she whispered.

"What? What do you want me stop?"

"Can't you feel it? Can't you feel it happening?"

"What? What's happening?"

She looked up at him, wanting to slap him again,

slap him awake. "Do you still love me, Neil? Do you still love us?"

She heard him quietly gasp.

"What are you saying? Of course I do."

"Then can't you feel what's happening between us? Can't you feel it? We can't pretend everything is fine. We can't!"

Neil said nothing.

"I don't know what you want me to do," he said a moment later, and his voice was pinched and hesitant.

"I don't want you to pretend anymore. I don't want to pretend anymore."

His arms loosened. "Pretend what?"

"That everything is perfect! That Chase is fine, that our marriage is fine."

"You think I'm pretending?" Neil dropped his arms. "You think everything about our life together has been an act?"

"That's not what I said. You know what I'm talking about, Neil. I'm talking about Chase and the fire. I'm talking about us!"

Neil took a step back, and his eyes glistened with disappointment. "All I've ever wanted was to make a good life for you, for our kids. What is wrong with that?" He punctuated the last five words with force.

Amanda looked up at him, into his eyes. "You did make a good life for us, Neil, but bad things happened anyway. Even while you were doing your best! It's not your fault. It's not anyone's fault."

He looked away from her, and in the glow of the streetlight, she could see that his eyes shimmered.

"I did everything I could," he said.

"That's all any of us can do. You're no better than the rest of us!"

Neil scanned the parking lot as if searching for a lost car.

"Chase needs us, Neil. He needs you."

Neil shook his head. "He doesn't want to talk to me."

Amanda sought his eyes. "You're wrong. He does want to talk to you, I'm sure of it. That's what he wanted last night. More than anything. You know I'm right."

"Last night? Last night was a . . ."

"A cry for help! I knew it, and I still walked away from him. He was begging you to open up to him, Neil."

"He was accusing me of not being there for him!"

"He was telling you how much he's missed you."

Neil scanned the lot and looked down at his feet. "Do we have to talk about this here?"

"Well, when do you suppose we'll talk about this, Neil?"

A second of angry silence hung between them.

Neil sighed heavily. "I don't know what to say to him now. I don't even know what came between us."

Amanda closed her eyes. "*You* came between you and Chase. You and your need to keep alive this illusion that we've got the perfect life." She opened her eyes. "I know, because I let the same distance come between you and me. We both did. And it's nearly finished us, Neil."

He'd been looking away, but he jerked his head back and studied her face. "What do you mean?"

"I began to imagine what it would be like to walk away." Fresh tears spilled from her eyes.

"Walk away? You mean leave me?"

"I couldn't handle imagining it, Neil. It felt like death. But I can't see us staying how we are, either. I just feel this horrible spinning no matter which way I look. It's like our world is crashing in around us, on all sides. That's what I want you to stop. I want you to see it. And stop it."

"Well, what if I can't stop it?" Still the anger, still the fear.

"I'm not asking you to fix something that can't be fixed! Just admit it's broken. I can learn to live with broken."

Neil paced a few steps away from her and then walked back. "I don't know how to tell Chase about what I tried to protect him from. What if he can't understand why I did it? What if we lose him?"

Amanda touched his arm. "Every day that we don't talk about this, we're losing him anyway. I'm sure of it, Neil."

He sighed heavily. "All right."

For several seconds, neither said anything. Neil looked over his shoulder at the gymnasium. "Do we have to go back in?" he said.

"I think it's almost over," she breathed.

Neil's cell phone began to vibrate in his pocket.

"Probably Delcey wondering where we are," Amanda said.

Neil pulled the phone out. "It's not Delcey." He flipped it open. "Yes?"

Even in the milky-white glow of the parking lot lights, Amanda could see the color instantly drain from her husband's face.

"Is everyone out of the house?" Neil said. "We have a son—he's seventeen. And our niece! Are they out of the house?"

Fear spiked through Amanda's body. "What? What's happening?"

Neil didn't answer her. "We'll be right there. We're, uh . . . God, we're twenty-five miles away. We'll get there as soon as we can. Tell the fire department there could be two teenagers inside the house!"

Hot fear crashed against her. "What happened?" she cried.

Neil reached down for her purse on the ground and thrust it at her. He grabbed her arm and began to run toward their car. "That was our security company. Our smoke alarms have gone off."

Amanda pictured the little white domes with their tiny scarlet lights scattered throughout the house. "Which ones?"

"All of them." Neil threw open the driver's door. "Call the house. Tell the kids to get out!"

With shaking hands, Amanda reached inside her purse for her phone. "Didn't the alarm company call the house?"

"No one . . . no one answered," Neil's voice trembled. "Call Chase's cell. Call Hal and Diana next door."

Her fingers closed around her phone and she pulled it out. "I missed a call! From the house!" Amanda slid into the car and slammed her door shut. She pressed the speed dial for her voice mail and waited breathless for it to connect. Neil started the car and shoved the gearshift into reverse. Seconds later she was listening to Tally's agitated voice telling her to call home as soon as she could. It was important.

Something wasn't right with Chase.

forty

It hadn't been difficult to locate the cemetery where Alyssa Tagg was buried. A Google search at an Internet café produced the results Chase wanted. A death index for Orange County that dated back to 1940 was one of the first hits on his search. Alyssa Rose Tagg's remains had been laid to rest at Whispering Cliffs Memorial Park in nearby Dana Point four days after the fire.

The decision to make the hour-and-a-half drive to her gravesite had been spontaneous, but once Chase left the house, he realized he'd wanted to do this from the moment he remembered what Ghost had done to the baby in the crib.

Chase's dreams from the night before had sent him reeling from the house before the sun rose. He couldn't remember the substance of the dreams, just how they made him feel. Alone. Afraid. Accountable. He'd grabbed the lighters and matchbooks strewn about his sheets and left the house in a daze of anger and fear. The missing minutes seemed within inches of his grasp, just on the other side of consciousness.

He'd driven downtown, parked his car in an Ace parking lot, and retraced his steps to the burned warehouse. For several crazed seconds he contemplated setting fire to the building next door for the sole purpose of challenging Ghost to a battle to the death. A battle for the truth.

But the moment the thought crossed his mind, Chase could sense Ghost's ardent willingness to happily meet him anytime, anyplace. He'd tugged at his pants pockets, removed the lighters and matchbooks, and flung them into the storm sewer.

Then he sat on the curb in the shadow of the hulking ruin for the better part of an hour.

There had to be a trigger that would trip the latch on that door to his memory. And he had to find it.

For the next several hours he'd walked the streets downtown, wandering without aim, intent on finding a way to remember what had been hidden from him.

A few minutes after two o'clock, a mother walked past him with a baby in a stroller, and at that moment it occurred to Chase to visit Alyssa Tagg's grave and, if nothing else, panhandle the heavens for forgiveness.

And if he didn't get it, he'd go back the next day. And the next.

But he'd needed money and his laptop. Those were the only reasons he'd returned home first. Extra clothes were an afterthought.

Chase had hoped to come home to an empty house, but Tally's presence hadn't complicated things like he thought it might. His cousin had instead unwittingly galvanized his plan to leave. An angry Tally swore to tell his parents everything he'd confided about the fire. Good. Finally, the silence would be broken.

Plus, his mother would see that the money in the tin was gone if she intended to finish what she started. She would know he'd read her hidden letter.

Seagulls soared overhead, calling out to one another as Chase strode across the parking lot at Whispering Hills.

A scattering of other cars revealed that he wasn't the only person needing to reconnect with the past. But there were no hearses, no long lines of cars shining in the sun; only diffused dots of humanity appeared on the gray and green landscape. The grounds were quiet except for the birds. A lone groundskeeper raked sycamore leaves into brown fringed piles.

Creamy stone pathways crisscrossed the shaded sloping lawns. Chase didn't know where he'd find Alyssa's headstone, so he started at one end of the park and traveled the rows, his eyes searching the names.

Ten minutes and four rows later, he came across a marble marker next to a giant oak. On the polished surface an etched lamb rested against a cross. Under the lamb, a name had been pounded into the stone.

Alyssa Rose Tagg
December 31, 1994 to May 19, 1995
Our beautiful baby girl—
A bud to bloom in heaven

He read the epitaph over and over, wishing to sail away on the expectation that allowed Alyssa's parents to think of heaven when a fiery hell had robbed them of their daughter.

Chase dropped slowly to his knees, staring at the headstone.

"Life sucks sometimes, doesn't it?" he whispered.

For several long moments he just knelt there, unaware of time and place, imagining what Alyssa's parents looked like. He couldn't remember them. He could only see the image of his own parents in his head.

It was oddly satisfying that his mother knew his outburst the night before had been a searing flash of transparency. She knew he remembered. And yet nothing had really changed. His worst fears were proving true.

Well, not his worst. Apparently his parents didn't *know* if he started the fire; they just wondered if he did. He laughed under his breath as he contemplated which was worse.

"You and your little sister sharing a joke?"

Chase's head snapped up. The groundskeeper, a rake in one hand and leaf bag in the other, stood a few feet away.

"Oh. She's not . . . She wasn't my sister."

"Family?"

Chase said nothing. He knew the man would mistake his silence for an answer.

"She was so young," the man said.

"Yes."

"Was she sick?"

"There was a fire." Chase said nothing else.

The man shook his head. "Oh my. That's too bad. I always hate it when I come to work and see a new little one's come to rest here. Doesn't seem fair."

"No."

The groundskeeper cocked his head. "I don't think I've seen you here before. You come here often?"

"I've never been here," Chase answered.

The man dropped his bag, then squatted down by Chase and extended his hand. Chase shook it. "I'm Rudy Girard," he said.

"Chase Janvier."

The man broke into a grin. "Janvier! That's French for—"

"January. Yeah."

"My last name is French too. Not as interesting as yours, though."

"Well, I don't know if it's that interesting."

"January's a month for new beginnings."

Chase blinked at the man.

"People think this is just a place where things stop," Rudy said. "But I know it's not true. Lots of things begin here. Good things. I've seen it happen."

"All right," Chase finally said.

"It's true." The man smiled for a moment and then said, "You look tired. You look sad. I just wanted you to know that."

Chase said nothing.

Rudy Girard grunted and stood. He nodded toward Alyssa's grave. "I see a man and his wife here at this grave sometimes. They have two daughters. One of them's named Molly, I'm pretty sure. I've heard them say her name. Not so sure about the other one's name. But you probably already know all that."

The groundskeeper mistook Chase's silent nod for a yes. The Taggs had two more daughters. Two.

"Okay," Rudy said. "Well, maybe I'll see you again sometime. Good-bye, Mr. Janvier."

Chase swallowed and his Adam's apple felt like a stone. "Bye."

The man picked up the lawn bag and ambled off, whistling. Chase watched him walk away. Chase sat back heavily against the tree that canopied Alyssa's grave. He tipped his head back against the trunk and stared at Alyssa's epitaph. His eyelids felt heavy.

A bud to bloom in heaven.

Chase closed his eyes, sensing the awful nearness of Alyssa's presence. He could see the bumper pads in her crib. The brown wooden rungs, twisted like long doughnuts. The smell of baby powder. The bluish hue of the room where they lay, curtains drawn, before the fire came.

Chase let his mind spin backward, placing himself in the room with the blue mats, back into the moments that he knew so far. He was supposed to be napping, but he couldn't sleep. He remembered thinking he was too old for naps. He had gotten up from his mat and peeked out the door. Keith was in the bathroom. Keith had model cars on his dresser. He saw himself walking into Keith's room and seeing something shiny on the bed. The lighter. Then he saw Keith coming into the bedroom. He yelled at him because Chase had the lighter in his hands. Keith told him the lighter wasn't for little kids and sent him back to his room.

But Chase went back. He felt his body go slack against the tree as he let the memory play itself out.

The boy with the stain on his shirt followed him back to the room. *Devin.* The name seemed to rush forward from a place in his mind that had been dark before. The boy's name was Devin.

Devin was in Keith's room with him, had followed Chase there. And followed him back a second time.

Chase fought to stay in the moment, but he was so tired. Restless sleep the night before, waking before the sun, walking the streets of downtown San Diego for hours, driving here, visually encountering Alyssa's grave . . .

Sleep overcame him as he rested against the tree.

The images in his head seemed to freeze, and

then slowly the pieces began to plunk down around him like pillows thrown down from twenty feet up. He saw the mats again and saw Devin standing at the closed door of the room where they were supposed to be napping. The lost minutes rained down on him, and he struggled not to gasp.

He saw the door in the room with the mats, and together he and Devin opened it wide. They tiptoed back to Keith's doorway and peeked inside. Keith flicked the lighter, and the flame bounced out of it.

He watched the baby-sitter's son touch the lighter to a cigarette he had in his mouth. Then he tossed the lighter on his bed and pushed back the curtain on his sliding door. He stepped out onto his balcony and slid the door shut, and the curtain swung back into place. Keith climbed down the balcony into the backyard. They saw him, through the fabric, jump down onto the patio.

Devin pushed the door open wide with his hand and walked into the room. They stood at Keith's bed and looked at the lighter.

Then Devin reached down and picked it up. He fingered it. Turned it over in his hand and worked the hinged top until he opened it. He ran his thumb over the mechanism the way they saw Keith do it. It took several tries, but finally a little flame appeared, and Devin and Chase laughed. They made it work. The lid slid back and the flame vanished.

"My uncle smokes cigarettes." Devin pointed to the pack of Marlboros that peeked out of a denim jacket slung over a chair. "He likes 'em." Devin reached into the jacket pocket and pulled the pack out.

"Those are Keith's," Chase heard himself say.

"I just want to see one." Devin pulled out a slim white cylinder and extended it to Chase. "Hold it."

"I don't want to."

Devin huffed, looked around the room, and then set the cigarette down on the bed. Again he ran his thumb over the mechanism and the flame appeared. Devin held the lighter to the cigarette perched on the bed, frowning as he tried to get the right angle.

"Ow! It's hot," Devin said, but he kept at it.

A wisp of gray smoke began to swirl up from the cigarette. Or maybe from the bed. Or maybe both. Devin was frowning at it when they heard Alyssa crying in the other room. If Alyssa kept crying, Miss Carol would come and they would get in trouble for being in Keith's room.

"Go back!" Devin commanded, letting the lighter snap shut and tossing it onto the bed.

"What about that?" Chase pointed to the cigarette and the plume of smoke now rising from it.

Devin picked up the cigarette and held it like a birthday candle. He blew on it and tossed it back on the bed. "I blew it out. Go! Before she comes!"

They ran back to the napping room and fell down on their mats.

"Shut up, Alyssa! Go to sleep!" Devin yelled.

Chase worried about the cigarette on the bed. What would Keith say about it when he saw it? Would he say something? What if he told Miss Carol? She'd be mad. She'd tell Chase's parents he'd been in Keith's room playing with cigarettes and the little silver thing with fire inside it. But maybe Keith wouldn't tell her. Maybe she didn't know he had those cigarettes . . .

The room faded then as if in fog; perhaps he really had napped for a few minutes. The next thing he knew, he was gasping for air and pennants of fire were flapping out of a square hole in the wall, reaching for Alyssa's crib.

Fire.

Alyssa was crying. Chase couldn't breathe. He couldn't see. He called out for his parents, and the breath on his tongue was hot. His eyes burned and his chest hurt. He crawled to the door, but Devin climbed on top of him, kicking him in the head as he reached for the doorknob. But Chase's body was in the way. The door wouldn't open.

Devin started pounding on the door with his fists, yelling.

He had to get out.

Had to get out.

Alyssa.

Chase pushed Devin away and grabbed the doorknob. The door swung open, and air filled the room . . .

A squawk from a seagull penetrated Chase's mind, and he awoke with a start. Sweat had beaded on his forehead and now trickled down his temples. He bolted upright, and his gaze fell on the little lamb to the left of Alyssa's name.

The dream had been more than a dream; the dream was a door.

He hadn't been the one to start the fire.

It wasn't him.

He sat forward on his knees and looked in the direction the gardener had gone. But Chase was alone in that little corner of the cemetery. He didn't know how much time had passed. He swung back around and breathed in the salted air and closed his eyes.

It wasn't him.

Relief and sorrow washed over him in twin waves. He opened his eyes and reached for Alyssa's name on her headstone. He ran his fingers across the etched letters.

Devin had been the one to hold the flame to the bedspread. Not him.

For several long moments, Chase knelt there on the grass, a stranger to the sensation of subtle release.

Not my fault. Not my fault.

He whispered the words, tried them on. Spoke them into the breeze that riffled through the branches above his head. Waited for them to whisk away the emptiness he still felt as he stared at Alyssa's name.

It wasn't his fault, but Alyssa had died anyway. He had crawled away from her, powerless to save her.

He hadn't known a cigarette wasn't like a candle. He hadn't known that when you open a door, you feed the fire.

"I'm sorry, Alyssa," he whispered.

Several minutes later he rose and began to walk back to his car. He passed a new headstone laden with fresh flowers. A long candle buried in red glass burned a plea that the departed not be forgotten. The flame swayed as if in prayer, whispering its grief in quiet, compliant meditation. A foe of no one.

Nameless.

A few minutes later he was in his car and headed south.

It took over an hour to get back to San Diego, but Chase drove unaware of passing time as he pondered the lost details that had been returned to him and the odd sensation of looseness he now felt.

He'd left the cemetery in sunlight, and now evening shadows were gathering. He was only faintly aware of the wailing of fire engines as he neared his neighborhood. The closer he got to home, the more strident the sirens became. A tiny thread of alarm wove its way across him. Chase turned onto the cross street, and immediately he could see fire engines coming from the other direction. Then he smelled the smoke. His eyes scanned the sky above him through his windshield. He turned down his own street and saw the amber glow of flames shooting out between the seams in the garage doors of his house.

The word fell from his lips in a rush of air. "Fire."

The woodshop was on fire. And the kitchen.

Tally.

Chase punched the accelerator and pulled up in front of the house, parking half on the lawn and half off. He dashed out of his car as the fire engines screamed their way down his street. A group of neighbors stood at a safe distance and yelled at him to stay back.

"Is Tally with you? Did you see Tally come out?" he yelled to them.

"Who's Tally?" said the neighbor from two doors down.

He couldn't see her anywhere.

Chase sprinted to the front door and threw it open, shouting Tally's name. Smoke and ash fogged the entry. Chase held an arm over his nose and mouth and stumbled in. Flames encircled the kitchen, and the doorway to the garage revealed an open, burning maw. Chase couldn't see the staircase or the living room.

"Tally!" he yelled. Spreading flames flanked the hallway to the laundry room and sewing room. "Tally!"

From behind he thought he heard her voice. *The stairs?* He turned toward the sound, then moved that direction and fell onto the first step.

"Tally!"

"Chase!" her voice wafted above the roar and smoke. He crawled up two steps and felt her leg.

"The dog! I can't find the dog," she sputtered.

"We've got to get out!"

He grabbed for her hands. He felt metal and plastic and fabric. His camera and something else. He didn't know what.

"Come on!" he yelled.

They began to crawl away, and suddenly a dash of fur and weight blew past them. Sammy was charging for the front door.

"This way!" Chase held Tally's hand and ran for the doorway, aware that she stumbled under the weight and encumbrance of what she carried. A fireman in full gear was now silhouetted against the opening, outlining their exit.

They staggered to the door, and a team of firefighters rushed forward. One firefighter grabbed them by the shoulders and propelled them forward to the far edge of the front lawn.

"Are you hurt?" the firefighter yelled.

Chase looked at Tally.

"I'm okay," she coughed. DVDs and a small box fell from her arms onto the grass at her feet. A few photographs fluttered out.

"We're all right," Chase said.

"Is there anyone else in the house?"

"No," Tally said.

The man rushed away. Chase looked at the black cases on the lawn, the overturned box of photos, and his camera that she held to her chest.

"What's all this?" he said.

"I had to go back for my dad's lighter in your room. Then I saw all your movies and stuff. And then I remembered your mom had all those old family photos on that buffet table in the dining room. Then I couldn't find the dog." She coughed and handed him the camera.

"Are you sure you're all right?"

She nodded. "Are you?"

"Yeah. I am."

"You came back."

He shrugged. "I finally got what I wanted."

She looked at him and waited.

"It wasn't me, Tally," he said quietly. "I didn't start the fire that killed Alyssa. It was the other kid in the room. It wasn't me."

"You . . . you don't seem that happy."

He shook his head. "It doesn't really change anything for that little girl."

Tally shrugged. "It changes things for you, doesn't it?"

He nodded. "Yeah. I guess."

"And what about . . . Ghost?" she said.

Chase looked over his shoulder as smoke rose into the twilight sky. "I'm not sure that I believe in ghosts anymore."

He began to tell her what happened to him at the cemetery as firefighters rushed past them into the ambitious, nameless inferno.

forty-one

She saw them drive up, hit a curb, and then stop the car in the middle of the street. Out spilled her aunt and uncle, and they ran under the ashy spill of a streetlight toward the house, now a smoldering dark mass flanked by spinning red, blue, and white emergency lights.

The house still stood, but the garage had disappeared into ruins, leaving the master bedroom above it to teeter on its floor joists. The front kitchen wall had morphed into a blackened skeleton, and all the downstairs windows had blown out. Glass glittered on the wet driveway. The laundry room and sewing room wall studs shone like obsidian when the firefighters' heavy-duty flashlights roved across them.

Chase stood near the melted and distorted garage doors several yards away, talking to a policeman. Tally was on her knees in the grass, putting photographs inside a box.

Amanda and Neil rushed to her and she stood up, a pile of photos in her hands.

"Where's Chase?" Amanda cried. Her aunt's eyes were shining with dread.

Neil scanned the charred scene. Tally could tell when her uncle's gaze landed on Chase, standing at the edge of the driveway, ten feet away from the start of the destruction.

"He's there." Neil seemed to swallow nails when he said it.

"Are you all right? What happened?" Amanda's face shimmered in the mix of early moonlight and streetlight and strobes. Her cheeks were wet.

"I'm okay. The garage caught fire. I don't know when. I fell asleep, and when I woke up the fire was in the kitchen. I left the door open. I . . ."

But Amanda was looking at Chase too and seemed not to have heard anything Tally said beyond "I'm okay."

Tally followed their gaze and knew where their thoughts had taken them. She knew at once what Amanda and Neil were assuming. That Chase, in an act of desperation or rage, had set fire to the house.

From across the pavement Chase turned toward them, as if he'd sensed his parents were near. He began to walk toward them and Amanda rushed forward.

Amanda threw her arms around her son, her

body shaking. "You're okay, you're okay," she murmured through hushed sobs.

"I'm fine, Mom."

"Chase." Neil's voice sounded thick with sadness, and even in the gathering blackness of night, Tally could see his anguish. "What happened?"

Before Chase could answer, the policeman Chase had been talking to took a step toward them. "Are you Mr. and Mrs. Janvier?"

"Yes." Neil raised his head. "I'm Neil Janvier."

"You had the woodworking equipment in the garage?"

Tally saw her uncle flinch. "I . . . I did. Why? What happened?"

The policeman nodded toward the garage. "Fire department says it looks like the fire started in the garage. Along the wall shared by the kitchen."

"But that wall is Type X drywall! It meets fire code."

"I hear the door to the kitchen was open."

Tally felt her face grow warm. "I forgot the door had to be kept closed!"

Amanda reached one arm out for her. "It's okay, Tally. It's not your fault. No one is blaming you."

"I'm sure the fire department will tell you more," the cop continued. "I'm just telling you what they told me. Maybe some equipment was left running?"

"No! I would never . . ." Her uncle seemed too aghast to finish his sentence.

"Hey, the important thing is you're all safe. I've seen worse outcomes with a house fire. And your son is something of a hero, although I'm not saying it's a good idea to go inside a burning house."

"What?" Amanda gasped.

"He saved your niece. Neighbors who saw him drive up told him not to go in. But he went in anyway. Brave. And stupid." The cop winked. The radio on his lapel squawked, and he turned to speak into it.

A firefighter emerged from the blackened front door and walked up to them. Soot marked his face. "You are Neil and Amanda Janvier?"

"Yes," Neil said quickly.

"I'm Captain Andrew Porter. Your son Chase here told us there are no other occupants of the home. Right? The two of you and your daughter were at a sporting event?"

"Yes . . . yes, that's right," Neil stammered.

"Well, that's something to be thankful for. It doesn't always end this way."

Amanda stifled a sob. "We are. So thankful."

"The fire has been extinguished," the captain continued. "And we've ascertained it began in the garage. Not sure how yet, but we can see that it started along the wall shared by the kitchen. It spread to the wood shavings and lumber and then intensified from there. We'll be able to see better in the morning. The flames entered the house through an open kitchen door and damaged or destroyed pretty much all of the first level. Half of your second level is intact, but there's major structural, water, and smoke damage. I think you'll be looking at a total loss."

"But we're okay." Amanda closed her eyes and inhaled deeply.

"Look, we'll be here for a while managing hot spots and making sure the fire doesn't flare up again," the captain said. "It's too early to go in and salvage anything, so the only thing you can do at this point is get yourself a place to stay tonight and come back tomorrow, and we'll see what can be removed from the house. The police will put tape around it for tonight."

"Yes. Thank you," Neil said.

The captain walked back toward the house, leaving the four of them in a small huddle.

For a moment no one said a word. Then Chase turned to his parents. "It wasn't me," he said.

A sob escaped from Amanda, and Neil opened his mouth to speak. Nothing came out at first, and then a low-toned squeak preceded his words. "You . . . We didn't . . ." But Neil didn't finish.

"No, I know you thought it was me. For a moment there you thought it was me." Chase sounded calm and in control. "And I know why you did. But I didn't start this fire. And I didn't start the one that killed Alyssa Tagg either."

Amanda reached out instinctively for someone

to steady her. She grabbed Tally's arm. "What?" she croaked.

Chase turned to his mother. "I didn't start it. It was the other boy in the room with me. I touched the lighter before Keith lit his cigarette. He took it from me and sent me back to the master bedroom where Alyssa, Devin, and I were supposed to be napping. But Devin and I went back into Keith's room after we saw him use the lighter. When Keith climbed down the balcony, Devin picked up the lighter and lit a cigarette on the bed. That's what started the fire. It wasn't anything I did or Keith did. It was Devin. He didn't know what he was doing."

"How long . . . have you known?" In the pearly streetlight, Tally could see tears shimmering in Neil's eyes.

"How long have I known it wasn't me? Or how long have I known there was a fire?"

"Chase . . . ," Amanda whispered.

"I finally remembered today that it wasn't me who started it. I had to go to Alyssa's gravesite to figure that out. And I've always known about the fire."

Amanda leaned into Neil as she continued to cry and whisper Chase's name.

"I . . . didn't think you remembered," Neil murmured. "I didn't want you to remember. That day . . . that day was a nightmare. I'm sorry, Chase. I'm . . ."

Neil's voice faded away, and he moved forward

to embrace his son as emotion overcame him. Her aunt leaned in over them and spread her arms. Tally wanted to give them privacy, but there was nowhere to go. She stood quietly with a blanket around her and waited.

"You went to Alyssa's grave?" Amanda said.

"I couldn't remember everything. And I needed to. I thought maybe I'd been the one . . . I had to know."

"But you weren't," Amanda murmured.

"But I didn't know. I thought it was me. And I know you thought it was me."

Neil grimaced and looked away. Her uncle's eyes were on the broken glass at his feet. He seemed unable to look away from the sparkling shards. "I thought I was protecting you, Chase."

"We're so sorry, Chase." Amanda's voice disappeared into a fresh sob. "Please forgive us! Please. Let us make it up to you. Please. Give us another chance, please?"

"Another chance," Chase echoed softly.

"Please!"

He reached into his back pocket. "I've made some mistakes of my own. I took this money from the laundry room today, from your secret place, Mom. I shouldn't have. I'm sorry."

Amanda gasped at the folded money in Chase's hand and then at her son. Tally saw her aunt's face blanch, and she seemed to falter for a second, as if she might faint.

"I was going to put it back in the tin above the washer when I got home tonight," Chase continued, his eyes never leaving his mother's. "But the laundry room is gone. It's all gone. It's all ashes now."

Amanda nodded slowly, her eyes still wide with fear and astonishment. Tally looked at Chase, and he said nothing. Not even with his eyes. Her aunt surely thought she was having a silent conversation with only one person—Chase. And it was to stay that way.

"It doesn't matter," Neil was mumbling. "It doesn't matter now."

Chase extended the money toward his mother. But she shook her head. "I don't want it back. I don't." She pushed the money back toward Chase. "I don't want it back." Her body seemed to relax as she moved the bills away from her, even as Chase's seemed to tense.

She believed her secret was safe. Safe with her son, safe in the ashes. Chase's shoulders seemed to sag just a bit at the whispering weight of it.

Tally stepped away from the three of them, sensing their need for privacy. As she moved, a sepia-tone photo fell from the pile she held in her hands. She bent to pick it up.

In the spill of streetlight, she saw in the photograph two women in woolen capes and nurses' hats standing on the steps of a brick building. One was her great-grandmother. Tally recognized the face; it was the same as the woman in the wedding picture Amanda had shown her. The other woman in the photo had fair hair; Tally didn't recognize her. The fair-haired girl had something affixed to her cape.

Tally peered closer.

It almost looked like a butterfly pin.

forty-two

Amanda stood at the base of the climbing structure in her classroom, her Sherwood Forest, and ran her hand along a smooth, latticed side. The reading tree was one of the first things Neil had made in the woodshop.

The tree was the only thing he'd made in the woodshop now left in her possession. The pie safe in the kitchen had been destroyed. Her sewing table. The coffee table in the living room was damaged beyond repair.

Everything else he'd made, he'd given away.

Neil hadn't mentioned the woodshop, neither its loss nor the part it played in reshaping every moment of their lives since Saturday evening.

"The kids will miss it," a voice said.

She turned.

Gary.

Amanda had been able to avoid being alone with Gary in the classroom all day. But the last student had left. An empty stillness permeated the room.

"I'm not taking it with me." She turned back to the tree and gave it a loving stroke.

"I really didn't think you'd come in today."

Amanda leaned toward the tree. "I needed to see my students. I had to tell them myself that I was okay."

"Are you?"

She turned from the tree and slowly walked back to her desk. "I'm getting there. The two-week break will help."

"So you're coming back." He didn't phrase it like a question.

Amanda looked up at him. Today he wore a Scooby Doo tie. Not one of her favorite cartoon characters. "I don't know what I'm going to do."

Gary took a step toward her, and Amanda felt her muscles tense. "I'm asking for a transfer, Amanda. You can come back here if you want."

"What did you say?"

"It makes the most sense. You have kids in this district. I don't. And I don't want to do to your marriage what I let my ex-wife do to mine. If I stay, I'd *want* to come between you and Neil. And I don't want to want it."

"I am really sorry—," Amanda began, but Gary cut her off.

"Look, I let you get close. I wanted you to. I knew the risks far better than you did. It's my fault."

"No, it's not."

"Anyway, I am sorry about what happened Friday night. It's not going to happen again." Gary picked up his briefcase and coffee cup. It was like he couldn't wait to be free of her.

"Wait. Where will you go?"

He shrugged. "There are plenty of schools that need long-term subs. I'm not worried."

"I wish I knew what to say."

He shook his head. "I don't want you to say anything."

"But you've been such a good . . ."

"Please. Don't. Don't say anything else."

She closed her mouth. Gary slung the strap of his briefcase over his shoulder and switched off his computer monitor. He came around to her desk. "Chase is okay?"

"He and Neil have been talking. They went out for coffee last night and didn't come back for two hours. I feel like maybe we're becoming a family again."

Again he slowly nodded. "And you're going to rebuild?"

"We are. We'll have to start over, from the foundation up. But the builder Neil has talked to said he can make it just the way it was. Better, even. There will be a smaller woodshop—much smaller—next to the garage from the backyard side."

"A woodshop."

"It's not what you think, Gary. Anything can

become what the old woodshop was to Neil. And we're going in for marriage counseling, just like you told me we should."

Gary stood silent for several seconds. Then he put out his hand. "Take care, Amanda. It was a pleasure to work with you. I really mean that."

She hesitated, then took the hand offered to her and shook it.

Gary took a step toward the classroom door, and as he swung it open, one of the third-grade teachers stepped inside.

"Oh, hey, Gary," the woman said, and then she spun around to face Amanda. "Amanda, I just got back from being out of town and heard what happened to your house! I'm so glad you are all okay! Do you need anything? Clothes? Shoes? Anything?"

"Thanks, Martha. I'm doing okay, but thanks." Amanda looked up at Gary as he inched toward the now-open door.

"How did it happen? I heard someone say it was caused by lightning."

"No. Not lightning. A mouse or rat chewed through the wiring on some electrical equipment, and it sparked on a pile of wood shavings. Neil is . . . was . . . had a woodshop in our garage. So there was a lot for the fire to feed on."

"How scary. So you have a place to stay?"

"We're in a hotel for a couple more days, and then we'll be renting a condo a couple of miles from here. It's furnished and really lovely. The kids are settling in okay, and we've got insurance money to buy new clothes. Delcey's loving that. And Tally actually seems like she's enjoying having new things."

Martha cocked her head. "Tally?"

"My niece. She's staying with us while my brother's in . . . in Europe."

"Oh. I didn't even know you had a brother. Did you, Gary?" But Martha didn't wait for him to answer. "What a crazy time to have a houseguest, huh?"

"You could say that."

"So your whole house is gone? You lost everything?"

Gary tipped his chin toward her and began to walk away. He did not look back.

"Not everything," she said.

forty-three

October 7
Pima County Human Services
Tucson, Arizona

Dear Mrs. Janvier,
Here is the second letter I phoned you about. Again, I appreciate your allowing me to open and read it. We are watching the Kolander house for your brother's return, and I will con-

tact you the moment he arrives. I did not read the other letter even though it is unsealed, since it is the letter your father wrote and has nothing to do with this situation. I just wanted you to know that.

Thanks for all your help with this. I know this all came at a difficult time with the loss of your house. Hope all is going well.

Nancy Fuentes

October 1

Hey, Tally-ho!

Guess what? You and I are spending Thanksgiving in Warsaw! I'm coming for you in a week or so, Tal, and we'll get you all packed up and ready to go. Tried calling you a bunch of times, but your grandma must've changed her number and not told me. Or maybe she needs a little help with the bill. I'll take care of that when I get there.

Now, I know I promised you a red Corvette and all, but we may have to wait on that. I haven't found that box of jewelry and money that belonged to Grandpa. The first time I looked for it, I kind of got chased away by neighbors, who called the police. I came back a second time after I met Anya—she's great. You'll love her. And she told me to just go up to the owners and tell them what I wanted to *do. So I did. Turns out they're decent people who lost family in the war just like we did. They helped me look. We dug right where Grandpa said it would be. And we dug a few feet away from that place—in every direction. No dice. Sorry, Tal. But hey, I haven't given up. These people, their name is Grocholski, have invited us—you and me—to come stay for a few weeks. The husband speaks very good English. The wife and Anya can sort of understand each other. Anya is from Ukraine. She went to school in London, though, so she sounds like the queen of England. She runs a ranch for orphaned and abandoned street children.*

Do you remember that job I had after Manhattan? Remember we were in Nashville and I was shoveling horse crap and you were so sad because I wasn't driving Mell's fancy cars anymore or drinking her expensive wine or wearing silk shirts? Who could've guessed that time in Nashville would fix me up for right now? Anya was in Warsaw same time I was, trying to convince her brother to come back to Ukraine and help her. Her ranch hand had just quit. But her brother didn't want to go. I met her at the train station.

Tal, I've been helping Anya at the ranch this last month so I can earn money for a plane ticket home, and I'm thinking we could make a go of it here for a little while if you want. It snows here—we're talking gobs of it. You've always told me you wanted to live where there was snow. I thought we'd stay here a bit and then poke around the Grocholskis' backyard some more and see what turns up. You can do that mail-order school thing like we did when we went to Switzerland.

I'm sorry I wasn't better about writing. And that I never could reach you by phone. I didn't think I'd be gone as long as I have been. I hope you've had a great time with your grandma and that you won't mind leaving Arizona behind.

Oh, hey, by the way, you can tell your grandma about the box I'm trying to find. I know I asked you to keep it a secret, but it's not like I found it or anything. And I probably should tell you, not that it matters, that the woman I thought was my grandmother was really someone else. It's a long story. It's all in Grandpa's letter, which I'm sending to you so nothing happens to it. I think your aunt Amanda will want to read it. I know she will. We should maybe stop in and see your aunt and uncle before we head out of the States. I know she'd love to see you again. You were just a kid last time she saw you.

Not sure when you'll get this, but I'm plan-

ning on arriving back in the States on October 20 or thereabouts. Start saying your good-byes, Tally-ho!

I'm coming for you.
Love, Dad

P.S. Hold on to Grandpa's letter for me. I sent it with this note. And, hey, the butterfly pin wrapped in tissue paper is for you. I know it needs some TLC, but I think it will clean up nice. Those little blue stones are sapphires, I think. It is the only piece of jewelry I've been able to find.

Fresno, California
June 2007

Dear Bart,
Unless you miraculously show up in the next couple of weeks, I don't think I'll have a chance to talk with you again. I know you don't want to hear any apologies or repri-mands, and to tell you the truth, I don't want to write any. So rest assured that's not what this letter is for.

As I lay here counting off the seconds, I know that I'm getting close to the end of my life. There are a few things I want at least one person to know before I die. You can decide if you think anyone else needs to know what I'm *going to tell you. For some reason it seems important that someone should know.*

I always appreciated that you and Amanda never pressed me to talk about the war or what happened to my father or what happened to your grandmother and me after we escaped the ghetto. It meant a great deal to both of us that we could start new lives here in America and that we didn't have to go traipsing about in the past.

But I need to tell you that the woman you knew as your grandmother was not really my mother. Not in the physical sense. By the time you came along, she was very much my mother—and had been for many years. My real mother died in the ghetto giving birth to my sister, Sabina. I have never told anyone what I am going to tell you. Bear with me.

A few days after my mother died, my father learned that he and I were scheduled to be on the next transport to Treblinka. People who were transported to Treblinka were never heard from again. There were rumors that most of the Jews sent to Treblinka were gassed within hours of arriving. I, of course, did not know that until I was older. My father knew enough of the horrors of Treblinka to want to get me and Sabina out of the ghetto. He arranged for me and my sister to be smuggled out of the ghetto through the sewers.

There were smuggling operations all over the ghetto for getting things in and getting things out.

I don't recall the names of the men who helped us inside the ghetto. But the names of the two women outside the ghetto were Sofia and Katrine. They were both nurses. Sofia had arranged for a family to take me and Sabina. Katrine was there to help Sofia get us to the meeting place.

I remember getting up when it was still night and watching as my father gave Sabina medicine to make her sleep. He tried not to cry when he said good-bye. He told me I was going on a little holiday with Sabina and that he would join us later. He kissed us both and waved good-bye, smiling all the while tears were sliding down his face. I believed I would soon see him again. A runner took us inside the sewers, where it was very dark and stinking. Sofia and Katrine met us on the other side, and the runner went back to the ghetto. Katrine wrapped Sabina in her cape and handed her to Sofia. Then she took my hand, and we made our way out.

We didn't see the Gestapo until it was too late. Soldiers had been tipped off by someone inside the ghetto. Sofia and Katrine ran into the streets, Sofia with my sister and Katrine with me. They separated to better their chances of escape. The Nazis missed this and only went after Katrine and me. As the soldiers got closer, Katrine lifted a sidewalk grate and lowered me inside, telling me not to make a sound and that she would come back for me. But she lost too many seconds securing my safety. The Nazis rounded a corner and came upon her. I watched from the grate as they shot Katrine as she ran. It was more than an hour before Sofia found me. I was still under the grate. I had not moved or made a sound. For many months after that I hardly spoke a word.

Sofia was unable to go back to her own apartment or the secret meeting place, so she asked me if I knew where my house was. I remembered I lived near a church with a cross. After hours of hiding and walking and looking for steeples, we did finally find my house. It had been looted and was empty but still standing. We were lucky there were no squatters.

The only item of value we had was Katrine's butterfly pin. It was pinned to the cape she wrapped Sabina in. Afraid looters would be back, Sofia asked me if I knew of a good hiding place for it. I told her where I had hidden the key to a strongbox of jewelry and gold I'd buried in the backyard. My father told me to bury the box when we knew the Nazis *would be coming to take us to the ghetto. I had placed the key on a ledge in the crawlspace between the second and third stories—it was a pocket too small for an adult to get into. I put the pin there with the key.*

We made one risky trip back to her apartment to get some clothes, some personal belongings, her photographs, and Katrine's engagement ring to use as a pretend wedding ring. Despite her best efforts to care for my baby sister, Sabina died two weeks after our escape. We attempted to keep a low profile, living out of only one room and not using any lights at night. But Nazi soldiers learned we were there, and before we managed to escape Warsaw, Sofia let the soldiers abuse her in exchange for letting us live. I didn't understand the sacrifices she'd made for me until I was much older.

When we finally secured our escape to England via her smuggling contacts, we had weathered several months in that house, enduring the most demeaning of circumstances. She and I never spoke of those months in the house again. Never.

When the war ended we came back to Warsaw to look for any of my mother's family. And any of Sofia's. But she could find none, and even if she had found my aunts and uncles, I didn't wish to leave her. We emi-

grated to the United States, she as Marta Bachmann. My mother.

After five years using the name Marta Bachmann, she had no desire to take back her own name. She'd ceased to be the girl she once was a long time before that, starting with those months in the house with the Nazis. I let her be who she wanted to be. This is who she was to me, anyway.

So now you know. You can decide who you will tell, if anyone.

I never went back for the strongbox of jewelry and gold that I buried in the backyard. It is under the third pine tree on the north side, out twenty paces or so. I was only six when I hid it. I have already told you where the key is.

My parents were quite well to do when Poland fell. I would imagine the contents of the box are worth a small fortune. It is yours if you want it.

I am tired, Bart. Tired and old, and I can't write anymore.

I want you to know I have always admired your capacity to see the glass half full. Always. There were so many years I could not even see the glass.

I hope you find all that you are looking for,
Kocham cię,
Edward Bachmann

forty-four

Spent wisteria vines dangled on the slats of the patio roof at La Vista del Paz, speckling the concrete below and the four people underneath with ameba-shaped shadows.

Chase and Tally sat in matching plastic lawn chairs across from Josef and Eliasz. Afghans were tucked about the old men's waists as they sat in their wheelchairs. A cool, early October breeze hinted of subtle changes to come.

"I am very sorry about your house," Josef said, and Eliasz nodded. "Eliasz and I know what it is like to have everything you own snatched away from you. It can leave you feeling off balance."

"Yeah, a little," Chase said. "I actually haven't minded that much. Other things were given back to me."

"Yes?" Josef looked hopeful. "What things?"

"My dad and I—we had pretty much stopped talking to each other before the fire. And it's different now between us."

"I understand. I was a boy your age once. So it is going well now with your father?"

"We're talking to each other again. And I'm learning things about him I didn't know before."

"Such as?"

"Why he gave away everything he made in the woodshop. He's always been a numbers guy. He's always felt this need to tip the scales in his favor. You know, give more than you take so you can somehow make up for the things that you can't make right."

"Ah, now there's an exercise to keep you hopping. No wonder he had no time for conversation. I am glad for you, Chase." Josef nodded. "What else was given back to you? Anything else?"

Chase knew what Josef hoped to hear. "My memory of the other fire. I got it back. The part I couldn't remember? It was given back to me."

"What other fire?" Eliasz said.

"Hush, *przyjaciel,* I told you about the other fire. You never listen to me."

"I listen. I just forget."

Josef turned to Chase. "So! Did God give it back to you?"

"I think maybe he did."

"And you were satisfied with what you remembered?"

"It wasn't me, Josef. I didn't start the fire that killed that baby. The other kid in the room with me was the one playing with the lighter."

"What baby?" Eliasz said.

Josef ignored him. "So it wasn't you."

"No."

"I wonder why you were unable to remember that all these years, if it wasn't your fault," Josef said.

"I don't know. But I do know I *felt* like it was my

fault. In some ways I still do. I saw that cigarette smoldering on the bed when we left the room. Somehow I knew it was wrong to leave it like that. But I didn't want to get caught sneaking around in Keith's room. I didn't want to get into trouble. And when flames came through the heating vent into our room, I knew we were all in terrible danger. And I couldn't reach Alyssa in her crib."

"So you chose not to remember. Set a guard around it to keep the memory hidden away?"

Ghost.

"I guess so."

"There is no shame in that, Chase. You were very young. Many in the ghetto, in Treblinka, had to do what you did. That is what all survivors must decide. We have to decide how much we will choose to remember and how much courage we are willing to expend to do so."

"I suppose."

"There is no supposing. It is the simple truth. We are the ones who know the flaws of the planet, yes? Who but us has the audacity to admit we are no match for a world in need of redemption? We choose how much we will carry away with us from the fire. Everyone else pretends they can't even see the ashes."

"Josef, what is all this serious talk?" Eliasz leaned back in his chair and closed his eyes. "I'm getting all worked up, and my massage therapist doesn't come on Tuesdays."

Josef waved a hand toward his friend. "This is good. I am indeed happy for you." He turned to Tally. "And you? Do you have good news? Have you heard from your father?"

Tally nodded. "He's coming home next week. I'm going to meet him in Tucson. Then he's taking me back to Warsaw for a few weeks, maybe a few months. We're spending Thanksgiving there."

"Oh! Then you will be leaving us. I should be happy for you. You will be leaving right away, then?"

"Yes."

"And how do you feel about spending some time in Warsaw? Does this excite you?"

"Well, my dad doesn't usually stay in one place very long, so I'll be okay with however long we stay there," Tally said. "But I've liked it here. I'm going to ask my dad if we can hang out here in San Diego when we get back. I only have two years left in high school. This would be a good place to spend them. I like having my family around me, even though everything isn't always perfect."

"Here, here," Eliasz said lazily, eyes still closed. His voice sounded like he was teetering on the verge of slumber.

"And then Eliasz and I would have a chance to meet your extraordinary father, no?"

"Sure."

"I like that plan. Don't you, Eliasz?" But Eliasz had drifted off to sleep.

Tally looked over to Chase and he nodded. She reached down into a bag at her feet and withdrew a photograph and a parcel wrapped in tissue paper. "Actually, Josef, we didn't just come here today to tell you I'm leaving for a little while," Tally said. "I came across something the night of the fire that I think you should see."

Tally handed him the photo of the two nurses.

Josef brought the photo close to his face. He eyes widened. "Where did you get this?" he breathed.

"Is that Katrine in the picture?" Chase asked.

"Where did you get this?" he repeated.

"The woman standing next to her is Sofia, isn't it?" Chase said.

Josef nodded wordlessly.

Chase leaned forward. "Josef, if you could know what happened to Katrine, would you want to know? Do you want to know what happened to her?"

Josef swallowed hard, and his eyes misted over as he looked up at Chase first and then Tally. "Where did you get this?"

"The woman you knew as Sofia is the woman our parents knew as Marta Bachmann," Tally answered.

"That's . . . that's impossible. The Gestapo killed Sofia when she and Katrine were running away. They shot her in the street!"

"No," Chase said gently. "They didn't shoot Sofia."

Chase said the words slowly, letting Josef adjust his mind to their meaning. When it appeared he understood, the old man screwed his eyes shut and brought a shaking hand to his face. Tally reached out and laid her hand on his shoulder.

"Katrine died saving our grandfather," Chase continued. "Remember when you told us someone inside the ghetto had sold you out? The Gestapo ambushed Sofia and Katrine as they left the sewers. The soldiers had been tipped off, just like you said. Sofia and Katrine ran. Katrine had my grandfather; Sofia had his baby sister. They split up. They were running through the streets of Warsaw, trying to get away. Katrine hid our grandfather under a sidewalk grate because he couldn't run as fast as an adult. The Nazis came upon her as she was running away without him."

Chase paused. Josef's body shook slightly with the cadence of silent tears. Tally stroked his shoulder.

"How do you know all this?" the old man whispered.

"My dad finally read the letter from his father. The letter explained everything," Tally replied.

Across from her, Josef was silent.

"You . . . you wanted to know, right?" Tally asked him.

Josef brushed away the tears and cleared his throat. His voice sounded thin and used up when he spoke. "You have no idea how much."

"I'm sorry about Katrine," Tally said, and Chase noticed her voice was also thick with emotion. "I'm sorry you had to hear what really happened to her."

Josef opened his mouth to say something and then shut it. He pointed to the picture of Katrine in his hand. Then he opened his mouth again. "But don't you see? This means she didn't learn to live without me like I had to learn to live without her. This means she didn't *choose* to learn to live without me. You've actually done me a tremendous kindness." His voice fell away again, and fresh tears sprang from his eyes. But this time he kept his eyes open. With shaking fingers he traced the outline of Katrine's face, frozen in a cheerful smile.

Chase nodded to Tally, and she began to unwrap the tissue-papered parcel in her hands. Josef looked up from the photograph at the sound of rustling paper. The old man watched as the paper fell away and the two butterflies—one large and one small—appeared in her palm.

"Oh," he whispered. "Where did you find it?" With a trembling hand he reached for the pin. Tally handed it to him.

"Katrine wrapped the baby in her cape," Chase replied. "The pin was attached to it when she handed the baby to Sofia. She and our grandpa hid the pin inside his family house and left it when they escaped to England. Tally's father just now found it in the house. It was still there. He sent it to her."

Josef smiled and held the pin up. The tiny pearls and sapphires caught the late-afternoon rays. He brought his other hand over the pin as if to hold it in an embrace. Then he stretched out his arm. "Thank you," he said.

"I want you to have it," Tally said.

Josef leaned forward, touching her with his outstretched arm. "And I want *you* to have it," he whispered. His hand trembled as he waited for her to take the pin. When she did, he sat back and exhaled deeply. "I would like to hold on to this. Just for a little while." He pointed to the photograph in his lap.

"That's a copy. It's yours," Chase said.

Josef nodded. "Thank you." He picked up the photo and brought it to his chest and closed his eyes.

Chase stood. "We should get going."

Josef slowly opened his eyes. He did not ask them to stay. But his eyes were kind.

"Oh, by the way, we got an A on our project," Chase said. "Thanks to Tally we didn't have to start over from the beginning. She saved the camera and the footage from the fire."

Josef smiled broadly. "An A! I am pleased for you both." He looked up at Tally. "Perhaps when you return from your trip to Warsaw, you can tell me what you thought of it. What it is like there now."

"Sure. I'd be happy to do that," she said.

"All right," Chase said. "See you later, Josef. Tell Eliasz good-bye for us." He and Tally turned to go.

"Wait!" Josef said quickly, as if a sudden thought occurred to him. "How did God give you back your memory of the fire? How did he do it?"

For a second Chase saw himself back at Alyssa's grave, hearing the gulls crying above him, feeling the cool grass beneath him, and contemplating for the first time the peculiar notion that his last name spelled out rebirth.

"He showed me in a dream." And he nodded toward Eliasz, whose closed eyes danced under his eyelids like water over stones.

ACKNOWLEDGMENTS

Writing is an art form for the soloist, but were it not for these remarkable people, I truly would have nothing meaningful to say.

Thank you, Bob—husband, confidant, partner in everything—for your patience and gentility. You are my hero. And to my kids, Stephanie, Josh, Justin, and Eric, thanks for being amazing young adults who keep me planted on solid ground.

I am grateful to my mother, Judy Horning, for willingly and lovingly reading with an honest eye the rough-cut version.

To the amazingly affirming crew at WaterBrook Multnomah, especially editors Shannon Marchese and Jessica Barnes, thank you for your creative insights into the human heart. You are geniuses.

To my agent, Chip MacGregor, thanks for your well-timed votes of confidence and cheering from the sidelines.

To Al Gansky, thank you for letting me peek inside the mind of a passionate woodworker.

To my beloved book club sisters, especially Debbie Ness and Barb Anderson, thank you for thinking me capable of greatness.

And to God, who gives beauty for ashes, I am indebted beyond words.

AUTHOR'S NOTE

The characters Josef Bliss, Eliasz Abramovicz, Katrine, and Sofia "Marta" Bachmann in *White Picket Fences* are fictional, but the Warsaw Ghetto, the carnage at Treblinka, and the smuggling of little ones out of the ghetto during World War II are historical events. One of the most well-known rescuers was Irena Sendler, a Catholic social worker who risked her life to save more than two thousand Jewish children during the Holocaust.

Irena was twenty-nine years old when the Germans invaded Poland and forced Polish Jews into a barbed-wire enclave known as the Warsaw Ghetto. Along with many other sympathizers, Irena took on an underground name, Jolanta, and joined an underground operation called Zegota to offer aid to the displaced and starving Jews. As the horrors of the ghetto heightened, Sendler and a small band of associates began whisking Jewish children away to safety. Sometimes they would use hidden compartments in ambulances. Sometimes the children were placed in coffins or gunny sacks. Sometimes they used a labyrinth of underground tunnels and basements. Sometimes they used forged documents and used the city's tram, if the tram operator for that day was a Zegota member.

Once outside the ghetto, the Jewish children were taken to Catholic homes and taught the Polish language so they could pass as Gentile Poles. Many priests and monks provided false baptismal certificates so that Jewish children could pass as Catholic born.

On the evening of October 20, 1943, informed Nazis came to Irena's apartment and began to bang on the door. A quick-thinking Irena passed the lists of locations of all the rescued children to a friend who was in the apartment with her. The friend hid the lists in her underwear as the Nazis broke through the door. The soldiers searched the apartment for several hours, looking for the names and locations of the estimated two thousand Jewish children that had been spirited away from the ghetto. They never found them.*

Irena was arrested, beaten, sent to Pawiak prison, and given the death sentence. A bribe from members of Zegota to her German captors allowed for her release, and she remained in hiding until after the war. The index of names was buried in jars under a tree until the war ended, though sadly, most of these children were not reunited with their parents because the vast majority of them had died during the war. In 2003 Ms. Sendler received the Jan Karski Award for valor and courage. She was also nominated for the Nobel Peace Prize. She died in 2008 at the age of ninety-eight. You can read more about her at www.irenasendler.org.

I love hearing from readers. Please visit me at www.susan meissner.com. You are the reason I write.

Susan Meissner

---

* Richard C. Lukas, "Irena Sendler: World War II's Polish Angel," *St. Anthony Messenger,* vol. 116, no. 3, August 2008.

AN INTERVIEW
WITH SUSAN MEISSNER

What led you to write White Picket Fences?
Several years ago I was a court-appointed advocate for children involved in protective services. There were times when I saw that despite the outward appearance of a less-than-perfect home, a child could be loved there. Just because a parent is unconventional or unsuccessful career-wise or makes choices that buck societal norms, it doesn't mean that he or she is by default a "bad" parent. Likewise, parents who we would traditionally call "good"—meaning they provide, they protect, they don't hit, they don't ridicule—can nevertheless make decisions regarding their children that have hugely negative effects, and yet their outward appearance would never lead anyone to suspect it. Even if you live behind a white picket fence, you still have to deal with the fallout of a living in a broken world. You can't hide from it. The perfect idyllic life is an illusion. Life is a weave of both delight and disappointment, and it's precisely these things that give it definition and depth. To ignore what is ugly is to cheapen what is beautiful.

You dovetailed a current day family drama with the Holocaust and the Warsaw Ghetto. Why the connection?

I think it's fair to say that the depth of the atrocities inflicted during the Holocaust wasn't fully appreciated until after the war. There was ugliness happening, if you will, and much of the West failed to see it—for whatever reason. Within the horror, though, people made brave choices, selfless choices. And there were survivors who had to choose what they would take with them from the ashes of their suffering. I wanted to explore how a person makes that decision. Even the decision to pretend it never happened is a decision regarding those ashes.

What interests you about the intersection of personal relationships and perceptions—a theme you wove into both The Shape of Mercy and White Picket Fences?

I see every great work of fiction being about human relationships. *Gone With the Wind* is so much more than just an epic story with the Civil War as a backdrop. It's a story of human relationships. Scarlett and Ashley, Scarlett and Rhett, Scarlett and Melanie, Scarlett and her father. It's within our closest relationships that our brightest virtues and worst flaws are exposed. That's why there is such tremendous story value within intimate human relationships. We are at our best and our worst when we are responding and reacting to the people who shape who we are. Human history is the story of relationships and what they teach us about what we value. And what we don't.

White Picket Fences is a different kind of novel than your acclaimed book, The Shape of Mercy, but there are some similarities too. Can you explain those?
As with *The Shape of Mercy,* there is a historical thread in *White Picket Fences,* though it is not as dominant. The invasion of Poland by the Nazis is woven into the story and provides the backdrop for Chase's and Tally's discoveries about hope, dreams, and redemption. This thread is enhanced by visits to a nursing home where Chase and Tally meet a man blind from birth who survived the occupation of Poland. It is also a story that draws its pathos from family dynamics and the near-universal desire we have to make straight what is crooked. There are two young protagonists in *White Picket Fences* as in *The Shape of Mercy,* as well as a third character, who, along with the two men in the nursing home, provide a similar multigenerational story thread.

Is there a reason why Tally's father, Bart, never makes a physical entrance in the story?
My intention was always to keep Bart's character a bit mysterious, enough so that readers have to

decide for themselves if Bart is a father figure worthy of any admiration. Whose perception of Bart will you believe? Tally's? Amanda's? Neil's? I wanted the reader to have the challenge and satisfaction of making that decision.

What is the motivation for Amanda's almost-affair with Gary? Readers aren't given reason to believe that Amanda is naturally prone toward such choices.
Amanda is actually an amalgam of so many individuals I know who derive strength and hope from a deep emotional connection to the person who loves them most. When we're worried, stressed, and afraid, most of us rely on that emotional bond with our significant other to affirm, uphold, and defend us from what wars against us. Amanda didn't have that emotional connection with Neil when the past reared its ugly head—and she didn't realize she didn't have it because up to this point she thought they had the perfect life. Amanda saw the mess and wanted desperately to clean it up. Neil saw it and wanted desperately to look the other way. They were both desperate. But apart.

It's interesting that Tally doesn't seem to grieve the absence of a mother. Why?
Tally is first and foremost Bart's daughter. And Bart is not one to brood over something he has no control over and can't change. The scene where

we glimpse Tally's perceptions of the women Bart has dated gives us some insights into how she's processed the fact that she doesn't have a mother. And because it's natural for us to want her to want a mother, I included in the last scene Tally's desire to come back to San Diego after she and Bart return from Warsaw. This lets us picture Tally being mothered by Amanda in the near future.

What do you hope readers come away with after reading White Picket Fences?
The pivotal moment in the story for me is when Josef says to Chase: "[This] is what all survivors must decide. We have to decide how much we will choose to remember and how much courage we are willing to expend to do so." It takes courage to acknowledge and remember what drove you to your knees or nearly killed you. If you choose to forget—that's assuming you actually can—then it seems to me you suffered for nothing. You are different, but you don't spend any time contemplating—or celebrating—how. I'd be happy if there was a takeaway for someone out there who needs to consider that.

About the Author

From early school-day projects to becoming editor of a local newspaper in Minnesota, Susan Meissner's love for writing has been apparent her entire life. She is the author of ten novels and lives with her family in San Diego. Find out more about her at www.susanmeissner.com.

Center Point Publishing
600 Brooks Road • PO Box 1
Thorndike ME 04986-0001 USA

(207) 568-3717

US & Canada:
1 800 929-9108
www.centerpointlargeprint.com